THEIR
DYING
EMBRACE

BOOKS BY HELEN PHIFER

Standalones

Lakeview House

The Vanishing Bookstore

THEIR
DYING
EMBRACE

HELEN PHIFER

bookouture

Published by Bookouture in 2025

An imprint of Storyfire Ltd.
Carmelite House
50 Victoria Embankment
London EC4Y 0DZ

www.bookouture.com

The authorised representative in the EEA is Hachette Ireland
8 Castlecourt Centre
Dublin 15 D15 XTP3
Ireland
(email: info@hbgi.ie)

ISBN: 978-1-83790-382-5
eBook ISBN: 978-1-83790-381-8

For Gina LoBue and Gilly Mahaffy, I hope you like your characters because I love them. Xx

ONE

Rosie Waite lay straight on the bed, staring up at the ceiling. The only sound was his incessant snores. She listened to him make a weird snorting kind of sound. It was pouring out of his mouth and nose like it was a thunderstorm rumbling in the distance over the tops of the Helvellyn mountain range behind their house. Her fingers were clenched into tight fists, and she wondered if he'd notice if she either punched him in the side of the head or put a pillow over his face.

She wasn't a violent person, but this was beyond a joke. He had come home from his work's team building evening as drunk as a skunk, and she had been furious with him. He'd promised her he wasn't drinking a lot, just a couple of lagers with the lads. He gave her the excuse that he didn't see them very often because he mainly worked from home; apparently, he just *had* to show his face, that kind of crap. She should have known it was all lies as soon as he'd spoken them out loud.

He had as much willpower as a rabbit in a field of carrots. It wasn't that she cared about him drinking. It was the fact that he'd promised they would get up early and drive to Manchester to go shopping for a dress for her birthday that was in two days.

She turned away from him and picked her phone up off the bedside table, opened Messenger and sent a long, ranting message to her best friend.

As she lay there staring into the darkness, waiting to see if Gina was awake enough to reply, she heard a thud come from the ceiling above her and held her breath.

Oh God, this was all she needed when he was comatose next to her.

She waited to see if it happened again, and sure enough there was a faint scraping, dragging sound.

Oh shit!

Rosie ducked her head under the covers, pulling the duvet around her, trying to block out any further noises that came from the attic. She'd heard noises like this before. She had wanted him to go up there again to take a look around and see if they had mice, or maybe a squirrel had found its way in there, but he had told her she was being stupid, and he wouldn't fit through the hatch. She wasn't being stupid and now he was too drunk to do anything, and the anger she had been feeling towards him was turning into full-blown animosity.

She sent Gina another message.

He's passed out oblivious to the world, stinking of stale beer and there's noises from up in the attic again. I can hear something moving around up there and I'm scared, what should I do?

Gina must be in bed because she didn't read either message, and Rosie wondered if she should call the police. Instead, she turned back to face him and shook his arm, then his shoulder a little more violently than she usually would and hissed down his ear.

'Wake up.'

His response was to mumble something incomprehensible, let out another snort and turn away from her.

Her body was frozen in fear. *Serves you right for watching scary movies when you're in the house on your own*, the voice of reason in her head told her. As she lay there questioning her film choice of *The Conjuring*, with the clock ticking, counting down the minutes, she hoped that Valak the Nun wasn't real. She didn't know what she'd do if that terrifying creature out of her worst nightmares glided across the bedroom floor.

Her phone pinged, making her jump out of her skin. It lit up the room, and as far as she could see it was all good, no evil nuns hiding in the corner.

Chuck a bucket of cold water over his head and tell him to go and check the attic out, but seriously Rosie, you live in a street with great big trees out the front. It will be a bird or a squirrel that's got in. Stop panicking, try get some sleep. Did you not get any of those earplugs I told you about? Xxx?

Rosie smiled, Gina was always the voice of reason and yes, she did buy some – they were still in her handbag downstairs.

Grabbing a couple of pillows, she thought she may as well go sleep on the sofa as far away from his snores as possible. She could make a hot chocolate and get cosy with her earplugs and hopefully get some sleep. Whatever animal was nesting in the attic could wait until tomorrow.

As she poured the milk into the mug, she heard soft footsteps above her head and tutted. She hoped he found the bathroom this time. Last time he'd been this drunk she'd caught him peeing all over the landing.

As she turned to cross the kitchen to put her mug in the microwave, she saw a dark shadow standing in the doorway. The mug slipped from her hand and smashed onto the tiled floor, spilling milk and spraying broken pieces of pottery all over.

Opening her mouth to scream she saw that there was no shadow: she was imagining it. A passing cloud over the moon must have caused it through the panes of glass in the window. She shook her head. Christ, she was not watching any more horror films, full stop. This was ridiculous. She yawned and decided she wasn't cleaning the mess up until the morning, and if he came down barefoot and stepped in it, well it was his own fault because if it wasn't for him, she wouldn't be up at this godforsaken hour scaring herself shitless.

She took the earplugs out of her handbag hanging off one of the kitchen chairs and ripped the packet open. Inserting them in her ears, she made herself another hot chocolate, sidestepping the mess on the floor, and went back into the living room where the bed she'd made up looked a lot more inviting than the one upstairs with him in it.

She couldn't hear a thing either which was a bonus, she thought, and let out a huge yawn.

She didn't notice the figure crouched in the darkest corner of the room or the glint of the moonlight reflecting off the long, narrow, pointed metal ice axe.

TWO

Morgan heard the sirens from the kitchen and rushed to look out of the front room window. They were far too close for her liking. Ben was in the kitchen making coffee, and she saw one, then two police vans speed past their house and stop a little further down. The sound of the heavy doors slamming echoed through the single-paned sash windows that Ben kept talking about replacing but hadn't got around to. Not wanting to look as nosey as her next-door neighbour, but unable to stop herself, she pressed her face to the window. They weren't that far down the street, next door but one. Kevin, their adopted cat, had already beaten her to it and was sitting on the windowsill, cleaning his paws, occasionally staring in the direction of all the action. She scratched behind his ears, and he let out a loud purr. Despite being a grouchy old thing that liked to be left alone, he was still happy to let them stroke him when he felt like it.

'What are you doing?'

She jumped at the sound of Ben's voice.

'Did you not hear those sirens?'

He shook his head, and droplets of water sprayed her, his hair still damp from his shower.

'Something's happened a few doors down, there's two vans.'

'Domestic, I will bet you two coffees on it.'

She turned and smiled at him. 'Nah, something worse than a domestic. I'm saying it's a break-in.'

He shrugged. 'Go out and ask them if you really want to know; it's the only way to find out seeing as how it's our day off. Where are we going today anyway?'

'Liverpool, I need some new Docs, and I want to browse the bookshops. And no, I'm not asking them anything, we are allowed to have a life outside of work.'

He smiled at her, that boyish grin that made his eyes crinkle and her heart happy. He was standing with his arms open wide and she fell into them. Nowhere felt as safe as in his arms, and then hammering on the door made them both break away from each other. Ben groaned, and Morgan shook her head.

'You answer it.'

'You, tell them we know nothing, and they can bugger off if it's house-to-house.'

'You better check the doorbell camera to be sure.'

'See, I keep telling you that you should be putting in to do your sergeant's exams.'

She gave him the middle finger and strode to the door. Opening it wide she saw the expression on Amber's face and all the warmth and happiness that had filled her heart moments ago fizzed away to be replaced with cold fingers of fear.

'What's wrong?'

'Murder, double murder, can you or Ben come take a look?'

Morgan felt her heart skip a beat as she tried to comprehend what Amber had just said. A double murder in one of the beautiful Victorian semis on this usually peaceful, treelined street was hard to comprehend. Morgan's head was telling her to say no, that they could phone the DS down in Barrow who was covering Rydal Falls today, but she couldn't, her heart wouldn't let her. This was their safe haven, and they knew most of the neighbours to say hi to which meant it was someone they knew. A double murder a few doors down from them was not the kind of thing you passed over for a day out shopping.

Ben came out of the front room.

Morgan turned to him. 'There's been a double murder.'

He looked as surprised as she had at the thought of two people being murdered a few doors away. 'Jesus, are you sure, Amber? Who is it?'

Amber shrugged. 'I don't know, I just got here, and their friend was crying in the street saying they're both dead, so Scotty has gone in to see and I came to get you guys. I know you're not in work, but it seems stupid waiting forever for the duty DS to come from Barrow. Could you not take over until they get here?'

'Who's the duty? Is it Will Ashworth?'

She shook her head. 'No, Gillian Mahaffy. I heard she's tough and doesn't take any crap.'

Morgan smiled. 'Maybe you should let her deal then, she can sort Marc out.'

'Are you coming to take a look?' Amber's eyes were almost pleading with her, and Morgan felt the all-too-familiar feeling of dread settle in the pit of her stomach and knew the crime scene was going to be terrible. She reached up to the side of her head where the skull fracture she'd suffered had only just healed enough that she could be out on active duty. Ben didn't miss it, though, even though she had done it subconsciously, and he gently moved her to one side.

'I'll go. Morgan, why don't you get sorted and go fill the car up with petrol? As soon as Gilly arrives, I'll pass it on to her.'

Morgan nodded but knew fine well that he wouldn't, that he couldn't, and she didn't feel any anger about it.

She watched him walk down the path with Amber towards the house two doors down. Scotty was standing outside with a woman who was sitting on the low dividing wall almost bent double, her shoulders shaking. She went inside and closed the door.

Morgan knew she wasn't ready to deal with another shocking crime scene so soon. But she couldn't ignore it even if she wanted to, as she felt a sense of duty towards her neighbours that couldn't be shrugged off, and she owed it to whoever the victims were to give this her best and catch the killer because it was far too close to home.

Tugging on her boots she grabbed the house keys out of the dish on the narrow hall table and locked the door behind her, jogging to catch up to Ben who sensed her behind him before she had the chance to speak.

He looked at her and gave her a half smile. Then introduced himself to the woman.

Morgan guessed she was in her mid-thirties.

Scotty began to speak. 'This is Gina LoBue, friend of the couple who live here. She found them and rang it in. I can confirm that two occupants are Foxtrot.'

Ben asked, 'Are paramedics on the way?' Neither he nor Morgan had radio handsets with them so they had no idea what protocols had been put into place.

He nodded. 'Yeah, they are.'

Gina had black hair that looked as if it had been in a neat chignon when she'd left her house this morning. Now there were wisps of hair sticking to her cheeks where the tears and mascara trails had trapped them. She was wearing a pair of cut-off jeans and a stripy long sleeve T-shirt, and she had small gold hoops in her ears. Tattoos were peeking out from the cuffs of her top.

Morgan thought she looked classy. She glanced down at her own fishnet tights, underneath her ripped shorts and her vintage witch T-shirt. She'd ordered the shirt especially from a store in Salem, Massachusetts, that she was in love with called Nocturne. Minutes ago, when she'd got dressed, she had smiled at her reflection, happy to be able to dress the way she loved and now she felt seriously underdressed compared to Gina and a little envious of her hand tattoos: they were a definite no in the police. She needn't have worried – the woman didn't give her a second glance.

Gina stared up at Ben, tears still rolling down her cheeks. 'This can't be happening, it really can't.' Her voice was low and there was the faint hint of a US accent.

Ben was crouching in front of her. 'Gina, can you tell me what you found?'

She looked at the open doorway with Scotty standing there blocking the view into the hall.

'I was just about to fall asleep last night when Rosie messaged me to say she could hear noises from the attic. Matt was drunk and snoring again so I told her it was probably a rodent or a squirrel, and she should put some earplugs in and sleep on the couch.' She sucked in a long breath and then let out a sob. 'Some squirrel it was to do that to them.'

Ben patted her arm. Morgan recalled the names Matt and Rosie, and knew instantly who they were. She and Ben had attended a summer BBQ less than a month ago, and met both of them there. One of the neighbours had thrown a get-to-know-each-other sort of thing that Ben had dragged her to, saying they should make an effort to get to know their neighbours. Matt had been funny; his jokes had made the long hour they had spent there more bearable; Rosie hadn't really spoken much to them, as she had been in the corner with a couple of women laughing loudly and drinking Prosecco by the bottle. The fact that she knew them made this all the more horrific.

'What happened when you got here?'

'I know Rosie keeps a spare key under that plant pot.' She pointed to a pale green pot with a dried-up rosemary plant inside of it. 'I phoned her, messaged her but she didn't pick up, didn't read her messages so I got a bit worried because Rosie's phone is glued to her hand. I always tell her she's going to need surgery to remove it. We were going for coffee this morning; she never missed our coffee dates.'

Morgan wondered what it would be like to have a friend to regularly go out on coffee dates with, then remembered she did have regular coffee dates with her colleagues and that was enough.

The woman bent forward again, sobbing. 'I think I'm going to faint; I feel awful.'

Ben looked to Amber to sit with her. Amber looked as if she'd rather do anything but. She did though, sitting next to the woman on the wall and awkwardly patting her back.

Ben lowered his voice and asked Scotty, 'Have you got any protective stuff in the van?'

'Yes, boss. A great box of it that I refilled yesterday because you never know around here.' He was looking at Gina.

Ben spoke even quieter to Amber. 'I think it might be better to get Gina home or sit her in the van.'

Amber's eyes narrowed, and she looked so angry Morgan wondered if she might throw a punch in Ben's direction. Amber stood up, taking hold of Gina's elbow, and guided her towards the van, shaking her head in Ben's direction.

Scotty waited until they were both inside before he spoke. 'Boy, she gets angrier the more I work with her. I have no idea what her problem is. Look, Ben, it's bad, there's a lot of blood, one of them must have been killed downstairs and dragged back up to the bathroom because there's a trail of blood from the living room, up the stairs and along the upstairs hallway. There's something else you should know.'

'What?'

'Actually, it might be better for you to see for yourselves, I can't do it justice.'

Morgan was staring at him to see if he was joking, but this wasn't anything to joke about.

'Just warning you because I crapped myself when I walked in and saw them.'

'Thanks, appreciate that. Morgan, you can wait this one out if you want.'

She shook her head. Yes, it was her day off, yes, she didn't really want to see the bodies if they were as bad as Scotty had said, but she wouldn't let Ben go in on his own. If he was going to have to think about this crime scene for the rest of his life, then so was she.

THREE

A line of perspiration trickled down Morgan's neck as soon as she pulled up the zipper on the crinkly white crime-scene suit. It was the modern equivalent of one of those eighties' style sauna suits that her mum Sylvia used to wear back in the day when she was trying to lose weight, which was crazy because Sylvia never needed to lose weight in the first place. Suited and booted she let Ben go first, wondering why they hadn't left for Liverpool an hour ago. Then she thought about the long, leisurely way they had made love because it was their day off, and knew that she wouldn't have missed that for anything. How swift, in the blink of an eye life could change and it wasn't always for the best.

The bitter tang of copper lingered in the air inside of the Victorian semi which was the same as theirs. Ben paused to take in the slick trail of blood that led from the living room up the cream carpeted stairs, and Morgan's stomach clenched into a tight knot at the thought of what they were about to face. It would never leave them; those memories would be imprinted forever in their minds. Ben motioned to the room the trail came out of, and she followed him, both of them keeping close to the wall opposite the blood so as not to contaminate any forensics. There was a chalky, beige-coloured sofa and one of the cushions had a huge dark red splotch of blood soaked into it. Morgan scanned the room. There were blood splatters all over the coffee table glass and on the wall behind the sofa. She spied a single, luminous orange earplug on the floor and felt a rush of coldness spread over her so fast she shivered.

'She never heard them coming. She had earplugs in, so she wouldn't have heard anything.' She pointed to the earplug, and Ben looked visibly paler than he had before they entered the house. This house was painted in pastel, chalky colours, very tasteful and classy. The similarities between this house and theirs made Morgan feel sick. Theirs was painted in slightly bolder colours, but it could have been their house they were standing in and that thought terrified her.

Ben pointed to the staircase, and she followed his lead, again walking as far away from the trail of blood as possible. Morgan had her hands tucked into her pockets, so she didn't reach out and touch anything, a tip she had picked up from Ben what seemed like years ago. The carpet was thick. She imagined what it would be like to be dragged up here, blood spilling out of the back of her head like someone had turned on a tap because she knew all too well from experience how much head wounds bled. Had whoever it was been unconscious? She hoped they had been. As they reached the top step, they followed the trail of blood along the hallway to the large bathroom where the door was open and two pale, rigid bodies, still dressed in their blood-soaked pyjamas, lay on the floor.

'Jesus,' whispered Ben, and Morgan thought that Jesus had nothing to do with this. They didn't go into the bathroom, there was no need. As Scotty had quite rightly said, both of them were clearly Foxtrot, police speak for dead.

Morgan stared in horror at the sight before them. Both bodies had what Morgan assumed were fatal head injuries, judging by the pools of thick, dark, congealing blood surrounding them. She crouched down and could see the point of contact where whatever object had been used to smash them in the back of the head had landed. The wounds were not very big compared to the amount of blood. If she had to guess, she would say a hammer or something similar had caused the wounds. There was a male and female, and even without the blood that was pooling around them, the pallor of their skin was enough to tell her they were no longer alive.

Their arms were reaching out for each other. It was so out of place. Their bodies must have been staged like that. But that wasn't the worst of it. Matt's dark brown eyes had a cloudy film over them, and they were wide open and staring at his partner Rosie; but it was their mouths that was the worst bit, and Morgan shuddered as her gaze fell onto the lower parts of their faces, both of them had huge black nails through their lips, sealing them shut forever.

'Hello.'

Wendy's voice broke the trance that both of them were in. Neither of them had uttered a word in the last five minutes as they'd taken in the horrific scene in front of them, and Ben had jumped letting out a high-pitched, 'Ah.'

Wendy shook her head. 'Why am I not in the least bit surprised to find the pair of you here, contaminating my scene? And to add insult you're not even on duty. What? Are you guys desperate for some action that you're gatecrashing on your days off?'

They both stepped aside so Wendy could see the bodies, and she cupped a hand to her face without touching her mouth and groaned. 'What is this fresh hell?'

Morgan thought that hell was probably an apt description of the sight in front of them and of what the victims had endured.

'We live two doors away, and Amber knocked for us.' Ben was defending their actions.

Wendy who could not tear her gaze away from the bodies didn't even answer. She turned around and retraced her footsteps back down the stairs, leaving them staring at each other. Morgan peered after her.

'Do you think she's okay?'

'Are any of us okay after looking at this? No wonder their friend is in such a state, it's horrific. We should go see what the plan is, if the boss wants us to work this or let DS Mahaffy run with it.'

Morgan wasn't about to argue with him and turned to go back downstairs. She paused at the top of the stairs and pointed to the narrow opening. 'We need to check that out.'

'We do, why?'

'Gina said Rosie had messaged her to say she could hear noises in the attic.'

Ben squeezed his eyes shut as if trying to process the enormity of the crime scene without losing his shit. He nodded and lifted a finger to his lips then pointed downstairs. Morgan knew he was wondering if the local police had searched it themselves. Could the killer be inside? They returned to the front garden.

'No one's been up there,' Scotty confirmed. 'The scene is awful, isn't it?'

'Dreadful,' replied Morgan. 'Who is going to check out the attic?'

At this Scotty shrugged. 'Why?'

'Gina said Rosie heard noises coming from up there, so we need to check it out.'

'That is way beyond my pay scale. Where is task force?'

Ben looked around and shrugged. 'Has anyone called for them? We haven't got radios, so we don't know what's happening.'

An ambulance was slowly driving down the street towards

them. 'At least paramedics can call it.' Scotty sounded optimistic, and Morgan wanted to throttle him. No wonder Amber got so moody working with him on a regular basis. He was lazy and far too cheerful for his own good.

Ben held out his hand. 'Give me your radio.'

Scotty didn't hesitate and unclipped it from his body armour, passing it to him with a smile. 'You can keep it, then I don't have to work.'

'Cheers, you're on scene guard anyway. You won't need it. Where's the crime-scene logbook? You can make a start by signing me, Morgan and Wendy in and out.'

Scotty's face was a picture, and Morgan had to turn so he couldn't see the smile on her face.

'Oh, yeah. There should be one in the van, I'll go get it.'

He sauntered off towards the van with his hands tucked into his body armour, looking as if he didn't have a care in the world, and for a moment Morgan envied him. She doubted he went home and lay in bed thinking about the crimes he'd dealt with, the victims, the families. He was in his own little bubble, and it wasn't a bad place to be.

FOUR

Marc arrived with Cain and did a double-take to see Ben and Morgan standing in the front garden, suited and booted. He strode towards them. 'Erm, it's your days off. Why are you here?'

Ben pointed at Morgan, who pointed to Amber. 'Amber came knocking for us.'

'Why? The duty DS is on her way from Barrow.'

'We live a few doors down.'

He frowned. 'Oh, yes, you do. Well, what do you want to do? Work this or go back to whatever you were going to do? Because I'm going to be straight with you, I don't know if the boss will authorise overtime for you both. The budget is already blown way beyond any reasonable allowance. You might not get paid; would you rather not disappear now and salvage what's left of the morning?'

Morgan thought that disappearing would be quite a good idea and looked at Ben to see what he was thinking. He was staring down at their house, and she knew he couldn't ignore what was happening this close to their home. And she didn't think she could either. It would be playing on her mind all day, not even a browse around her beloved bookshops would blot it out completely.

'I'm happy to work it for time in lieu.'

Morgan knew this was the equivalent of saying for free because the likelihood of either of them ever getting to take all the time off in lieu they had accrued over the past year was practically zero. Marc turned to Morgan, and she nodded.

'Yeah, same here.' She blocked out the image of the coffee and donut she had been looking forward to at the huge Waterstones in Liverpool city centre, surrounded by books and nice people who also liked books and probably never dreamed of killing anyone and putting nails through their lips.

'Are you sure? You don't sound it.'

She smiled at Marc; he was more astute than she gave him credit for. 'Of course I am. It's not like we can switch off with this on our doorstep.'

'Welcome back to being on fully active duty, Morgan. May as well start as you mean to go on, eh?' He leaned closer to elbow her in the side, and she smiled at him. He was definitely thawing and getting more like them, a touch more relaxed and gaining a sense of humour that was an absolute must working in Rydal Falls CID, or at least he would be until he went back inside.

'Thanks, boss.'

He nodded. 'Plan of action then? Should I go in and take a peek?'

Ben looked around for Wendy and saw her hovering at the side of the CSI van, fiddling with her camera. 'Best wait until Wendy's been in first, and we need to get someone to check the attic out. It hasn't been searched. A witness claims one of the deceased complained about hearing noises up there last night.'

Marc nodded. 'No problem, task force is on the way. I already requested them. I'll wait for DS Mahaffy to arrive and brief her on the scene and her wasted journey.'

Ben didn't hear, he had already gone to speak to Wendy.

'Hey, are you okay?'

She looked up at him and nodded. 'I'm good, it was just a shock. I mean we deal with horrific deaths all the time, but I didn't expect that.'

'Me either, the nail through the lips is not something I've ever seen or heard of.'

'No, I have this phobia about mouth piercings.'

'You do?'

She shuddered. 'I do, I don't know how people have their lips or tongues pierced. It makes me cringe just thinking about the pain and catching it when you're eating. So to see something so brutal and out of place creeped me out a little bit, but I'm good now. I'm going to need help though with this one.'

Ben reached out and patted her shoulder. 'No worries, we'll get someone else travelling to give you a hand, but I need a task force officer to go in with you. We need to check the attic out and make sure it's clear. Morgan thinks the killer could be up there.'

She smiled at him, her eyes a little blurry with tears. 'Why does that not surprise me? Thanks, Ben, I think I'm getting soft in my old age.'

He laughed. 'You are definitely neither soft nor old, you're younger than me. How do you think I feel?'

This made her laugh. 'Do you ever question your career choice, like seriously?'

He lowered his voice. 'Almost every single day that I walk into the CID office and see all those younger people sitting at their desks who don't have aching knees or an addiction to coffee.'

'Yeah, me too, mate. Try working with Joe, I don't even know half of the stuff he's talking about most of the time. It's like he's speaking a different language.'

A van full of officers dressed in full tactical gear turned up, and Marc hurried over to brief them. Choosing one of them he pointed in the direction of where they were standing. They both smiled at him, and Wendy began walking towards the house.

Ben called after her, 'Do you want me to come inside with you as well? I promise to keep out of the way.'

'No, I bloody don't. You're a good guy, but you always get in the way. Thanks, though I appreciate the gesture and besides I have an armed babysitter now. I'm good.'

'Can you document it as speedy as possible so we can get someone to clear the attic, then you can take your time.'

'You don't ask for much, do you?'

Ben shrugged, and she turned to the officer standing behind her. 'Follow me, step where I step and do not touch a single thing.'

He nodded and with that she walked into the hallway, the bright flash of the camera illuminating her way and the armed officer following behind.

FIVE

Declan's white Audi pulled into the street followed by another white car, this one driven by a woman with cropped bleach-blonde hair, black eyeliner and bright red lipstick. Morgan knew she was going to like her before she even stepped out of the car, even though there was a look of confusion on her face, and she was staring directly at Morgan, one eyebrow slightly raised.

Cain had sauntered over to where she was standing. He said, 'Oh shit. Have you met her before?'

Morgan shook her head.

'She's going to be mad as hell that she's driven all this way to find you and Ben parading around like you own the place.'

'Really?' She looked up at his face to see if he was being serious, and he nodded.

'She's even tougher than you. I worked with her once and she scared the shit out of me.'

Morgan grinned at him. 'You're such a big softie underneath that huge exterior, Cain.'

'Am not, just don't know how to cope with you feisty women.'

The car door slammed shut, and Cain turned to hurry towards Al, the task force inspector, who was talking to Ben and Marc.

Morgan smiled at the woman and nodded appreciatively at her Doc Marten boots.

'Morning, I'm DS Gillian Mahaffy, the duty sergeant. Who's in charge here and what on earth is going on?'

'Good morning, ma'am, I'm DC Morgan Brookes.' Morgan reached out a hand to shake Gillian's, who took it and gave her a curt shake.

'Ah, *the* Morgan Brookes. It's a pleasure to meet you, how's your head?'

Morgan smiled. 'Thankfully a lot harder than it should be and on the mend.' The DS had a northern accent with a slight Northern Irish undertone, not that Morgan was an expert on them, but the soft lilt was there, a little like Declan's who got more pronounced the more excited he got.

'Good, that's very good.'

Morgan pointed to Ben. 'Ma'am, that's DS Matthews. We're here because we live a few doors down and the responding officer came knocking.'

'Gilly, please, I forget who people are talking to when they call me ma'am, it's so old-fashioned. So, why am I here then?'

'Ah, we're not technically on duty. It's our day off.'

Ben noticed the arrival of the DS and came striding over. 'Ben.' He shook her hand briefly too. 'Has Morgan updated you?'

'Gilly, and she was just about to; I was asking why I'm here.'

Marc came sauntering over and smiled at her. 'Good to see you again, Gillian. How are you keeping?'

'Inspector, I'd be great if I had a reason to be here, do you even need me?'

He shrugged. 'There's been a bit of a mix-up, we were just discussing who would be best to run with this case.'

Morgan noticed that the sergeant hadn't insist Marc called her Gilly, which made her realise she must have met him before and had yet to give him a reason to.

'I suppose it should be you as you're on duty and covering, but Ben and Morgan have both agreed they would work it if you're happy with that.'

Gilly looked at the scene and shrugged. 'I kind of feel I should, but it would make sense if you did because it's your area. I'm happy to do what you want, Ben.'

Morgan had to turn away to hide the smile that was threatening to break out across her face. Marc looked a little put out and strode away to talk to Declan who was approaching.

Ben nodded. 'I could do with your expertise; a second pair of eyes, maybe see what you think. I'm also happy to run with it if you're busy.'

She nodded. 'I'm happy to assist, let me get suited up.'

Gilly went back to the car to get dressed, and Morgan whispered, 'You don't need me then?'

Poor Ben looked horrified, and his expression showed it.

'I'm joking, I'll just wait around to see what needs to be done. It's only fair you give her a crack at it after driving all this way.'

Wendy came out of the front door followed by the armed officer. 'You're good to search the attic. I've documented everything. The attic opening is the opposite end to where the bodies are; so as long as you don't trample through the blood and ruin my forensics it's okay.'

The task force officer beckoned Al across. 'Boss, the attic hatch is tiny. None of us is getting up there even if we remove the body armour.' He looked around, studying every person on the front street that was there in a professional capacity then pointed to Morgan. 'She'll probably fit through the hatch.'

Ben began shaking his head, but Morgan smiled at him. 'I'm okay, happy to take a look.'

'No, you don't have a taser or anything.'

Al intervened. 'I'll have Tony here follow her up and be standing right behind her. If she sees anyone, we'll pull her straight out. If they won't give themselves up then we'll have to make the opening big enough to get through.'

Ben looked at Morgan his eyes pleading with her to say no, but she looked towards Al instead.

'Have you got a ladder?' She knew Ben had several in the garden shed, but purposely didn't ask him because he would have said no.

'Of course, we always come ready equipped for loft inspections.'

She didn't know if he was joking or not, but then the van doors slid open, and an officer began to manhandle a ladder out of it. She was impressed, seriously impressed.

'Come on, me, you and Tony will go in, so we don't cause too much damage. I'll hold the ladder, and Tony will be ready to take over if you need him.'

Before Ben could disagree, Morgan was sandwiched between both men and back inside the house that seemed to smell even worse than when they'd arrived, or was that her imagination? Al positioned the ladder under the hatch, and Tony passed her a torch.

'All you need to do is pop the hatch off, stick your head through and have a quick look around.'

Morgan lifted two fingers to touch the side of her head where her hair was stubbly and felt the rough scar to remind herself to be careful. Then, not seeing any point in hesitating, she began to climb the rungs. Using the palms of her gloved hands she pressed firmly against the wooden hatch until it moved, silently. She had expected it to groan or stick but it didn't. It was on hinges, and they must have been well oiled because it opened smoothly and silently. Standing on the top rung she felt her knees wobble a little. She didn't like heights, but she wasn't wimping out in front of these two. Pressing the switch on the torch, she hoisted herself up and leaned on her elbows, scanning the space. There was nobody up there or at least she couldn't see anyone. She listened for signs of movement. There was none and she pulled herself through the rest of the way.

'Hang on, Morgan.'

She heard Tony's heavy footsteps climbing the ladders behind her, and he stuck his head through the hole. She laughed at the sight of his floating head. There was no way he'd get through the hole, and she wondered who out of Rosie and Matt came up here. There were the usual stacks of cardboard boxes and plastic containers full of Christmas decorations that almost everyone stores in their attics. There was a pinprick of light coming up through the floorboards at the far end of the space, and she walked across to kneel down and look at it. She felt her heart skip a beat. The tiny hole looked down into the bathroom where she could quite clearly see the two bodies, and she let out a small screech.

'Everything okay?'

'Fine, fine, sorry. There are holes that look directly down at the bodies. I wonder if our killer was up here enjoying the view. Oh God.'

She stood up quickly, realising that she might have just totally fucked up any forensics, and bumped into a stack of boxes that quivered as she reached out her hands to steady them. She saw some cushions on the floor behind them, several empty water bottles, crisp packets and a piece of folded-up paper. Taking out her phone she photographed everything then picked up the paper carefully between her gloved fingers. Unfolding it she read the note several times to make sure she was reading it right.

IF YOU FOUND THIS
YOU ARE NEXT TO DIE

The paper slipped from her fingers and floated down to the floor where it landed next to her feet.

'Talk to me, Morgan, what's happening, what is that?'

Tony's voice was loud, so loud that it filled the space, and she turned to look at him.

'A death threat.'

Al's voice filtered up through the hatch. 'Morgan, get out of there; we'll get someone to go up and process the scene.'

She walked away from the note, backing up, too scared to turn her back on the attic space in case someone was still up here. When she reached the hatch, Tony moved back down to allow her to get through onto the ladders. She struggled to get back through the narrow opening because her entire body was shaking, terrified the moment she looked away someone would come at her with an axe and chop off her head. Then she felt strong hands grip her legs and guide them onto the step. She felt the safety of the metal underneath her boots and allowed herself to breathe out, not realising she'd been holding her breath since she read the note. When she was off the ladder, she found herself looking at Al's concerned face.

'Whoever killed them has been up there watching them, they left a note too.'

'Jesus, what did it say?'

She didn't need to focus; the words were burned into the back of her mind as if someone had written them with a soldering iron. 'If you found this you are next to die.'

'Seriously?'

She nodded, and the colour drained from his face.

'It's just an empty threat, Morgan, it doesn't mean anything. It might have been meant for the victims.'

She nodded again, struggling to find her voice. Ben was going to have a nervous breakdown over this, and she wished for once she hadn't volunteered to do the right thing.

SIX

Ben waited for Gilly to join him at the front door. Declan was waiting with him. Both men stooping towards each other, voices low at the horror of what had happened in this nice, mostly quiet, suburban street.

'You know what they say?'

Ben had no idea and shrugged; he wasn't even in the mood to give it his best guess. 'No, I don't.'

'Oh, you are extra grouchy this morning. Well, I'll put you out of your misery and save you guessing.'

'Please do and I'm not grouchy, it's our day off. We were supposed to be going to Liverpool, away from here and all the stress.'

'Ah, you are forgiven. I'd be angry too if I got dragged to work on my day off. Oh, well would you figure that one out, stupid me. It is my day off and yet here I am, again.'

Ben shrugged. 'Sorry, mate. Nothing to do with me this time.'

'For a change. Well, I'll continue, should I? Don't want to keep you in suspense. They say that too many cooks spoil the broth.'

Ben stared at him, his head shaking. 'Is that the best you have?'

Declan grinned, his shoulders giving a slight shrug. 'Yes, but it's early and why are there so many of you? What's Gilly doing here if you're here? I bet she's not too happy about that.'

'Gilly is getting paid and on shift, unlike you two losers.' She was standing behind them, had managed to walk up to them without them realising.

Both Ben and Declan laughed, and Declan nodded. 'That is true, you won't have to wait until next month to be rewarded for the fruits of your labours.'

Ben looked at him. 'Excuse the cheesy quote king, he's on one today.'

She smiled at them both. 'Declan, it's good to see you again even with those awful clichés rolling off your tongue.'

He laughed. 'You too, Gilly, it's been a while since I had the pleasure of your company. The good people of Barrow seem to be laying off killing each other for the time being. Unlike the people in Rydal Falls who can't keep their murderous hands off each other. You're doing a great job keeping them reined in, unlike someone I could mention.'

'Nah, they're just scared of me. Ben, you're far too nice.' She winked at them both, and Ben smiled. 'Are we ready?'

Declan and Gilly nodded, and they switched from light-hearted banter back to serious professionals in the blink of an eye. Ben didn't always agree with Declan's humour, but it was his coping mechanism for what he had to deal with on a daily basis, and if it helped him get through then there was no harm in it.

Morgan came out of the doorway, her complexion much paler than minutes ago. He knew then something had happened. Al and Tony followed her out, Al pausing to speak to him. He nodded at Gilly and Declan.

'Morning. Ben, there's a lot of evidence up in that attic.

Morgan found a peephole that looks directly into the bathroom. She said it's clear that someone has been up there watching them.'

'Jesus, that's terrifying. How did they get in and out?'

Al shrugged. 'I think Joe is going to be the best to send up there; he should fit through the hatch, and he can process the evidence.'

'Sounds reasonable.'

'There's one more thing.'

Ben thought, *isn't there always?* 'What?'

'There was a note, Morgan said it was a death threat.'

'To whom?'

'The people who lived there, I should imagine, but it said something like if you find this, you're next.'

Al nodded then walked in the direction of the van to wait with the rest of his team to be given the go-ahead to do a full search of the property, gardens and street. Ben felt the coffee he had downed before coming here churn in his stomach, the bitter taste in the back of his throat. It didn't mean that Morgan was next. Whoever had written that had no idea who was going to find it, it was just a coincidence that it had been her, but still that uneasy feeling of dread began to settle across his shoulder blades. To think someone had been hiding in one of their neighbours' attics. He glanced at Morgan who was chatting to Wendy. She wasn't looking in his direction.

Declan clasped his elbow. 'Are we ready, my friend?'

'Yes, of course.'

Ben led them into the house, his mind a whirlwind of questions. How did the killer get access to the attic without getting caught? How did they manage to spend hours up there when the victims were in the house? Why did they leave that note?

Declan's eyes fixated on the trail of blood, and Gilly muttered, 'Dear God, that's bad.'

Ben was kind of adjusting to the horror of it all, and he

nodded. That was the problem with this job, the things that no human had any right to witness, he saw on a regular basis. The awful stuff that should shock and tip most people over the edge didn't bother him anymore; his thoughts and feelings were sufficiently numbed so he could deal with the macabre. That was the whole reason he had fallen so hard for Morgan; she had woken up feelings inside of him that he no longer thought had existed. She had roused him out of the blackness that had taken over his life, had saved him in more ways than she could ever know and now, he was terrified of losing her. He couldn't live without her in his life and yet she too often found herself in situations where she was fighting for hers.

'Ben.'

Gilly's voice roused him from his thoughts. 'Yes?'

'Who was killed down here, do we know that?'

He stared at the mug of what looked like hot chocolate on the coffee table, a thick skin of milk across it. The disarray of blankets and pillows, the single earplug on the floor and the huge bloom of almost black blood stained into the cushion.

'We believe it was Rosie. She had messaged her friend to say Matt was snoring, she could hear noises in the attic, and she couldn't sleep.'

Gilly nodded, pointing to the earplug. 'Was she wearing those?'

He shrugged. 'Possibly.'

Declan shuddered. 'So, she didn't hear them approaching. This is like something out of a nineties' horror movie. I'm glad it's not Halloween or we'd be looking for a Michael Myers wannabe.'

Ben pointed upstairs. 'They're both in the bathroom. The bodies have been clearly staged, there is no doubt about that. I'm assuming Matt was killed in the bedroom, though we haven't even looked in there yet as Wendy was kind of angry at us that we were already here, but we had to check.'

He led them upstairs to the bathroom, standing to one side so Declan could examine the bodies, while Gilly stood on the other.

'Have you ever seen anything like this?' she asked him.

'Not quite like this, but unfortunately I've seen a lot more horrific crime scenes than I'd like.' His mind showed him a picture of the beautiful Cora Dalton's lifeless body – draped across the huge stone at Castlerigg Stone Circle, blood dripping down her slashed throat, surrounded by grazing sheep – and he had to blink hard to dislodge it, needing to chase that one away before it clouded his judgement of this scene.

She nodded at him. 'I'm going to be honest, I haven't. I've seen plenty of domestic arguments that have gone wrong and led to a partner being killed, lots of fatal drug overdoses, but murders like this, not one. I don't think I'm qualified to deal with it and do it justice, Ben.'

'There's only one way to get the experience though, Gilly.'

She shrugged. 'I'm happy to assist, that's not a problem, but I don't want to be the lead if it's okay with you. It seems point-less when I'd be covering it from Barrow and you're practically neighbours with the victims.'

He smiled at her. He didn't blame her: if he could let someone else run with this one, he would have been tempted, too. But ultimately, he knew that he owed it to Rosie and Matt. They had seemed like a nice couple when he'd met them last month. Both always waved or shouted hi when they passed in the street, and they had so much to look forward to in life, they should not be dead, murdered, and their bodies left like this for a loved one to discover.

SEVEN

Morgan was leaning against the side of the CSI van, still unable to process the thought of someone stalking Rosie and Matt in their own home.

'Morgan, is that you?'

She turned around to see Mrs Walker standing there, her slight frame pressing against the police tape, waving at her, and she groaned inwardly but walked towards her anyway. Mrs Walker lived in the house between Ben's and the victims'; she never missed anything that happened in the street, much to most people's annoyance.

'Morgan, what's going on?'

'There has been a double murder.' There was no point in trying to skirt around it, Mrs Walker would have the information soon enough and she might be a key witness. She usually knew everything that was going on in the street. The woman had the decency to look horrified.

'Are Rosie and Matt okay?'

'No, I'm sorry, unfortunately they are the victims.'

'Oh, no, no that's not right. It can't be, I'm supposed to be checking on the house today. They're going to Manchester.

Rosie asked if I could take any parcels in that might get thrown on the doorstep.'

Morgan had no idea they were so close. She hadn't known the couple well enough for them to ask her to keep an eye on their house. 'When did you last speak to Rosie?'

'Last night, she knocked on my door around eight. I know because *Coronation Street* had just finished.'

All the colour had drained from Mrs Walker's face and she looked much frailer than usual.

'Why don't you go home, and I'll come speak to you as soon as I can.'

She nodded, turned and walked back to her house without saying another word, which surprised Morgan. The woman's shoulders were stooped along with her head, and she thought that she must have been quite close to Rosie and was probably in shock. She wasn't needed at this moment in time, so she went to the van and stripped off all of her protective clothing, dropping it into a brown paper sack. Wendy took it from her and wrote her name on it in permanent marker.

'Where are you going?'

'To speak to that lady, she might have some information.'

And with that she ducked under the tape. It wasn't lost on Morgan that Rosie and Matt, too, had planned a day out of Rydal Falls. What were the chances of that? Two couples living near to each other, both wanting to go shopping, neither of them making it because two of them were dead and the other two were investigating their deaths.

She caught up with Mrs Walker as she was going back inside her house.

'Mrs Walker.'

She turned and stared at her. 'Yes, dear.'

'I thought I could make you a pot of tea and we could have a chat.'

'You did? Thank you. That's very thoughtful of you and yes, we could.'

'Can I come in?'

Mrs Walker nodded, and Morgan stepped inside the coolness of the airy hallway. It was so bright in here, the white walls and paintwork made it look sterile and it reminded her of the hospital. She followed her down to the kitchen, where Mrs Walker had a small pine table with two chairs. It was strange looking at Mrs Walker's kitchen, the same layout as Ben's only it was very eighties with bright orange pine cabinets and a white marble worktop. His was very noughties with lemon cupboards that she kept threatening to paint black.

'Should I make the tea?'

Mrs Walker shook her head. 'I can't abide the stuff; I'd rather have coffee. There's a bag of ground coffee and a cafetière in the cupboard; mugs are there too.'

Morgan smiled to herself; she would never have thought that Mrs Walker didn't drink tea. She had imagined that she sat in her bay window all day long, with her mug of tea, watching everybody going in and out and she felt bad for judging the woman so harshly when she didn't even know her. Boiling the kettle, she put the ground coffee into the cafetière and took two mugs from the cupboard. Then taking the milk out of the fridge she poured a little in each mug, then put them all on the table. Mrs Walker smiled at her, though her cheeks glistened with fresh tears.

'This is nice, thank you. I wish we had been able to do this before—' She didn't finish her sentence; her voice had caught in the back of her throat.

'I work really long days and evenings; I don't get many days off. In fact, today is my day off and—' It was her turn to stop talking. She didn't want to sound as if she was whining about their neighbours being murdered.

'I know you do, both you and Ben are rarely at home, and I do worry about you both. I read the newspapers and see how hard you work, all the horrible people you deal with. How's your head now? I saw him bring you home from the hospital that day with a dressing on it and I felt so bad for you. I know everyone thinks I'm a nosey old bat, and I am. I'm not going to lie, but it's because I care about you all. I don't even know most of the neighbours other than to say hello to, but I like to make sure everyone is safe, their cars and houses are safe... and I feel terrible because out of everyone in this street Rosie and Matt were the only two to really give me the time of day, and I've let them down so much because —' She swallowed the lump in her throat and shook her head.

'You have no reason to blame yourself for anything, Mrs Walker. This is not on you, it's on the sick individual who did this to them.'

'Annie, my first name is Annie.'

Morgan smiled at her, then pushed the plunger down slowly in the pot of coffee, pouring the smooth, heavenly smelling liquid into the two mugs, passing one to Annie.

'You might be able to help me though.'

'How?'

'I need as much information about Rosie and Matt as you can give to me.'

Annie took a sip of her coffee and nodded appreciatively. 'You made that just right.'

'I'm a coffee addict.'

Annie laughed. 'Me too. I wouldn't expect anything less the stress you must be under with your job. How do you do it? How do you go into horrible crime scenes and be able to sleep at night?'

Morgan shrugged. 'I don't know, I just do. Someone has to do it, and I feel privileged that I am able to be a voice for the victims who in no way deserved what happened to them. I guess I sleep when the bad guys are safely locked up and behind bars. Until that happens, then coffee is my best friend and saviour rolled into one.'

Annie smiled at her. 'Bless you. Well, this is what I know about Rosie and Matt. Rosie is a teaching assistant at Priory Grove, and Matt is an independent mortgage advisor; he works from home a lot. He goes out for a run three times a week usually around six, and no, I'm not in the window watching everyone at that awful hour, Rosie told me. It's Rosie who I get on with, we both hit it off, which was nice. The day they moved in she saw me looking out of the window and came to introduce herself. She is so pretty, so lovely, kind, helpful, sweet and even more of a dreadful gossip than I am.'

She laughed, and Morgan smiled. 'She sounds fun.'

Annie nodded. 'She is, was. Oh my, it's really hard to speak of her in the past tense.' This time the tears flowed, and she didn't try to stop them.

Morgan sipped her coffee to give her a moment.

Annie stood up and tore off a couple of sheets of kitchen roll to blow her nose with. 'It's the shock, you know.'

Morgan nodded. She reached out and patted the woman's hand, she did know, all too well.

'Did Rosie ever mention hearing noises from the attic?'

Annie nodded with a movement so sharp Morgan heard a bone in her neck crack, and she cringed. 'Yes, yes, she did. She said Matt couldn't fit up there so she went up there last week but couldn't see anything. I told her maybe a bird had got in. Every year without fail I get two little sparrows who go into the attic through a loose slate. They nest up there and then the eggs hatch. What a racket they make but they have been doing it for years, and even when I had the roof fixed, I told the builder to leave that one alone. I didn't have the heart to block it up, as it's quite amazing to see them flying in and out. So, I told her it was probably something like that, up in the eaves.'

Morgan didn't want to tell Annie what she had found, that wasn't public knowledge.

'Have you heard anything in your attic lately?'

She shook her head. 'No, they've been and gone, the birds won't be back until next year now.'

'Do you ever go up there, Annie?'

'I have no need to, love, all that's up in my attic are boxes of painful memories and probably a lot of feathers and bird crap.'

She smiled at her, wondering what Annie's life had been like. She wasn't that old, maybe in her late sixties. 'What about Rosie's and Matt's families, do you know them or where they live?'

'I don't, Rosie's parents live away, no idea where and as far as I know Matt's mum died a few years ago, so it's just his dad and he works away a lot. I think he's a contractor for BAE Systems.'

'Don't worry, we'll find them.'

'And give them the worst news of their lives.'

Morgan nodded. 'Yes, no doubt about that and it never gets any easier, knowing that you're about to ruin someone's life that way. What about friends or visitors, did you notice anyone going to their house lately?'

'Only woman I ever see there is the friend Gina, she's from the States,' Rosie said. 'I've been neglecting my duties lately and haven't been watching as much. I started reading again and have been so lost in the world of Detective Josie Quinn I might not have noticed if they had.'

Morgan agreed. 'Reading is great, I can't get enough of it. I love Lisa Regan's books; she's so brilliant. Just a thought, but can I check your attic, Annie?'

'If you want to, love, but I don't know what you're hoping to find up there. Help yourself, I have one of those pull-down ladders, there's a hook thing propped up in the corner next to the wardrobe.'

Morgan went upstairs, turning on the lights as she did, and stared at the hatch. *What are you doing, Morgan, there's nobody up there,* she whispered to herself, but she had to check. She had this irrational fear that maybe whoever had been hiding in Rosie's attic might have access to the others somehow and, if they did, what did that mean for her and Ben? What if someone had been in their attic space, watching them whilst they showered? A full-blown body shudder ran down the length of her spine. She grabbed the pole and hooked it into the catch on the attic door, stepping to one side to let the ladders slide down. Her mouth was dry and yet the palms of her hands were slick with sweat, and her heart was hammering against her ribcage. She stared up into the blackness of the hole.

'Morgan.'

Cain's voice called to her from the bottom of the stairs, and she almost collapsed to her knees with shock.

'Upstairs.'

His pounding footsteps were like music to her ears.

'What are you doing? Ben's having a shit fit out there, he sent everyone looking for you.'

'Why?'

'I wonder, let me see.' He pressed a finger against his lips. 'Hmn, who is it who regularly gets into scraps with violent killers?' He spoke into the radio he was holding. 'Found her, in next door.'

She looked at the fading yellow bruises around both of his eyes where he'd got a broken nose only a couple of weeks ago.

'Says you?'

'Yeah, but you really get into it with them, mine was a case of mistaken identity.' He pointed to the attic. 'Why?'

'We need to check that the attics aren't connected to each other. Remember those houses that were, the other year, and the killer fled through the one next door?'

'I do, I suppose it's a valid point.'

'Well, seeing as how you're here now, you can go up and take a look.' She gave him her sweetest smile.

'Nah, I don't think so.'

'I did the one next door.'

'Yeah, with two armed guards behind you. You want to send me up there all on my own with you for backup? Besides, I'm claustrophobic, I hate attics.'

'Sometimes I think you're such a wimp, Cain Robson.'

She began to climb the ladders, ignoring her racing heart and the fact that her palms were so slick with sweat it was hard to grip the metal rungs. When she reached the top, she stood up and tugged on the cord. A single bulb lit up the space which was full of dust, boxes, bird crap and feathers. There were no fresh trails or footprints in the dust, and only half of the floor had been boarded out. She couldn't see any way that the killer could get from one attic to the other and felt the breath she'd been holding whoosh out of her mouth.

EIGHT

Task force had been left guarding the crime scene and the cordoned-off street whilst Wendy, Joe and the crime scene manager from headquarters processed it. Morgan had run inside their house to change out of her shorts and grab her jacket, stopping to feed Kevin a quick pouch of food. She knew he would lick the jelly off and leave the rest, preferring his luxury cat feeder full of biscuits and Dreamies. Ben slipped the treats in there when he thought she wasn't looking, which amused her no end because he had been the one to say he never wanted a pet, or Kevin, who they had technically adopted after Des's murder when no one else could take him. His white cat hairs drove her insane because her wardrobe consisted of all black clothes, but he was worth the pain. He was so happy doing his own thing and was more judgemental of them both than their parents had ever been. Morgan was sure he rolled his eyes at them especially the time Ben had brought her home from the hospital after her head injury. He had watched them from the third step up with a look of pure disgust at the state of her. He came to rub himself against her legs, and she gave him a quick scratch behind the ears.

'Sorry, it's going to be chaos again and you're going to be on your own for a while.' He began to purr loudly, and she laughed. 'I honestly think you prefer having the house to yourself, cat, don't miss me too much.'

When she got in the car Ben pointed to the hairs stuck to her black leggings. 'Kevin give you a hard time again?'

She laughed but leaned forward to brush them off. 'Kevin is ecstatic he has the house to himself; we couldn't have ended up with a better pet if we'd chosen it ourselves.'

'Cats, they're the total opposite of dogs; I love dogs though.'

She turned to him. 'You do? You said you didn't like pets.'

'I don't have the time for pets is more the problem.'

'I can see you walking a dog when you're retired. Can we get one like Caesar?'

'I'm terrified of him, he's like a devil dog. He actually scares the shit out of me. He's all muscle, more than I am, and almost as big as me. I'm more of a golden retriever kind of guy, just so you know.'

Morgan grinned at him. 'You are?'

'For sure, so you know if you get any ideas in the future about getting a puppy or anything. I like gentle, non-human-eating dogs.'

She snorted with laughter that was short-lived when she caught a glimpse in the wing mirror of the crime scene behind her, bringing her back down to reality with a huge bump.

'Ben, this is bad.'

He nodded. 'It is.'

'Does it not bother you how close to our house it was?'

'Yes, very much. Which is why we're on the way to a briefing at the station instead of Liverpool. What did nosey Nellie have to say about it?'

'Mrs Walker is called Annie, and I feel bad for her.'

'Why?'

'She's lonely, she's really very nice to talk to and she was very good friends with Rosie. She's devastated and feels bad she missed whatever happened.'

'Ah, you have a soft spot for her. You're a right softie when it comes to older people, Morgan, I would never have thought that.'

She glanced at him. 'Exactly.'

'Ouch, that's mean. I'm not that much older than you.'

She laughed. 'You said it and no, I'm not, I have a lot of respect for older people. I think we're too quick to judge them. Look at us, we always avoid her because she's watching out of her window, but she's just lonely and thinks she's helping.'

'Okay, point taken. Did she have anything useful to say?'

'Not really, I checked her attic and it's not been used recently.'

'I can tell you for certain there is no access through ours to our neighbours'. I made sure of that when I bought it years ago.'

'Good.'

'See, older and wiser.'

'Hahaha, you can drop the older stuff now.'

The station loomed into view and Ben pulled close to the entry point so Morgan could swipe her card against it. He drove through the gates before they'd had chance to even open halfway, they were so slow. They walked into the station and Morgan let out a huge yawn. She was tired. What had started out as a very pleasurable morning had soon turned into one of huge stress.

Madds came striding out of the duty sergeant's office, took one look at them and shook his head.

'You two are like grim reapers in reverse. Is this your hobby? Do you purposely go looking for dead people?'

'You can blame Amber; your staff are the ones responsible for us being here.'

'Why?'

Morgan wasn't going to get into it with him, but Ben was

happy to. 'She came knocking for us when she found the bodies.'

Madds swore under his breath and shook his head. 'Right, well, sorry about that. I'll have a word with her; she shouldn't have.'

'It's fine, we couldn't exactly ignore it.'

'Are you still complaining, Madds?'

All three of them turned to see Gilly striding towards them. She nodded in Madds's direction. 'Never changes, do you? How are you, Paul?'

He said, 'Not bad, Gilly, yourself?'

She shrugged. 'Not sure, but I'll find out one way or the other pretty soon. So, where's the briefing?'

'Blue room.' Three voices echoed in unison, and she laughed.

'Ah, the pink room that hasn't been blue for how many years? Eight, nine.'

'That's the one, same old. You know how nicknames stick in this place,' replied Ben.

She nodded. 'Well, someone point me in the direction of a half-decent cup of coffee and then I'll meet you up there.'

Morgan smiled. 'I'll make the coffee and bring it in, how do you like it?'

'Strong, dark, like my men.'

Morgan laughed, heading upstairs to go and make a round of drinks, leaving Ben with Gilly. She walked into the office to see Amy staring out of the window. She had startled when Morgan had walked in, and she was sure she had been crying judging by her red, puffy eyes.

'Morning, are you okay?'

Amy nodded. 'I'm fine, hay fever.'

Morgan didn't say anything else; she knew – or as far as she knew – that Amy didn't suffer from hay fever and never had because she had never complained about it or taken antihistamines once whilst they were in work.

'What are you doing here anyway?'

'We live a couple of doors away from the victims.'

'Jesus, yes, you do. I didn't realise it was that close to your house. Oh that's bad, did you know them well?'

'Not really, we only met them properly about a month ago. Just kind of waved and smiled at each other in passing.'

'Still, that must have been a shock for you.' Amy had blown her nose several times and dabbed at her eyes before turning to look at Morgan.

'Yes, it was, still is to be honest. Amber came to get us when she realised the duty DS was in Barrow.'

'Bloody hell, that was good of her. Did you not tell her to bugger off; it's your days off?'

'I couldn't, I'm too nosey for my own good and I needed to know what had happened anyway. There's a briefing anytime, I'm brewing up, want a coffee?'

Amy mimed puking. 'No, can't stand the stuff anymore, it makes me feel sick, which is a right pain because how am I supposed to put up with Cain and the rest of you with no caffeine in my system?'

Morgan smiled at her. 'Oh no, that's pants.'

'Yeah, it is. All I want to drink is full-fat Coke and I don't think it's good for the baby, you know, all that sugar. It might come out with an addiction to fizzy pop.'

'What about cordial or water?'

'Could you survive working in here off water?'

'Absolutely not, point taken. Decaf?'

'Jesus, that's even worse. I've got a can of pop. I'm trying to limit myself to two a day so I'm good, but thanks.' Amy stood up. She had the slightest bump that was barely visible, and Morgan thought was so cute.

'Stop staring.'

'I'm not, I just think it's amazing.'

Amy rolled her eyes. 'Yeah, well you better not get pregnant just yet because the whole world will fall to bits if you're not out there chasing psychos.'

Morgan knew Amy was joking but she didn't laugh. Chasing psychos was beginning to wear her down more than any of them knew.

———

Morgan had a tray with mugs of coffee balanced on it, a bowl of sugar and the milk carton out of the fridge that she'd sniffed a couple of times to make sure it was drinkable. It felt as if she was the only one who gave a shit about fresh milk in this place; the others were quite happy to drink it when it was on the turn with flakes of milk swirling around in their mugs like a snow-storm. She placed it on the table and pointed. 'Help yourselves.'

They did. Gilly was first to grab a mug, and Ben, Cain and Al followed. Ben had an evidence bag on the desk in front of him, and she felt a cold chill when she realised it was the note from the attic. When everyone had mugs in front of them, he held it up, waving it in the air.

'Anyone want to tell me what this means or why it was put there?'

Gilly held out her hand and took it from him. 'Oh, crap this isn't good.'

She passed it to Cain who looked at it, then straight at Morgan, Al took it next and stared at it before passing it to Marc, who had walked in looking flustered with his own mug of coffee. He looked at the tray, pointed to his mug and winked at Morgan which made her snort with laughter. He was definitely thawing, there was no doubt about it, he was losing his edgy city attitude and she was beginning to think he might just be okay.

'What's in the bag, pass the parcel?'

Ben looked so shocked that the boss had cracked a joke, he had to sit down and take a moment. 'I wish it was, sir, it's the note Morgan found up in the attic of the victims' house.'

Marc took it from Al and studied it then gave it back to Ben. 'That, my friends, is in my opinion quite worrying.'

Everyone looked in his direction, Ben nodded. 'I think we are all of the same opinion. Who do you think it's aimed at?'

'Clearly the occupants of the house, it was in their attic. I don't see how it could be aimed at anyone else.'

Morgan didn't agree, and she shook her head. 'I think the killer left it there for whoever discovered the bodies.'

'Who discovered them, wasn't it the friend?'

She nodded. 'Yes, but she didn't go up in the attic, did she? So she didn't find the note, just her friends who were very dead.'

'What do we know about the friend? Is she on the level? Are we thinking she could be connected? Or do we need to be putting a guard on her?'

Morgan thought about Gina, how she had looked devastated. She didn't look like the kind of person to kill her friends in such a violent way. She wasn't very tall and didn't look strong enough; how could she have dragged them into the bathroom? There wasn't a bit of blood on her either, not that she couldn't have gone home and changed, but she didn't see Gina being responsible for this.

Ben beat her to it. 'We will get a full statement from her, of course, but she's not hitting my radar as a suspect at the moment.'

Marc shrugged. 'I saw her, me either, but you know. Can't rule someone out just because they're a bit good-looking.'

Cain arched an eyebrow at Marc, and Morgan had to cup a hand over her mouth again. Why was she acting so childish? She shook her head at Cain and turned to look at Ben before he worked out they were being stupid and disrespectful. Gilly ignored them all and looked up from the notebook she was writing in.

'The note is disturbing; we need to clarify who it was meant for. Can we ask Gina if she ever went into the attic, had any reason to? I think we should check that it wasn't meant for her to find because if it was, she could be the next target.'

Ben nodded, and Gilly continued. 'I also think we need to concentrate on the possibility of the note being left for the police. The killer knew that the house would get searched. It was inevitable once the bodies were discovered. I hate to say this, but you and Morgan live a couple of doors away, so do you think the killer targeted Rosie and Matt because of the proximity to your address? Morgan, you have had your fair share of run-ins with violent criminals, and it's possible they saw this as a direct challenge. I don't think we should be ignoring this and there should be somebody keeping an eye on your house. Do you have precautions against anyone getting inside of the house? You both work long hours, and you're going to be working even longer ones, maybe the killer knew this, and it was all a decoy to get you both out of your own home so they could do the same again.'

Now all eyes were on Gilly, and she shrugged. 'Sorry, it has to be mentioned. We can't ignore it. It's a big coincidence and I don't like them one little bit.'

'Bollocks,' was Ben's reply. He was staring at Morgan, and she wanted to stand up and walk out, pretend that none of this was happening and start their day again. She didn't, instead she shrugged.

'We have a burglar alarm and a Ring doorbell, cameras out the back, and the house is secure. There is no way in unless anyone has a key and the code. Annoyingly, I went through the footage and there's nothing that can help us with the case. But it rules out any tampering with our own attic.'

Gilly leaned forward. 'Does anyone have a key and the code?'

Ben shook his head. 'Just me and Morgan. Thanks for your concern, Gilly, I appreciate it, but I don't think the person who did this did it to scare me and Morgan or to target us.'

'I hope not, I'm just stating the obvious. I want you both to be aware of the possibilities regarding your safety. I wouldn't sleep if I hadn't brought it to your attention.'

Marc was watching Gilly intently. 'Yes, well thanks for that. Point taken, I'm sure they'll both up their observations when going in and out of the house. Any prints, forensics that have come to light?'

Ben pointed to the smartboard behind him and a close-up of the mouths of the victims. 'Nothing from the mattress or any debris in the attic. CSI are still working the scene, but up to now nothing outstanding. We need to find out where the nails came from. If we could trace those, we might be able to pick up CCTV footage of the person buying them. Whoever did it must have a stomach of steel to be able to hammer them through. Which brings me to the murder weapon, did they smash the back of their heads in with a hammer then use it for the nails, we need to locate that asap.'

Morgan said, 'I don't think they'd have needed to use a hammer. It kind of looks like a piercing. If they were dead, the killer was probably able to pull the top lip out and push the nail through.'

The colour drained from Cain's face, and he squeezed his eyes shut for a moment. She carried on. 'In fact, someone who does body piercing could do that without blinking, and they would have the clamps too, to pull the lips out whilst they did it.'

Ben wrote *body piercer* down in his notebook. 'Do we have any body piercers in Rydal Falls?'

Morgan shook her head. 'Kendal, used to be one in Bowness

but I'm not sure if they're still there. It's been a while since I went there.'

Marc looked her up and down. 'What have you had pierced?'

She was tempted to say her nipples, but Ben would kill her, and the thought made her squirm. 'My tragus, my ears, belly button, but I took that out before I joined the job.'

'Tragus, what's that?'

She pointed to the tiny diamanté stud in the middle of her ear.

'Oh, thank God for that. I was thinking you were going to point to some female body part I'd never heard of.'

Cain's shoulders were shaking next to her, and she knew he was on dangerous ground, one step away from a fully blown, highly inappropriate burst of laughter. She didn't look his way.

'We should see if Rosie or Matt had any piercings; it's worth looking in to. I wonder how easy it is to pierce cleanly,' Morgan said, picking up the photos of Rosie's face. 'Can you learn how to pierce on the internet? Can you buy all the equipment online?'

'Ben, add that to your list.' Marc couldn't tear his gaze from Gilly, who he noticed had lots of piercings in her ears.

'Already have, boss, patrols have gone to inform next of kin. So, that's in the process of being taken care of. We also need to find out who their friends are, speak to work colleagues and get as much information about Rosie and Matt as possible. Morgan interviewed the only neighbour who seems to know them well. Nothing suspicious to report. Me and Morgan will attend the post-mortems, but that is going to take up a considerable amount of time unless someone else volunteers and we do one PM each. Any offers?' Ben's eyes scanned the room. There was only really Gilly and Cain, maybe Marc if he could spare the time.

Gilly nodded. 'I'll do one.'

'Thank you, would you like one of my staff to come with you?'

'Not a problem, have you got anyone you can spare? When are we releasing the bodies?'

'No. It's going to be some time yet before we can release them. The pathologist has said he'll clear the schedule for first thing tomorrow morning, so if you want to get to the mortuary around eight thirty – and, Cain, are you free tomorrow?'

'Not really, boss, can Amy not do it? She's stuck in the office. It will give her a chance to get out for a bit.'

Ben shrugged. 'She's pregnant, Cain, is that wise?'

'Exactly, she's not ill. She's tougher than she looks, I'll tell her.'

Morgan looked at him. 'Yeah, make sure you tell her you volunteered her as well.'

Gilly was smiling to herself. 'Will do, I'll report back to you. Do you need me for anything else today, it seems as if you have it covered?'

'No, thank you. I appreciate your help and input, Gilly.'

She nodded and stood up. 'I'll see you tomorrow.' Then placed her empty mug on the tray, and walking out she didn't look back, and Morgan wished she was walking out with her.

NINE

Morgan followed Cain into the office wanting to make sure he told Amy he had volunteered her to attend the post-mortem with Gilly tomorrow, but she wasn't there.

'Must be in the loo, she's never out of the bathroom.'

'How would you know that, Cain?'

'Because she's staying at mine for a bit. Her and Jack have called it a day and she didn't want to stay in the flat, so I said she was welcome at mine.'

Morgan smiled at him. 'You are full of surprises today; bless her, I didn't realise things were that bad between them.'

'Yep, some men are arseholes. I've never liked him.'

Amy walked in. 'Never liked who?'

Morgan felt her cheeks begin to burn and looked away. Cain pointed to a torn, tattered picture of one of their regular master criminals whose speciality was stealing from sheds and outhouses. 'Him, bloody Adam Dickson.'

'He's in prison.'

'I know, I still don't like him.'

Amy looked at Morgan and rolled her eyes in Cain's direction, making her smile.

'Cain has something to tell you.'

Amy sat down and stared at Cain, narrowing her eyes. 'What have you done now?'

'Nothing, always ready with the accusations, Amy. I just made a little suggestion in the briefing, that's all.'

'About what?'

'That you might be fed up with being stuck in this office and appreciate a bit of a change of scenery.'

'I am but tell me you didn't volunteer me for a post-mortem, because that's not the kind of change I'm after.' Amy was glaring at him, and Cain's cheeks flushed even redder than Morgan's.

'I might have.'

'Piss off, Cain, I can't stomach coffee, I've gone off my favourite takeaways and you think I can stand at a post-mortem for four hours with no caffeine in my system without puking.'

Amy looked at Morgan. 'Is he for real, or am I hallucinating?'

'It's okay, Amy, I'll do it.' Morgan didn't know if Ben could spare her for almost an entire shift, but she was willing to do it.

'I don't expect you to, Morgan. Why can't you do it, Cain?'

'I'm on a late shift and I was planning to take Angela shopping.'

'Tell me I'm dreaming, Morgan, and that he isn't a walking death wish.'

'Sadly, you are not dreaming.'

Cain lowered his gaze. 'I wanted to buy her a ring.'

Amy tilted her head. 'Buy her one next week or after the post-mortem.'

'We have an appointment at Fulton's in Keswick.'

Amy crossed her arms. 'And?'

'It's for a special ring.'

'Oh, wow. Are you getting engaged, Cain?' asked Morgan.

He nodded. 'I wanted to surprise her, they're getting champagne and everything for us.'

Amy's gaze softened. 'You're mad, Cain, but that's kind of sweet too. You're forgiven, this job takes up all our time and ruins most special days. I'll do it this once. Congratulations.'

'I didn't want to tell anyone in case she said no.'

Morgan hugged him. 'Why would she say no? You're a nice guy, a bit of a pain but you have a good heart.'

He hugged her back and she relished being in his arms, the warmth of them soothing her already tired soul.

'Jesus, put her down. You can't keep your hands off her.' Ben was laughing as he walked straight past them into his office and shut the door before anyone could stop him.

Cain let her go.

'Well, I'll see what she says tomorrow. It's not like we have to get married. I just wanted her to know how madly in love with her I am.'

Amy mimed being sick then held up her hands. 'Enough, I'll go to the post-mortem if you shut up now.'

A loud knock on the glass came from Ben's office, and Morgan saw him peering through the blinds at the three of them, beckoning her with his finger.

Cain whispered, 'You're being summoned.' And she smiled at him.

She walked in, moved a stack of files off the vacant chair and sat down. 'It's all going on out there.'

'I don't want to know, those two can bicker all they want. Can Amy do the post-mortem?'

'Yes, she said she would.'

'Oh, great. That's something ticked off the list. I'm going back to the scene; do you want to come? I feel as if we're missing something, and then I want to go and talk to Gina, now she's had time to process what's happened. Actually, we'll go there first.'

'Fine by me.'

He smiled at her. 'I think Marc was wanting to go speak to Gina so let's slip out before he realises. Twice now he's mentioned she's attractive. I don't want him getting himself all worked up and in trouble. You know how hot-headed he can be. He's just starting to fit in and I'd hate for him to do something unprofessional and get moved out of the department.'

'I agree, I was thinking earlier how he's mellowed a lot. I guess we've worn him down and turned him to our way of working.'

'It took long enough.' Ben winked at her, his blue eyes crinkling at the corners, and she felt a rush of love for him so intense she wondered if they could make it through all of this and come out unscathed. Had Rosie looked at Matt that way? What plans for the future did they have? Her heart hurt just thinking about all the lost opportunities that had been ripped away from them. Would they have had children, grandchildren? Would she and Ben ever have them? She didn't want to at the moment, but she knew Ben would like them.

'Anyway, if we get that ticked off at least it's done.'

She nodded, hadn't realised he'd still been talking to her, and she hoped he hadn't noticed she wasn't paying attention.

'It's so sad.'

Ben nodded. 'It is. It's scary to think they weren't that far away from us; I want to find who did this like an hour ago.'

'Me too, to be honest. Ben, do you think it's a coincidence they lived so near, were our neighbours?'

He didn't answer and she understood that he couldn't, because as much as they would like to believe it had nothing to do with them or her, that seed of thought was planted in their minds and if they didn't stop it soon it was going to grow bigger and stronger. What meaning did the posing of the bodies have, was it something only the killer could understand or was this a message too? What creeped her out the most was the thought that this was so personal. It had to be someone who knew Matt and Rosie. What kind of person could do this?

TEN

Gina lived in an apartment in a newly converted mansion house that overlooked Lake Windermere. It was on the outskirts of Bowness, and the landscaped formal gardens looked like something out of the Chelsea Flower Show.

'Nice.' Ben was looking around as she drove down the long driveway to get to the house. 'I wonder what Gina does for a living?'

Morgan sighed. 'Whatever it is, we're in the wrong job, this is beautiful.'

Ben's hand softly patted her knee. 'We could probably afford something like this if we sold the house and got a joint mortgage. Would you like to live here?'

Morgan followed where Ben was looking. 'I would, but you never know who your neighbours are going to be and I don't think they'd appreciate the hours we keep and the drama. Besides, I love your house, it's beautiful.'

'*Our* house and I guess we would struggle to fit in. They wouldn't want the drama that's associated with being our neighbours.' He winked at her, and she laughed.

'You're so sweet though, thank you. It's nice to dream, but I wouldn't expect you to sell your home and get into more debt just because of these beautiful gardens, the breathtaking view of the lake and the stunning house.'

'We could stroll around these gardens and have picnics by the shore. Kevin would be in his element.'

'Now who's the one fantasising? The reality is we'd never actually do any of that because we're always so busy working.'

'Spoil sport.' But Ben was laughing.

'Maybe one day when we decide to pursue a calmer way of life instead of deranged killers.'

He squeezed her knee. 'One day, it's a promise.'

He parked next to a brand-new Aston Martin and sighed. 'Look at that car.'

'I'd rather look at you.'

He leaned across, pressing his lips against hers briefly then pulled away. 'Come on, let's pretend we're looking at the apartments if anyone asks.'

Morgan laughed, slamming the door shut of the white Ford Focus hire car. 'What? in this car? Dream on, poor boy.'

The granite steps leading up to the arched Gothic front door had been restored, all the years of grime removed. Morgan had seen the before photos of the mansion, had driven past it enough times and admired it from afar. It was beautiful before even, when it was in a state of disrepair; in fact she loved it more when it had looked unloved. The door opened into a huge entrance hall, where low-hanging cut-glass chandeliers lit it up as sunlight caught the crystal teardrops and hundreds of tiny rainbows filled up the space. She whispered, 'Wow.' There was a curved grand staircase that was the focal point of the hallway, and she imagined how beautiful it would be to walk down those stairs in a ballgown or a wedding dress, then she looked at the carved wooden spindles and thought how sturdy they were, how they could easily hold the weight of a body as it hung from them, and she shuddered. She knew how that felt, had almost died that way when she'd been hanged from the staircase in her old apartment.

'Which apartment is Gina's?' Ben's voice echoed around the space, and he whispered, 'Blimey, it's like a cave.'

There was a row of postal boxes on one wall underneath a huge sideboard. 'Six people live in this.' She stepped closer. Gina's was on the top row. 'She lives in number six.' There was a lift a little further along. Ben pointed to the boxes. 'One to three are downstairs. Do you want to ride up in style?'

Morgan shook her head. 'No, I want to walk up those stairs and pretend I'm Scarlett O'Hara.'

He smirked at her. 'Why, ma'am, you would need a huge, hooped dress and a pair of dainty shoes to pull that look off. I'm not so sure the boots and black ensemble quite cut it.'

'Shush, a girl can dream.'

She was already walking up the stairs, and Ben followed. On this floor there were two apartments – four and five – and another, smaller staircase, not quite so grand, led up to the next floor.

'Gina has the penthouse,' he whispered. 'We should have taken the lift.'

They went up to the next floor which would have been the servants' quarters back in the day. A whir and click as a camera tracked their movements broke the temporary silence they had fallen into, and Morgan pointed to it. 'At least she has good security.'

The door to Gina's apartment opened and a man in a dark grey pinstriped suit was staring at them. 'Can I help you?'

'We're here to speak to Gina. Is she home?'

He looked at Ben, who was in suit trousers, shirt and tie, then at Morgan.

'You are?'

Morgan smiled at him. 'Detectives Matthews and Brookes from Rydal Falls police.'

'Jacob France,' the man replied. He opened the door and pointed into the biggest room that Morgan had ever seen. It went on forever and in the middle of the Gothic-styled room was a huge black velvet sofa where Gina was curled up in a ball, a box of tissues next to her and a large glass of what was either water or gin in her hand. She waved the glass towards Morgan.

'Come in.'

Morgan didn't know where to look first, the walls were painted in a warm black and every decorative detail was gold or gold gilt. On a huge mantel were so many brass candlesticks she couldn't count them, and she let out a small sigh. Of all the beautiful houses, flats, apartments she had ever been in through her work, this one was the one – she was in love. Ben was oblivious to any of it. He was focused on Gina which he so rightly should have been.

The guy with the suit crossed the vast room in big strides and picked up a Louis Vuitton laptop bag. 'Do you need me to stay, Gina?'

She shook her head. 'I'm good, thanks for stopping by, Jacob.'

He leaned down, pecked her on the cheek and gave her a quick squeeze. 'Call me if you need me, okay?'

'I will.'

He nodded at Ben and Morgan then strode his way out of the apartment in those big strides and then he was gone, the door closing softly behind him.

Morgan couldn't help herself. 'Gina, this is stunning.'

Gina smiled at her. 'It is, thank you. I designed it all myself, had the best time scouring all the flea markets and antique shops with Rosie for all the bits.'

An angry-looking taxidermy badger mounted on a wooden

plinth was glaring at her, and there were birds too, under glass cloches – a magpie, crow and a beautiful raven.

Gina pointed to the badger. 'Don't mind Fred, he's still pissed he got shot by the farmer. I fell in love with him the moment I set eyes on him; Rosie hated him but he's my kind of guy.'

Morgan said, 'How are you? That must have been a terrible shock for you finding your friends that way.'

She nodded. 'I still can't believe it.' Her eyes filled with tears that she tried to blink away, and she looked down at the glass in her hand. 'Can I get you guys a drink?'

Ben shook his head. 'No, thank you, we're on duty.'

'Oh, it's not alcohol it's water.' She smiled at him. 'As much as I'd like to blot all of this out with a bottle of gin, I haven't got the time for the hangover. I don't want to be grieving and hanging as Rosie liked to say.'

'We just want to ask you a few questions,' Morgan said. 'Get a picture of who Rosie was. It will help us find who did this.' Gina nodded. 'You and Rosie were close; how did you meet?'

'Facebook Marketplace.'

Morgan couldn't have been more surprised. 'Really?'

Gina nodded again. 'She was selling some of my favourite candlesticks, and Magic over there.' She pointed to the taxidermy magpie.

Morgan tried to imagine those things in Rosie's house, which was the complete opposite end of the rainbow spectrum to Gina's.

'They belonged to her aunt, family heirlooms that no one wanted except for me. We just clicked straight away. She was funny and wouldn't touch the bird without a pair of those ridiculous bright yellow rubber gloves on in case she got germs from him.' Gina paused and dabbed her eyes with a tissue. 'I'm going to miss her so much. She was my best friend since I came here from the States. I've had a few friends, but nobody like Rosie.'

'That's so sad, I'm so sorry. Do you know why someone would want to do this to them?'

She shook her head. 'Who in their right mind would want to do that to anyone?'

Morgan glanced at Ben; *yes who would?*

'How long have you lived in the UK?'

Gina paused. 'Around ten years, I moved here for work and fell in love with the vibe.'

'Where did you move from?'

'Los Angeles.'

'Wow, you prefer here to there?' Morgan tried to imagine what it would be like to live in LA compared to here and couldn't. She had always loved the States, would give anything to be able to move there, especially to Salem where Ben kept promising they would go for their next holiday.

'I like the slower pace of life over here. The threat of violence is so much greater back home, or it was until now. Who do you think did this to them and why?'

Ben answered, 'That is what we're working on finding out, Gina. We need to know everything about them so we can get a picture of what their life was like. Did they have any relationship problems, work problems, family upsets?'

Gina nodded. 'Good, that's good. I'll tell you everything I know. They were pretty happy with each other, as happy as any couple in a relationship is. Rosie didn't have any lovers and as far as I know neither did Matt, although I was Rosie's friend. They didn't see a lot of their family, no disputes that I know of. Rosie loved her job at the school, although she did talk a lot about going to school herself to do an interior design course.' Gina paused, plucked a tissue from the box next to her and dabbed at her eyes then inhaled deeply. 'Boy, this is harder than I ever imagined it could be.'

Morgan asked, 'You imagined it would be easy talking about your dead friends before it happened?'

Gina shook her head. 'No, I listen to a lot of true crime podcasts and I used to host one, they're my thing, and I read a lot of true crime too. I always wondered how the family and friends coped after a tragedy and now I know. I would do anything to take that back and not be sitting here talking to you both. I'd do anything not to have gone into their house this morning and found them like that. Do you think I'll ever be able to forget that image? Because right now it's all I can see. Who does that? It's so cruel.'

This time Gina let the tears flow, and Morgan felt bad for asking her that question, but she had to know if this had been something that Gina had been thinking about, because if it had that would mean she was now their number one person of interest, and the murders were premeditated.

Ben changed the subject. 'Is Jacob your partner?'

Gina shrugged. 'No. He would like to be but he's my assistant and friend.'

'Where do you work?'

Gina pointed to the gold desk in the corner of the room. 'Here, I work from home.'

'What do you do?'

'I produce podcasts. I work with a lot of true crime shows.'

Ben's eyes looked as if they were about to pop out of his head. 'And that pays well enough for all of this?'

Gina laughed. 'It contributes, I had a wealthy ex-husband who was happy to share that wealth once we divorced.'

Morgan nodded. 'That was nice.'

'I'm, what's that word you Brits use? Kidding, winding you up. He was a miserable bastard and didn't want to give me anything, but we didn't sign a prenup and he cheated on me, several times. Then he died and I had a good lawyer and did okay.'

Morgan looked around and thought she did more than okay, but she liked Gina. She was fun and if she was honest, she envied her a little. 'So, Jacob is what, your personal assistant?'

'Yes, he's my PA. He does all the parts I don't want to so I can go spend time with Rosie. I can't believe she's gone, just like that.'

'So, you have no idea who would want to see them dead?' Ben was looking at her with an expression of hope on his face, and Morgan got it, they had nothing to go on and needed something to work with.

'I don't, I'm sorry. I wish that I did. I would drag them to the station myself.'

'How did you get along with Matt?' Ben asked her.

Gina shrugged. 'Fine, we were okay. I don't think he liked me as much as Rosie did. I think he thought I was a bad influence on her.'

'Why?'

'She started listening to true crime podcasts because of me. We would spend every Sunday thrifting, or scouring the antique shops as Rosie called it. I think he was a little jealous, but Rosie said she'd ask him to come along, and he said he'd rather poke his own eyes out. What is it with you Brits? I hear that a lot. She also loved coming here and we'd have our own little book club meetings every couple of weeks that involved wine, food and talking about books we'd read. We both love reading.'

Morgan thought she would give anything to be able to do all of those things with Rosie and Gina. It sounded like her idea of heaven.

'Wow, that's amazing. I love true crime, reading, and antique shopping.'

Gina smiled at her. 'Maybe in a few weeks we could do that, when you've caught the killer, or killers. Do you think there could have been two of them?'

Ben shrugged. 'It's hard to say at the moment, we're not ruling anything out, but we have very little to go on. You have no reason to believe that anyone would want to do this to them?' He asked again.

Gina shook her head. 'The only thing that I can think of was the noises from the attic.'

Both Morgan and Ben leaned closer to Gina, their body language showing how interested they were to hear about it.

'Rosie had mentioned a couple of times hearing noises up there, I kept telling her it was rodents or birds. They live on a street that's lined with trees; it happens. I feel bad, she thought the house was haunted but I told her it was more likely to be a squirrel.'

'Do you know if she checked the attic out?' Morgan was leaning so far over she looked as if she might fall off the edge of the seat.

'She said she put her head through the hatch, saw nothing and got the hell out of there. She was convinced it was a ghost.' Gina laughed, but it didn't reach her eyes.

'We found evidence that someone had been up there, watching them from the attic space.'

Gina's hand clamped across her mouth, and she shook her head. 'Holy shit, you have to be kidding?'

'I'm afraid so.'

'That's terrifying, I feel so bad. I kept telling her it was okay, but it wasn't.'

Morgan reached out and patted Gina's knee. 'You can't blame yourself; this isn't on you. If you think of anything that might be useful even if it seems not that important, can you let me know?'

She pulled out her notepad with a couple of pale yellow Post-it notes attached to the back and wrote her phone number on it, then passed it to Gina. 'You can call or leave a message any time, I'll get back to you.'

Gina looked at it and nodded. 'What happens now?'

Ben stood up. 'We work hard to find the person who did this. Do you know any of the family members, other friends?'

'No, I only knew Rosie and Matt.'

'No worries, take care, Gina.'

She stood up and reached out for their hands, shaking them both in turn, then walked them to the door.

ELEVEN

Morgan paused before getting back into the car, turning slowly to take in the view down to the lake. Windemere, although always busy in the summer with boats, canoes, paddleboarders, swimmers, yachts and steamers, was still one of her favourite spots. Standing in the lush greenery on the opposite side of the lake was what looked like the ruins of a grand stone castle but was actually Claife Viewing Station. It was built in the 1790s for visitors to take in the beautiful vistas of the lake and fells surrounding it, that could be seen from the second floor.

Before it had all gone wrong, and their lives had been turned upside down, her father Stan used to take her to visit on chilly autumn days when it wasn't overcrowded with tourists. They would get the ferry across and spend hours exploring the views and the woods around it. They would play hide and seek along the woodland trails, collect conkers and warmly coloured leaves for her to take home. Morgan sighed, once again wishing she could have told him he'd been a good dad and how much she regretted the years they hadn't spoken much due to his downward spiralling drink problem and her animosity at his selfishness. The poor guy had doted on Morgan's mother, and when Sylvia took her life it had left him broken. At the time, Morgan had been so consumed by her own grief she didn't see it like she could now. After getting to know Ben, who had been through the same thing with his wife, Cindy, she had so much more empathy for Stan now than she had back then. She closed her eyes and whispered, *sorry, Stan.*

Ben's voice filled the air as he called out from inside the car, 'Are you good, Morgan?'

She blinked a couple of times, clearing the tears. 'Yeah, I'm just admiring the view.'

'Well, can you admire from inside the car, please.'

She smiled at him. 'Yes, boss.' But got inside and gave one last look behind her at the beautiful mansion before turning to stare at the drive ahead of them.

'Were you daydreaming about being lady of the manor?'

'Something like that.'

His warm hand cupped her chin and turned her face to look at him. 'One day, Morgan, I will make you lady of the manor, but for now you'll always be the lady of my heart.'

She kissed his hand. 'I love you so much, Ben, thank you, but you don't need to do that. We can do it together.'

He shrugged. 'I can do romantic on occasion.'

This made her laugh. 'You can; me too.'

He smiled at her and began to drive away from the house of her dreams. Gina was really living the kind of life she would love, and she envied her a little more than she'd ever admit. Gina didn't give off any bad vibes. What would she have to gain from killing her best friend? It didn't make sense so, for now, Morgan pushed her to the bottom of the non-existent suspect list.

For the first time since Morgan had moved in with Ben she didn't want to turn into their street. As he approached it, she felt a small tick as the pulse begin to pound in the side of her head, which was still a bit of a mess after being attacked. Sam was now on scene guard, but she waved at them and lifted the police tape high enough for the car to drive under. They both waved back and parked in the vacant space near to their house. Kevin was sitting in the front window watching the activity, and Morgan smiled. 'He has such a great life.'

'Who?'

'Kevin.'

Ben glanced at their house and grinned. 'Good, I'm glad someone does. Do you want to do some more door knocking, speak to the neighbours? They might be more comfortable talking to you if they recognise you.'

'What are you doing?'

'I need to go back inside and look at the scene again, if Wendy and crew will let me.'

She knew he was trying to protect her, and she appreciated that, and she didn't feel the need to revisit the scene. Once had been more than enough to last a lifetime.

———

She strode towards the house on the other side of Rosie and Matt's. She waved to the guy who was watching out of the window; what was his name? Didn't he organise the street BBQ? He threw open the door. 'Morgan, good to see you.'

She found this a little off-putting; she wasn't here to ask him for the recipe for his jerk chicken. 'Hi.' She ran through a list of names and found the one she hoped it was. 'Daniel, how are you?'

He nodded his head in the direction of next door. 'Better if I knew what was going on. Have they had the mother of all domestics?'

'Has nobody spoken to you?'

'I've literally just got home from work five minutes ago, had to leave the car at the end of the street and walk down. I wasn't sure who to ask. Martin is away on a course, so he isn't here to fill me in like he usually does on the street drama.'

'Is there a lot of drama on the street?' It was the first Morgan had heard about it, then she noticed the faint blush creeping up from the collar of his shirt and she realised he probably meant her. She didn't press further, and he just smiled at her.

'Come in.'

Next door, Ben was now suited and booted, chatting to Wendy, and Carl the crime scene manager.

She slipped into the hallway, and Daniel closed the door behind her. 'So, what's the gossip then? Will they be coming to the next get-together as a couple or will they have split up and gone their separate ways? I thought we could have a street Halloween party and all dress up, that would be so much fun.'

She wondered how to break the news to him, he seemed to be enjoying the drama a little too much. 'They won't be going anywhere ever again, Daniel, they are dead.'

His bottom lip fell open and to give him his due he looked genuinely shocked by that news.

'What? How are they dead? I saw Rosie last night and Matt earlier on in the day.'

She thought she could have been a little more tactful and pointed to the living room. 'Should we take a seat?'

He nodded emphatically. 'Yes, sorry, where are my manners?' And she followed him into his very taupe living room. 'I'm sorry, Morgan, could you explain what you meant because that's just ridiculous?'

'A friend found their bodies earlier. I'm afraid they were murdered.' She let that sink in and watched as Daniel's face went through a range of emotions.

'Somebody killed them. Was it someone they knew; how and why?'

'You've taken my questions out of my mouth; this is what we are trying to find out.'

'Sorry, we watch a lot of cop dramas on the TV. Martin is obsessed with *Happy Valley*. He reckons that—' He stopped talking, his already pink cheeks now positively glowing.

'That I'm the real-life version of Catherine Cawood.'

He nodded, and she smiled. 'I've heard that before.'

'We don't gossip about you all the time, but it's a little bit of excitement when your face pops up in the paper or on Google. Sorry, Morgan, I'm not being disrespectful. We thank you for your bravery and your service.'

At this she smiled. 'I feel as if I should be getting a medal or a certificate from you, Daniel.'

'You deserve a row of medals and I'm a terrible gossip. I bet you thought that old Annie was the worst with her curtain twitching, but now you've realised she's tame compared to me.'

'Annie is quite lovely; I spoke to her earlier. As are you. I really need to know if you saw or heard anything at all from next door after you last saw Rosie. What time was that?'

He nodded. 'It was about quarter to nine. I went to pick up a pizza and she was going in the door. She waved to me, and I waved back, then she shut the door. I didn't think anything of it. We never heard a thing. We ate the pizza, polished off a bottle of red wine and went to bed. Martin would have told me if he'd heard any noise from next door, and I was out for the count.'

'What about when you woke up. Did you hear anything then or see anyone leaving the house?'

He shook his head. 'I'm sorry, the only thing I saw was her friend knocking this morning, but I was going out to work. I only had a half day today, thank God, so I did my four hours and came back just now. That's not much help, is it?'

'Not really, but that's not your fault.'

'How were they killed? I mean, how did someone get into their house, kill two people and we managed to sleep through it all? Was it quick? Did they not know a thing? God, I hope they didn't. If I was going to be murdered in my bed, I'd rather not know about it.'

'Those detective shows have really paid off.' She smiled at him.

He laughed. 'Sorry.'

'Don't be sorry, I'll tell you what I can. We believe that someone has been watching them. We don't know how long for or why but there was evidence up in the attic that someone had been up there. Rosie was killed downstairs and Matt in his bed, but we don't know how or why just yet.'

Daniel was shaking his head in slow motion. 'Awful, it's awful. You mean like a stalker?'

She let out a long sigh. 'At this point it looks that way, but nothing is confirmed, and this is between you, me and Martin.'

'Of course, I won't tell a soul, except for him.'

'Thank you, have you noticed anyone hanging around who doesn't live in the street, anything odd?'

'I wish I could tell you I had, but I haven't.'

'Do you use your attic much, have you been up there lately?'

She watched what little colour was left drain from his face as he thought about what she was asking him.

'Not really, we keep the Christmas decs up there. Oh God, do you think someone is up there watching us as well?' His voice was high-pitched.

'No, but it would be good to check it out in case.'

'Can you? I'm a wimp.'

'Well, I can, but I wouldn't know if anything was out of place. Why don't we do it together.'

He stood up, and leaving the room he came back holding a hammer. 'I saw once that if you use a household item to assault an intruder it's not as bad as stabbing them.'

Despite the seriousness of the situation, Morgan couldn't stop the grin that stretched across her face. 'That's true, although if it's life or death and all you can find is a knife, then use that.'

He nodded. 'Follow me, I should go first, shouldn't I?'

They went upstairs to where the attic hatch was – it was the same in all the houses along the street – and stood underneath it.

'How do you access it?'

He pointed to a bedroom. 'There's a ladder in there.' Ducking through the door he came back out with a stepladder. He put it in place, stepped on the bottom rung and turned to her. 'Morgan, I'm sorry, I'm scared, and I don't think you should be going up there either. Are there no armed police hanging around you can send up?'

'They're busy searching, but it's okay. I'll do it.'

They swapped places.

'Have you got a torch?'

'There's a pull string near to the hatch. I got Martin to make it longer so we didn't have to scrabble around in the dark.'

'When was the last time you were up here?'

'January, to put the decs away.'

She climbed to the top, pushed open the hatch and fumbled around for the string. Finding it after a couple of missed attempts, she tugged it hard, and a bright light filled the space. Peering through she couldn't see anything out of place.

'Looks okay, I'll just give it a once-over.'

'Be careful. What do I do if someone attacks you?'

'Run outside for help. My boss is next door and there are police officers all over.'

'Right, okay, I can do that.'

She pulled herself up and walked around. There was nothing up here, nobody had made themselves a den. She checked to see if there was any way next door could be accessed. It couldn't, the walls were solid. She expelled the breath she'd been holding and climbed back down.

Daniel was clutching his chest. 'I have never been so scared in all my life. How did you do that, were you not scared?'

'A little, but I guess I'm used to it. When you speak to Martin can you ask him if he heard or saw anything unusual on the street recently?'

'Of course, Morgan, I'll ring him right now and let you know. I'm so sorry about Rosie and Matt, they seemed so nice. Although he did snore quite loudly. It didn't wake me, but Martin sometimes mentioned it in the morning. Are you sure she didn't beat him over the head to stop his snoring?'

'Quite sure, thanks, Daniel.'

'Wish I knew something helpful.'

She left him still clutching his hammer and went back outside, glad to be out in the daylight. She'd had enough of dark creepy attics for one day.

TWELVE

Ben stood at the doorway to the bathroom staring at the bodies, unable to tear his gaze away from the black nails that had been put through their lips. The more he stared the more he could see the dried blood that had crusted around them. On first glance he had found his eyes unable to focus on their lips for more than a second, but he was forcing himself to look, to study them and try to figure out what the reason behind it was because it had to have meant something to the killer.

'Anything?'

His feet almost left the floor for the second time; he hadn't heard Wendy come up behind him again. She was in stealth mode today.

Ben was clutching his chest. 'Jesus, could you not do that?'

'Ben, I sound like a tornado ripped through a crisp packet factory walking around in these bloody suits; next door probably heard me rustling up those stairs. You were in a world of your own.'

He smiled at her. 'I was, point taken and no, I have nothing. What do you think it means, the nail through the lips? Did the killer want to silence them forever, stop the noise, stop them talking?'

'Sounds good to me, stop them from talking perhaps.'

'Stop them talking to who, each other, the killer?'

'That's not for me to say, you're the detective, you're the quizmaster, you get to figure out the clues.'

'Sometimes it's too hard to do that.'

'Yeah, tell that to Marc who is outside causing havoc wanting to know if anyone has visited the witness who found the bodies. He's like a dog on heat.'

'Crap.'

Wendy nodded. 'We're almost done. You can get the bodies moved to the mortuary if you're happy to do so. The undertakers are going to struggle to get them separated, as their arms will be pretty rigid by now.'

He closed his eyes, his stomach churning at the thought of whoever got the job of trying to separate the bodies, and had to swallow down some bile that was rising up his throat. He was a seasoned professional; he shouldn't be feeling like a rookie. He realised he'd lost count of the murders he had dealt with and felt sad. He could remember every single victim and the horrible way they had died, but couldn't pluck a number off the top of his head and that was a terrible sign. He nodded at Wendy, and was about to walk away when he saw a glint of something underneath Rosie's outstretched arm. Bending down to take a closer look he realised he could see a couple of gold links.

'Have you got a torch?'

She passed him one, and he shone it at the gold. 'Look at that, it's hard to see because it's coated in thick blood but...'

Wendy was crouched next to him. 'Well, bloody hell. I can't believe I missed it.' She leaned forwards with a pair of tweezers and plucked the chain out of the mess of thick, gloopy, blackish-brown blood. Ben squinted his eyes as she held it up.

'What is it?'

'Looks like a medallion, maybe a St Christopher, although I can't really say until the congealed blood is cleaned off. I haven't seen anyone wearing one of these in forever.'

'Do you think it belonged to either of them?'

The chain was snapped. 'Hard to say, but they're more of a man thing I reckon.'

Ben looked at Matt's neck, then Rosie's, but there weren't any marks on the skin to show that something had grazed it when it had been pulled off.

'Maybe it belonged to the killer and Rosie managed to snap it off.'

Ben looked at Rosie with her eyes wide open. She had been staring at something in horror when she'd taken her final breath. 'Good girl, Rosie, did you try to leave us a clue?'

He stood up, his knees creaking far too loud in the silence. Wendy was holding up an evidence bag, about to deposit the chain inside it. Taking out his phone he snapped a couple of pictures then nodded. 'Thanks, Wendy, be interesting to see what exactly it is and maybe' – he put his palms together in a prayer position – 'just maybe it will have DNA from the killer who is on the database, and we can go arrest this sick bastard before the end of the day.'

Wendy gave him the saddest smile he'd ever seen, and he knew she was humouring him. 'Let's hope so, Ben.'

He also knew he was grasping at straws, that likely there would be nothing of forensic value on it, but what the hell, he was going to try and think positive. He'd seen Morgan listening to a book on her phone called *The Power of Positive Thinking* and had read the blurb on Amazon. She'd also talked about it and as much as he was more of a practical kind of guy, he would take all the help he could get. The thought that someone had stalked Rosie and Matt inside of their own house had unlocked some deep-seated fear within him; that and the close proximity to his own house creeped him out way too much.

THIRTEEN

They reconvened back at the station. Marc was pacing up and down the office like he was a big cat at the zoo walking along the fence waiting for feeding time. Amy stood up.

'Boss, sit down, you're giving me vertigo. I'll go get you a brew or something. Do you need a herbal tea, because you definitely don't need any more caffeine. You're buzzing your tits off without it.'

He sat down on the nearest chair and pursed his lips, blowing out a long breath. Morgan glanced at Ben, who didn't know what was going on. She sat down behind her desk and waited for the fireworks to start.

It was Ben who asked, 'What's the matter, Marc?'

Marc was back on his feet, picking up a whiteboard pen, and Morgan was transported back to her school days where her favourite English teacher, Mr Mayes, would jump onto unsuspecting pupils' desks to get their attention. She wondered if Marc could jump that high in his tapered suit trousers.

'The matter is those two bodies; how did it happen?'

Amy slipped out of the door. She hadn't been there, had not

witnessed any of it, so it was safe enough for her to go and make coffee for everyone. Morgan envied her being spared the horror of the crime scene. Although she would see the photographs soon enough, it was somehow easier to look at dreadful scenes through pictures. There was no stench of clotting blood, urine, or anything else untoward to assault your senses.

Ben shrugged. 'I don't get what you mean. It happened because some maniac decided to kill them.'

Marc was shaking his head. 'How did said maniac get into their lovely house and hide up in the attic without them noticing? If that was your house, Ben, wouldn't you have noticed something odd, out of place, heard noises?'

Morgan held her hand up and quickly put it back down; she was acting like a school kid.

'Sir, Rosie did hear noises and told Gina about them, so you can't say they didn't notice.'

His head snapped in her direction, his eyes sparkling with emotion. 'Yes, she did, but why did she not check it out properly? Why not call the cops to go check it out?'

Morgan tried to keep her cool, but sometimes he wound her up too much and she could feel herself on the verge of arguing with him. 'Gina said she thought it was rodents or a bird. The hatch isn't very big, which was why Matt didn't go up there; so whoever got up there wasn't a huge person. I mean, let's be realistic, if you heard a noise in your attic what would your first thought be? A bird, or animal, ghosts even, but you wouldn't even add killer to the list, would you?'

He was nodding. 'No, that's true, but if there's anything we've learned the last couple of years, it's that there is evil hiding everywhere.'

Ben's face was a picture. He looked both concerned and confused at Marc's outburst.

'Boss, what are you trying to say? That they knew someone was living in their attic? Where are we going with this?'

Marc shrugged. 'No bloody idea and that's the problem, it's all a bit too much.'

He sat back down. Amy came into the room backwards, pushing the door open with her bottom, carrying a tray with mugs on it. Cain stood up, motioned twirling his finger at the side of his head then nodded in Marc's direction. 'I'll go find some biscuits.'

'Good luck with that, Cain, everyone on this floor locks them away now because you keep eating them.'

'Ha, not everyone. There's two student officers who were brewing up downstairs as I walked in and just blatantly put a full packet of biscuits in the communal brew cupboard, so you know what that means?'

Amy put the tray down, glaring at Cain. 'It means keep your hands off. I'm surprised Madds hasn't had you arrested for theft yet.'

'It means that they are for anyone if they're in the communal brew cupboard. Sharing is caring and the boss needs something to soothe his soul; a digestive will do the trick.' He disappeared leaving Amy shaking her head at him, Marc staring into space and Ben staring at Morgan.

Morgan stood up and picked up a pen for the board, and uncapping it she began to write.

- *Rosie heard sounds in attic – when did they begin?*

- *Told Gina and Matt – Gina told her it was animals; Matt wasn't bothered he came home drunk and fell asleep. Likely didn't hear anything.*

- *Rosie went downstairs to sleep on the sofa – was killed in the living room on the sofa, killer was already in the house. Sounds were the killer moving around the attic.*

- *Both attacked with a sharp object to be confirmed to the back of the head, killing them.*

- *Dragged Rosie back upstairs, why? Why not leave her where she was and risk waking Matt up?*

- *The letter – who was that for?*

She turned to Ben. 'Matt was a big guy, at least six foot, and if I had to guess, about twenty stone. If he heard the killer, he could have taken him out no problem. He can't have heard anything because the blood spatter on the bed shows that was where he was killed. Then dragged off the bed the short distance to the bathroom. Whoever it was, they're strong. Imagine trying to drag Cain's body out of his bed and along the floor?'

Cain walked in with a packet of biscuits. 'What about my body?'

'You're a big guy, it would be hard to drag you so how did the killer manage to drag Matt?'

Cain shrugged. Morgan screwed her eyes shut searching her brain for some logical answer. She continued.

'Maybe he was even stronger than Matt? Or whoever it was, they were on some psychotic rampage, they were happy enough to commit cold-blooded murder, they were probably on some kind of adrenaline kick which gave them super strength. You hear about it, don't you? I read once that a kid got trapped under a car and their mum who had never been to the gym or lifted weights managed to lift the car up on her own to free him.'

Marc shrugged. 'Yeah, that's very possible, highly unlikely but you never know.'

Cain was tearing open the packet of biscuits; he took five then passed them around. 'Or they could have used a skateboard or something to slide him along with. You can get those pads, can't you, to put under heavy furniture, would they work under a body? I mean it's the same principle, isn't it? Moving an inanimate object from one room to the other.'

Morgan took a biscuit and snapped it in half, pushing it into her mouth.

'The nails must have been inserted with precision, but why?'

Cain began to talk through his mouthful of mushed-up biscuit. 'They were the final nail in the coffin.'

Amy gasped, leaned across and slapped his shoulder. 'Cain.'

Morgan couldn't believe he had found a cliché so appropriate to the situation. 'You're awful, Cain.'

He winked at her. 'Hey, I am what I am.'

'Yeah, a biscuit thief and terrible comedian.'

He held out his hands. 'I'll take it.'

Marc shook his head and stood up. 'Focus; can we do that? I still need to know how the killer got access into that house?'

'The key? Gina said there was a spare key under a plant pot. If she knew about it then other people might have too.' Morgan wrote *spare key* on the board. 'Whoever it was could have collected the key, took it to get a copy cut at the ironmongers or the supermarket and put the original back in time before either of them knew it was missing. They could have entered and hid in the attic days before killing them. The rubbish up there suggests they were in the attic for days. Certainly not weeks. Unless they left it to get more food.'

'Yes, that's good, Morgan. That's more like it. What are we thinking about this friend Gina then?' asked Ben.

Everyone shook their head at the same time, and Morgan felt a tiny prickle of doubt at the back of her mind. Gina might not have wanted them dead or have killed them, but it didn't mean she wasn't completely out of the question. Marc was still pacing although he had slowed down a little to sip from his mug of coffee.

'I wanted to talk to Gina; however, what did she have to say?' He was staring at Ben.

'She was nice, she has a very nice apartment, an excellent job that pays her well and she doesn't seem to have any motive to want her friends dead. I mean what's the point of throwing everything away? And she truly doesn't come across as the psychopathic type of killer a person needs to be to commit this level of crime. She's not strong enough to drag and position their bodies.'

'Husband or partner?'

'Ex-husband, but he's dead, no partner. She has an assistant to help her run her business.'

Marc nodded. 'What line of business is she in?'

'Podcast producer with a rich, dead ex-husband.'

'Interesting.'

Morgan glanced at Amy who mimed sticking a finger down her throat at Marc.

'What about her PA?' she asked.

'We'd have to interview him, he was in a rush to go to a meeting when we got there. Nothing to suggest he's involved.'

Marc sighed. 'You're not being overly helpful here. Cain and Ben, I want you to bring me suspects we can work with.'

'Well, sir, it's only been a few hours. We have a lot of work to do.'

'You do. I'm off to a meeting with the superintendent. Let me know if you have any updates for me.'

And with that he strolled out of the office, taking his coffee with him.

Ben sat down on the corner of the desk, and Cain let out a small whoop of delight.

'Thought he'd never go; he's got a right bee in his bonnet.'

'Cain.' Both Amy and Morgan spoke his name at the same time.

'What? It's hard, okay? I can't help myself, they just creep out of my mouth.'

Morgan grinned at him.

'Oh, I nearly forgot,' Ben added. 'When I went back in the second time, I noticed some kind of necklace in the pool of blood next to Rosie. Wendy has taken it to be tested but it looked like some kind of St Christopher she thought.'

'What's a St Christopher?' asked Morgan.

'It's like a small medallion that is supposed to keep you safe when you travel.'

She closed her eyes; it sounded familiar.

'They're a bit old-fashioned though so maybe it belonged to the killer and maybe he's older than we're thinking.'

'How old are we thinking?'

'Well, he's not that old if he's strong enough to drag bodies around like that. They can't have a bad back or a bad knee like me. Look, all we have at the moment is what ifs and that's not enough. We're going to have speak to both Rosie's and Matt's work colleagues, family and friends. Then we're going to check every single house in the street for cameras and dashcam footage; we need to find someone who saw a person who wasn't either of the victims going into that house. We should also speak to any local piercers and see if they knew of the victims, just in case.'

'I can't figure out how the killer got those nails in. I don't think it's the type of skill you can learn online,' Cain added helpfully.

'Great. So, Amy, can you try and get a list of the people we need to speak to regarding them, family, friends, etc. Cain and Morgan can you find out where the piercing studios are and give them a visit.'

'Yes, boss.'

Ben leaned over and took three more biscuits out of the packet. 'Oh and, Cain, you can buy some biscuits to replace these whilst you're out before Madds realises you stole them.'

He left them to it and walked into his office, closing the door behind him.

FOURTEEN

Morgan let Cain drive. She had googled the list of piercers nearest to Rydal Falls and had come up with one in Bowness and three in Kendal. They headed to Kendal first; the first two were closed and the last one they tried, Cobweb & Crow, was open. It was a tattoo studio and as they walked inside the music was loud, there was also a heavily pierced woman with gorgeous dark green and black hair in two space buns, sitting on a stool behind the reception desk. Her eyes lifted up from her phone to look at them. Morgan fit right in; she had pushed up the sleeves of her shirt so her tattoos were visible, but Cain looked out of place and the woman, after looking him up and down, turned back to Morgan.

'Can I help you?'

Morgan smiled at her. 'I hope so, I'm Detective Morgan Brookes and this is my colleague, Detective Cain Robson.'

She held out her hand and the woman took it, giving her a firm handshake. 'Raven Castle.'

Morgan tilted her head slightly.

'For real, I was destined to be a Goth chick from day one. My mum owns the shop and is the tattoo queen of Kendal.'

'That's a cool name and a cool mum.'

'Yeah, she can be. Not that she ever hardly tattoos me though, I'm always last on her list. Sorry, too much info. How can I help you both?'

'Do you have a body piercer here?'

'You're looking at her, what are you after?' Raven paused then turned to Cain. 'Sorry, that was rude of me, is it you who wants a piercing?'

He shook his head rapidly. 'No, thanks.'

Morgan laughed. 'Actually, I'd love my forward helix done. When can you fit me in?'

'Now. I'm bored out of my skull. Come out back and I'll grab you a form to fill in.'

She walked through a beaded curtain, and Cain looked at Morgan in horror. He whispered, 'You're not; what's a forward helix?'

Raven stuck her head back through. 'You can come back too, Cain.'

'Argh, no thanks. I'm good. Morgan, I'll wait for you in the car.' He exited the shop much quicker than he walked in.

'Ignore him, he's a wimp.'

She walked through the curtain, and Raven pointed to a small room.

'Take a seat whilst I grab the forms.'

The room was very white, bright and sterile. It smelled strongly of antiseptic. There was a large comfy reclining chair and Morgan climbed onto it feeling relaxed and not at all nervous. Raven gave her a clipboard with a form on which she quickly filled out, ticking all the relevant boxes. She signed it and handed it back.

Raven skimmed through it. 'You know, I don't want this to sound rude or anything, but I would never have pegged you as a copper. Your mate yes, he screams cop, but you look nothing like one.'

Morgan grinned at her. 'Good, I hope I never do. I was born a Goth too and yes, he does, bless him. He's a good guy though.'

'He looks it. He's big, isn't he? Is he married?'

'He's newly engaged. Sorry, he's out of bounds.'

'Ah, just my luck. It would have been interesting to date a detective, especially a big dude who is good-looking too.'

'Not that interesting, we are always at work or thinking about it and very rarely get time off to do any fun stuff.'

Raven had gloved up and tied a plastic apron around herself. 'I bet. Is there a lot of crime in this area?'

'Too much.'

Morgan stopped speaking as Raven began to clean the top of her ear, not wanting to put her off. It took a couple of minutes, and Morgan was the proud owner of a forward helix piercing that had stung a little as the needle had gone through the cartilage of her ear. She waited until the stud was in place before speaking again.

'That's it, you're all done.'

'Wow, thank you. That was quick.'

'I'm fast.'

'That's good. Actually, I'm not just here for this.' She pointed to her very red ear.

'I figured not, but you know I can't resist a piercing. You're my first detective.'

'I am? I'm honoured. Do you know a Rosie Waite or a Matt Smith?'

'I don't think so, at least not personally as in friends or anything like that.'

'Could they have visited to get piercings or tattoos by your mum?'

Morgan hadn't noticed any obvious tattoos on either body, but it didn't mean that there weren't any. Not everyone had them in noticeable places, some people had discreet ones, especially if their job didn't approve of them. She typed Rosie's name into Instagram and found a picture of them both smiling at the BBQ last month.

'I'd have to check the records; can you hang on and I'll take a quick look on the database?'

'Of course, that would be amazing.'

Raven passed her a sheet of paper. 'This is your aftercare, bathe it in salt water twice a day, and don't touch it with your fingers. No prodding or poking it, and any problems come back to see me.'

'I won't, thanks.'

Morgan folded up the sheet of paper and tucked it into her pocket, following Raven back out into the small reception area.

Raven was tapping on the keyboard and exclaimed. 'Oh, I did have a customer in for a piercing a couple of weeks ago called Matt Smith. Where does he live? Is it Rydal Falls?'

Morgan's jaw went slack, and she had to shut it quickly because Raven wasn't the only person who had been judgy today. 'Is this him?'

Raven nodded. 'Yes, that's the guy.'

'What did he get?'

'His daith.'

'Where's that?'

Raven pointed to a big board on the wall showing an ear diagram with a multitude of every piercing available. 'That one there, through the bit of your ear below the forward helix. It's for migraines. I remember him now; he looked as comfortable as your colleague when he walked in, but he was nice and said his headaches were so bad he thought he'd give it a go. I told him it was nothing to be scared about and that a daith piercing was my most popular next to noses.'

'Oh, wow, that's interesting, thank you. Can you tell me the date, please?'

Raven looked at the computer screen. 'Oh, yes, how could I forget? It was Friday the thirteenth, and he kept making jokes about it being bad luck and was his ear going to fall off. He was a bit of all right too, nice looking, funny. What's he done, is he a master criminal? Does he run a drug ring all over the county? He was asking me loads of questions about the piercing process and the needles, which was a bit odd.'

Morgan wondered if she should, but then thought that it was surely already all over Facebook. 'I'm afraid he's dead.'

Raven's already pale face went even paler. 'Oh God, it wasn't the piercing, was it?'

'No, definitely not.'

'Thank God for that, I mean that's awful. How tragic, he wasn't much older than me.'

Morgan thought that Raven had a very good memory now it had been jogged, then stopped herself, his date of birth would be on the form he'd filled out just like hers was. A strange feeling washed over her, and she felt herself tipping forwards.

'Oh, are you okay? You're not going to faint, are you? You've gone very pale.' Raven rushed around and guided her to the window seat. Unwrapping a lollipop she shoved it in Morgan's mouth. 'Delayed reaction to the piercing, suck on that. A bit of sugar will do you good.'

Morgan felt stupid but smiled at her. Her feeling faint had nothing to do with the piercing, but more to do with the realisation that Matt had been here and had died a few weeks later. Could Matt have done this to himself? Killing Rosie then positioning them that way after mutilating himself? No, that was impossible. Perhaps he had an accomplice? But why? Why go to so much trouble to murder Rosie like this, when he could have killed her in a far less messy way? She looked at Raven. Morgan had hoped to find out more from Raven, but this case was getting stranger and stranger.

FIFTEEN

As Morgan left the shop her legs felt a little shaky. She had crunched the end of the lollipop off before she walked out so Cain didn't think she'd passed out at getting her ear pierced. He'd never let her live it down. Especially as how she had done all of this in work's time. As she got into the car he was grinning at her.

'Tell me you didn't do it?'

'I can't, because I did.' Morgan lifted her hair out of the way so he could see the angry skin beneath the thick titanium stud.

'Whoa, you're madder than you look, Brookes. The boss won't like it.'

'The boss doesn't have to know and besides it was an intel-gathering exercise.'

'Yeah, well by the time we visit the other three shops your ears are going to be throbbing and shining like a red beacon. That's above and beyond the call of duty.'

'The boss doesn't need to know, does he, Cain?'

'But he's your partner out of work, won't he notice?'

'What I do with my body has nothing to do with Ben, it all belongs to me. If you grass me up for doing it in work's time, you can get yourself out of all those scrapes you manage to get into.'

Cain turned to her, his eyes wide. 'You honestly think I would grass you up to the boss? Morgan that hurts.' He was clutching his chest with one hand. 'I'd never, you're my friend. I wouldn't get you in trouble, I was winding you up.'

She winked at him. 'I know you wouldn't, at least not on purpose anyway. So, that was very useful.'

'It was, I thought we were just clutching at straws.'

'Cain.'

He shrugged. 'I told you they roll off my tongue, I'm a natural at it.'

'Who do you think out of Rosie and Matt came to see Raven for a piercing?'

His eyes narrowed. 'Probably Rosie, but then again it could have been Matt.'

'You can only pick one.'

'Rosie.'

'It was Matt.'

'No way, crap I was going to say him but then changed my mind at the last minute. What the hell did he get pierced? Do I even want to know?'

'His daith, it's the bit of cartilage inside your ear. Apparently, it's good for stopping migraines. He suffered with headaches.'

'So, Raven is an expert at piercing, and she knew Matt. That's interesting, she gave me the impression that she could pierce anything dead or alive, so do you think she could have the motive to kill them?'

'And that my friend is the question. Does she have the motive? She did say she thought he was attractive. Maybe she was jealous? Or maybe Matt went there for the knowledge of how to pierce, and he killed Rosie first, then Raven killed him.'

Cain was nodding. 'Possibly, but highly unlikely, Morgan. It makes me shudder thinking about that. There are other ways to kill someone, far less painful and messy. This must be much more personal.'

'Yeah, I know. I'm just putting that theory out there to see what it sounded like.'

'Sounded pants to be honest, but the only problem I have with it all is Raven was tiny, wasn't she? How would she have got her up the stairs?'

'You talked about psychotic rage back at the office, or maybe she didn't work alone and had an accomplice.'

'Think we better go back and do some digging on Raven Castle and her mum. At least your ears have been saved.'

Morgan was staring at her ear in the small mirror on the sun visor, and she murmured, 'What are you on about?'

'If you found a worthy suspect at shop one, you don't have to go through it all again in the rest of the shops, do you? No more piercings.'

She laughed loudly. 'I didn't intend to get any more, but thanks. Let's see what Ben has to say. He might want the rest of the shops checking out anyway.'

'If he does, he can send the PCSOs, we're too busy now with this.'

Snapping the visor back into place she looked at him. 'Yes, let's hope Raven turns out to be a viable lead.'

He pulled out into the traffic then glanced her way. 'Ah, no way.'

'What?'

'You liked her, didn't you? You're going to be gutted if she's a mad killer.'

'Yes, I like her, and I hope she isn't, but life would be sweet if she was.'

They drove back to the station in silence, Morgan thinking about how Gina had told her Matt was sometimes in a bad mood with Rosie for very little reason.

SIXTEEN

Theo loved his job as parish priest of Rydal Falls. What he didn't love was the nastiness that went on with the retired women who all turned up once a fortnight for flower arranging and fundraising. He usually managed to escape the flower arranging nights, but unfortunately for him the fundraising meetings were obligatory. All he could think about was what time Declan would finish work tonight. He wanted to surprise him with a proper home-cooked roast dinner, but if they didn't wrap up this bloody fuss around the autumn bring-and-buy sale, he would never get the roast potatoes put in on time for them to be cooked.

'Isn't that right, vicar?'

'Huh?' He realised that Mrs Decker was staring intently at him.

'I mean if we can't agree on the simplest of things this is never going to work.'

He nodded. 'Quite.' He looked at the rest of the women who were all watching him, but he had no idea what they had been arguing about.

'Can you run that by me again, just to make sure I got the

gist of it?' He thought he'd rather be anywhere than here and
didn't think God or Jesus would argue with him over that decision if they had to sit through this on a biweekly basis. Mrs
Decker coughed, loudly, as if to make sure he was paying attention this time.

'We thought it would be fun to do a calendar for next year,
or at least some of us did.'

Theo tried not to groan out loud, oh dear Lord, had they
been watching *Calendar Girls*?

'What kind of calendar?'

'Why? A photographic one of our flower arrangements,
what else would it be?'

He glanced over at the six-foot Jesus on the cross above the
altar and nodded his thanks to him for keeping them under
control, and them not suggesting posing topless with nothing
but Chelsea buns to cover their nudity.

'That sounds like a great idea.'

'Well, it would be if there were only twelve of us, but there
are fifteen and if I'm not mistaken there are only twelve months
in a year, vicar, so three of us are not going to have our work
featured and it's not fair to whoever those three are.'

He stared at Miss McKenzie and muttered, 'Oh fuck.'

All fifteen women let out gasps, and he lifted his hands in
the air. 'Sorry, ladies, forgive that slip. I'm tired and I don't
know what to say.'

Mrs Decker smiled at him. 'Of course, you must get fed up
with listening to us go on. I think if we put the names in a hat,
you could pull twelve out, that would be the fairest way to do it.'

He nodded. 'Have you got twelve photos of your flower
arrangements?'

'Well, probably. Or we could have a competition between
ourselves, and you could pick the twelve best arrangements to
go in the calendar.'

Theo thought he would rather poke his own eyes out with a

stick than put himself through that and the aftermath of bitterness and sniping it would cause between them. 'Can I have a think about it?'

'Yes, of course. You see what you think and let us know before the next meeting. We don't have long to get it arranged.'

He stood up. 'I'm sorry, ladies, I need to leave. I'll come back and lock up the church after you've finished.'

He smiled at them then strode towards the door before they could stop him. As he walked outside, closing it behind him, he looked up at the sky. It looked like a painting, it was so beautiful, full of dusky orange and the clouds were streaked with pink. He leaned against the side of the church, closed his eyes and inhaled deeply.

'Tough gig?'

He straightened up and looked in the direction of the woman who had spoken. She was holding a bunch of flowers in her hands.

'Ladies fundraising meeting.'

The woman who looked much younger than the ladies inside the church raised an eyebrow. 'I'd get out of here whilst you can.'

He laughed. 'I intend to. Nice flowers.'

She smiled at him. 'It's my friend's birthday.' She pointed to the newer gravestones at the back of the churchyard, and he nodded.

'Birthdays are hard, aren't they? I always find I miss my mum more on her birthday than any other day except maybe for New Year's Eve. I find that totally depressing.'

'Me too, it's the worst, especially when your best friend is dead and you're single.'

Theo nodded, giving her a sympathetic smile. 'I'll leave you in peace, good evening.'

'Good evening.'

He walked towards the low wall that separated the churchyard from the vicarage and jumped over it, hurrying towards his red front door before Mrs Decker decided to follow him. He had the patience of a saint, but he was hungry and tired. He wanted a quick shower, then he was going to put his new Beetlejuice pyjamas on that Declan had brought him home the other day. They had rather odd-looking characters that looked as if they'd all been to Turkey for plastic surgery, but it was the thought that counted. Then he was going to make that roast. Declan had messaged earlier to say today had been rough, and he wanted to make sure he came home to a large glass of red wine and a hearty supper. Theo supposed he should be thankful that bickering women were the hardest thing he had to cope with, unlike Declan who had to deal with death day in, day out, and rarely complained.

By the time he heard Declan's car outside as he parked on the drive, the potatoes were almost ready, the chicken was carved and the veg had been cooked to perfection. His mum had been a good cook, she'd been a chef in a bistro that had become so popular in Birmingham that customers booked months in advance, and he thought she maybe would have been surprised at his change in career after her death, but proud of his cooking skills.

———

Ben was alone in the office and sitting at Morgan's desk scrolling through photos of the crime scene when she and Cain walked in. She didn't question that he was working at her space. She wouldn't care who was sitting there.

'Where's Amy? We have some research for her.' Cain breezed in and flung himself down on his chair that groaned loudly.

Ben looked up at them. He looked as if he was in some kind of daze.

'Oh, she's gone home.'

'What? Why?'

'She didn't feel well.'

Cain tutted. 'Talk about milking this pregnancy for all she can get.'

Ben glared at him. 'Having a migraine has nothing to do with having a baby. Did you find anything?'

His tone sounded as if he was begging for some break, and Morgan smiled at him, wanting to ease his pain. 'We might have, a couple of the piercing studios weren't open, but we struck lucky at the third one in Kendal. There was a girl there who pierced Matt Smith a couple of weeks ago.'

Ben frowned. 'How young was she? I mean how old do you have to be to be a body piercer?'

Morgan realised that Raven was probably around the same age as her so not that young, it was more a case of Morgan feeling older, way beyond her years.

'I didn't get her date of birth, but she looked around my age.'

Cain laughed. 'Well, you're not a girl, Morgan.'

Both Ben and Morgan said, 'Shut up,' in unison.

'And what did he get pierced?'

'His daith, it helps with migraines.'

'We should take Amy tomorrow, stop her from skiving off work,' Cain muttered.

Ben turned to look at him. 'Cain, she's not skiving. If you looked the way she did I'd send you home too.' He turned back to Morgan. 'Do you think she could be involved?'

'Hard to say. I don't think so, but she said Matt was handsome. She must have a thing for big men or need glasses because she thought Cain was too.'

Cain grinned at this piece of information, and Ben shook his head.

'Does she have motive? Can we find out if there was more to it than her just fancying him?'

'Probably, Cain thinks she's too small to have done the murders and moved the bodies, but she could have had help.'

Ben was nodding. 'This is great, it's a lead and a viable one at that. If we can connect her to Matt and Rosie even more then we might have our killer or a link to our killer. Is there anything else we can do tonight apart from start running the checks on Raven Castle?'

Morgan shook her head then paused. 'Actually, I can't help thinking that Matt might have been involved too. Before he died, of course. Raven mentioned he was asking about the logistics of piercings. What if he learned how to do it? What if he killed Rosie? Was working with Raven? And Raven turned on him?'

Ben turned to her and shrugged. 'I like that you're thinking outside the box, but that's quite convoluted, Morgan. Next thing you'll be telling me he smashed his own head in. We'll leave that for now unless something turns up to lead us back to that line of thinking.'

'Cool, I'll update Gilly and then we'll call it a day. Unless you find something that gives us cause to make an arrest. Tomorrow is going to be full-on with the post-mortems.'

He stood up to let Morgan take over on the computer, and she glanced at the photo that Ben had been staring at. She shuddered. The horror of what her neighbours had endured would be permanently etched into her mind and it creeped her out more than anything else had up to now.

SEVENTEEN

Declan had walked through the door and laughed to see Theo standing there in the pyjamas with a large glass of red wine in his hand. 'Hey, how are you?'

'Better now that I'm here. Those pyjamas, what's going on with their faces? I didn't notice that in the shop.'

He was grinning, and it made Theo feel blessed and grateful that he had found this amazing man at a time in his life when he'd almost given up on love. Declan dropped his bag and wrapped his arms around Theo. Holding him tight, he kissed him as if he hadn't seen him in weeks, then let go.

Theo wiped a hand across his brow.

'Wow, are you hungry or do you want to call it a night?'

'I love you, Theo, but I'm starving, and I can smell real food. Did you cook a roast dinner?'

Theo beamed at him. 'I did, I'm just about to take the potatoes out of the oven.'

'When are we getting married? I am not ever letting you go.'

Theo laughed. 'Ah, well. Hopefully they won't decide to move me for a long time. I wouldn't want to get your hopes up and then have to dash them because they were posting me to the Shetland Islands.'

Declan looked sad. 'Don't say that. I don't know what I'd do if you had to move away.'

'Me either, let's not talk about that. How are you, how bad was it?'

'On a scale of one to ten it was a hundred, but I don't want to talk about that either. What have you been up to that made you shower, get ready for bed and open a bottle of wine so early?'

'Women's fundraising meeting.'

'Oh feck, was it bad?'

Theo nodded. 'Terrible, they are thinking of doing a calendar.'

Declan held his hand up. 'Stop right there, I don't think I can take anymore.'

Theo laughed, took hold of Declan's hand and led him into the kitchen, where he had set the table with candles. It was cosy and the look on Declan's face made all the effort of cooking worthwhile. 'Do you need to shower?'

He shook his head. 'Already had one at the hospital.'

'Right, well do you want to go put your PJs on whilst I dish up?'

He took a large gulp of wine and put the glass down on the table. 'Be right back.'

They ate and chatted about everything but work. Declan had almost finished the bottle of wine, and he pointed to the wine rack. 'Should we open another bottle?'

Theo yawned. 'You can, but I'm good. I don't want a red wine hangover in the morning. I have a visit to the retirement home planned.'

'You're right, I won't either. I have a lot to do. It's just so tempting to get hammered and forget it all. Hey, let's send Ben a picture to cheer him up. I imagine he's as fed up as we are.'

Declan walked around to where Theo was sitting and stood behind him, phone in hand. Grinning he snapped a picture of them both in their matching pyjamas and sent it to Ben, who replied almost instantly.

Nice, where did you buy those? Temu?

Declan and Theo both roared with laughter and Theo asked, 'Does he even know what that is? I thought he was a bit of a dinosaur with shopping and technology.'

'Ah, he was until Morgan came along and changed his way of thinking.' He sent it to Morgan in case they weren't together, and she replied instantly with a laughing face emoji and

That's your Christmas Card pic.

Theo stood up and Declan took hold of his hand as he tugged him upstairs to bed.

————

Declan had fallen asleep almost instantly, lulled by a full stomach and three glasses of red wine, but not Theo. He felt unsettled and turned on his side to stare out of the moonlit window that looked onto the floodlit church and swore.

'Bloody hell,' he whispered; he'd forgot to lock up. There was little chance of someone going in and stealing the collection box at the back of the church because there was only pennies in it, but what if they did? Or what if someone trashed the place?

He threw back the duvet cover and went downstairs. He slipped his feet into a pair of knackered Vans, not even bothering to push them all the way in, and grabbed the set of church keys off the sideboard he kept them on. That glorious sunset had turned into a chilly, star-speckled sky, the moon was almost full, and it was quite beautiful.

Stepping over the wall he wished he'd thought to bring a torch with him. He locked the church door and turned away.

But as he did, he heard a noise from inside the entrance and felt his heart begin to beat a little too fast.

Crap, is someone in there? What if I've just locked some homeless person inside who was trying to keep warm for the night?

His body taut, shoulders stiff he turned around and looked at the keys in his hand. Walking back towards the door he pressed his ear against the centuries-old oak, pushed his fingers against the rough wood whilst trying to listen if someone was moving around.

He had run a busy church a lot bigger than this in inner-city Birmingham, where it was always noisy and brightly lit. Lots of drug addicts and homeless people coming and going all hours, but he was never alone in that church, there were always volunteers, Samaritans, someone would be there all hours of the day and night. His mouth felt dry, this was too quiet. The body of one of Morgan's colleagues had been found on the steps inside, and not that long ago he had discovered the body of a teenage girl in a ditch near to the far wall. This beautiful small stone church had seen more tragedy than the last ever had. The keys felt heavy in his hand, and he didn't want to go inside in case someone was in there, or what if there was a dead body? He could go back and wake Declan up, but he didn't have the heart to.

Snap out of it, Theo, you're being ridiculous. But he couldn't walk away without checking, and he swore under his breath as he inserted the keys and swung the door open. He turned the torch on his phone on and called out.

'Hey, is anyone in here before I lock up and go back to bed?'

The silence that greeted him was so heavy he could feel it

pressing on his shoulders, but there was nothing to indicate that someone was inside except for the yellow glow that came from underneath the ladies' toilet door. He shook his head. He could leave it, he should leave it, but this place cost a fortune to light and heat; the electricity bill was enough to make the giant statue of Jesus weep.

He sighed, and swore at an invisible Mrs Decker who had promised him she would make sure all lights were off before they left. The church hall that meetings were usually held in was out of bounds until it was fully repaired. The insurance for the fire that had been set there by a crazed killer had caused more problems than it was worth.

He strode towards the toilet, feeling a little better there were no apparent bodies, no homeless people and no one loitering around except for in his imagination. He reached the toilet and threw open the door. It was empty. Flicking off the light he pushed the door closed and turned to walk away. He was almost back at the entrance door when he felt the presence of someone behind him... and then a sharp pain cracked in the back of his head, making him sink to his knees.

He felt the rough slate under his knees and a pressure so immense in the back of his head it felt as if it had exploded. Lifting his fingers to feel it, they touched something warm and sticky. He knew what the smell was and before he could look at his own blood-stained fingertips he collapsed onto the cold floor, the coolness of the dark grey slate pressing against one cheek before he slipped unconscious.

EIGHTEEN

Morgan couldn't sleep. Usually she had no problem going to sleep, it was the staying asleep that caused her trouble, but stupidly she had let Raven pierce the side of her ear that she normally slept on and now it was burning and throbbing so much she couldn't put any pressure on it.

Ben had been too quiet, and she hadn't the energy to talk much either. She felt as if she was all spent up. As she lay there, she heard the slightest noise above her head and her entire body froze.

She knew it was impossible, no one could be up in the attic. The burglar alarm had been armed when they'd come home, but still the thought creeped her out and she strained to listen to any further movement. None came and she wondered if it was Kevin wandering around and the noise had come from a different direction altogether. She was likely being paranoid. It had been an upsetting day.

Coming home to see the house still under scene guard had been more than a little unsettling. She could see the moon from her window and stared it. Almost full it was illuminating the sky like a giant spotlight. As if thinking about him had summoned him from wherever he was, Kevin jumped onto her feet and she felt the duvet sink down as he began to try and make a bed for himself. She moved her legs, and he continued to paw the empty space where her legs had been to get comfortable. Now she had Ben who was gently snoring on one side and the cat who would soon start purring or cleaning himself on the other.

Morgan knew she should get up and go and sleep on the sofa where she could get some peace, but an image of Rosie Waite's blood-stained sofa cushions filled her head, and she knew she couldn't go down there on her own if she wanted to. She was almost relieved when her phone began to vibrate and snatched it off the bedside table so as not to disturb Ben. She answered to Declan screaming and crying Theo's name and shot out of bed, accidentally throwing Kevin across the room.

At her sudden movement Ben sat up too and switched on the light.

'Declan, talk to me, what's going on?'

Morgan didn't know if Theo had hit him or was trying to hit him. She would never in a million years have guessed Declan's next words.

'Oh God, he's dying, please, Morgan, he's dying.'

Ben heard his best friend's pleas and began hurriedly dressing. Both of them tugging on jogging pants and sweatshirts they kept near to the bed in case of emergency call-outs. Declan was sobbing down the phone.

'Where are you?'

'Oh God, why? Theo, please can you hear me.'

'Declan, where are you?' Morgan shouted at her friend, so loud that Kevin jumped an inch off the floor.

'The church.'

Ben nodded and the pair of them ran downstairs, shoving feet into trainers, not even fastening them properly, unbolting the door and running for Ben's car which was much faster than Morgan's.

'Declan, have you called an ambulance? Are the police on the way?'

'Yes.'

The pain and misery in their friend's voice shook her to the core. 'Five minutes, tops, we're on our way. Don't hang up, keep the line open okay.'

He didn't answer. She could hear him sobbing and wondered what the fuck had happened.

———

Ben drove far too fast along the quiet roads, where there was no other traffic, and he screeched to a halt outside the church, abandoning his car with the engine running and headlights illuminating the entrance. The door was wide open, and Declan was kneeling on the floor cradling Theo's lifeless body. There was blood pooling on the tiles, and Declan was covered in it. He looked up at them both, eyes wide with shock and horror.

Ben knelt next to him. 'What happened?'

Sirens in the distance got louder, and Morgan ran to wave the paramedics to where Theo was lying.

Declan looked at him, shaking his head.

'I don't know, I woke up and he wasn't there. I called out for him, but he wasn't home, so I came to check the church, and I found him like this. Someone did this to him, someone attacked him from behind.'

Two paramedics ran to where Declan was cradling Theo's lifeless body and looked at the scene in horror. Ben took hold of Declan's arm. 'We need to let them work.'

Declan nodded. Gently laying Theo's head down on the floor, he stood up, his new pyjamas soaked through with deep crimson bloodstains.

Morgan felt the world begin to sway – so much blood on other people sometimes made her feel faint – but she shook herself, she wouldn't do this now, her friends needed her.

Ben was leading Declan inside the church. It was as if the darkness swallowed them whole inside of there, and she looked around for the light switches so the paramedics could see what they were doing. Flipping them all down the whole building was flooded with warm white light, and she found herself silently praying for God or Jesus to help Theo. One of the paramedics began ripping open packets of gauze, wads and wads of it, to put pressure on the wound at the back of his head whilst the other was trying to get a line in.

'What can I do?' Morgan asked the woman who was struggling with one hand to keep the pressure on and open the packets.

She pointed to her kit bag. 'Open as many of them as there is and then start passing me bandages to secure it.'

Morgan did as she was asked, glad to be able to keep herself busy. She couldn't look at Theo's deathly white face but whispered, 'Is he alive?'

The paramedic who had managed to get a cannula in, nodded. 'Barely, he's got a weak pulse. We need to get him to hospital ASAP; he's lost a lot of blood.'

More sirens, heavy boots pounding along the gravel path to get to the church as three officers arrived, took one look at the scene and kept their distance to let the paramedics work.

'Can you hold this?'

She took hold of the IV bag of fluids as he ran to get a trolley from the back of the ambulance. It took three officers and two paramedics to get Theo safely onto the trolley and into the back, and the whole time Morgan kept hold of the fluids and found herself in the back too. She looked over at Declan who was now staring at the empty space where Theo had lain minutes earlier and the pooling blood he'd left behind. Ben had hold of

Declan's elbow, who was leaning heavily onto him, and he gave her the thumbs up just before the ambulance doors slammed shut.

The paramedic who was working on Theo glanced at her. 'Are you okay to come with us? We didn't give you a choice.'

'Fine, I'm off duty but Theo is my friend.'

'Sorry, this can't be nice for you. His partner is distraught. Did he do this?'

Morgan caught herself for the briefest of moments – could Declan have done this? Then shook her head. 'No way, they are madly in love with each other. I don't think they ever argue at all. Declan is a forensic pathologist, he's not a violent person.'

'I thought I knew his face; I didn't want to say anything because you know this is a terrible situation for him. What happened then? Because somebody has clearly attacked the patient with something sharp and heavy.'

Morgan shrugged. 'You know as much as I do, you arrived seconds after we did.' The ambulance was going fast down the winding lanes to get Theo to hospital, but it was still a bit of a trek.

'Where are we going?'

'Westmorland, they can stabilise him and airlift him to Preston to the trauma unit.'

She took out her phone and typed *Westmorland* into it and sent it to Ben, so he knew where to come and find them.

'Can you keep his head stabilised for me whilst we're on these windy roads?'

Morgan reached down gently to keep a hand on either side of the foam that was holding his head in place, and she bent down and brushed her lips against Theo's forehead.

'Keep fighting, Theo, we'll be there soon.'

Tears began to flow down her cheeks, but she couldn't lift her sleeve to wipe them away and tried to brush them against her shoulder.

NINETEEN

Ben was unsure what to do for the first time in a very long time. He looked at his friend who had gone from sobbing to silent as the shock began to settle over Declan's body.

'I want to go with Theo, Ben.'

'I know and we will, but I'm going to have to take those god-awful pyjamas off you, Declan.'

'What for?'

Ben dry swallowed; his throat was parched. 'Evidence.'

Declan looked into Ben's eyes. 'Evidence, you don't think I did this?'

Ben shook his head. 'Absolutely not, but you know the protocol, Declan. We have a serious assault on Theo, and you're covered in his blood. You could have the attacker's blood on you. Did you see a weapon anywhere?'

'No, all I saw was Theo lying there bleeding profusely and looking as if he was dying.' The words caught in the back of Declan's throat and a sob came out. 'I can't do this, Ben; you can fuck protocol. I need to get to the hospital with Theo.'

Ben squeezed his eyes shut for a second and wondered about the times he'd been in similar situations with Morgan being the one bleeding to death. He had never been a suspect; it had always thankfully been someone else.

'I know and you will, let's get you out of those; you can't go anywhere in them. They are soaked through with blood and pretty soon it will start to dry and start to smell. I'll get you something to wear, I have some overalls in the back of the—'

'No way am I going to the hospital to see Theo looking like a criminal. Do you know how much gossip that will cause?'

'Wait here, I'll go grab your clothes from inside.'

Declan nodded. His eyes were sparkling with tears and fury. Ben had never seen him this way and he wanted to hug him and tell him it was okay, but he couldn't. Despite Declan being his best friend, he couldn't totally risk losing any forensic evidence. He didn't for one minute believe that he had done this to Theo – for one thing it reminded him too much of the crime scene from this morning. He looked around for any signs of a weapon or a note.

'Wait here, you can't go back inside the house.'

Declan glared at him, but didn't argue with him. Ben wasn't even suited or booted, but shouted to the officers who were waiting for CSI and a supervisor to attend. 'Be two minutes, he needs some clothes.'

Then he was over the wall and jogging to go inside the vicarage that smelled of roast chicken and nothing untoward. The lights were on, and he could see no blood, no signs of an argument, no overturned furniture, broken pottery; there were two empty wine glasses on the coffee table in the lounge and he felt his heart break for Declan. Theo had looked terrible. He hoped he was going to be okay. Ben ran upstairs to the bedroom and grabbed a set of clothes and a pair of trainers out of the wardrobe, no idea if they were Theo's or Declan's, but they were around the same size, so it didn't matter. He quickly checked each room and found nothing out of place. In record time he was back at the church, where he took Declan inside and put the clothes on the nearest pew.

'Take them off and drop them on the floor. Wendy or whoever is on call will bag them up.'

Declan's eyes were red and swollen. 'Can I at least wash my hands?'

They were covered in blood. 'Not until they've been swabbed. You know it's my job. I don't think for one minute you could hurt Theo, but don't you want me to be able to prove it too?'

He nodded. 'What am I going to do about them?'

Ben shouted, 'I need some gloves.'

One of the officers tossed a rolled-up pair in his direction, and he gave them to Declan who snapped them on. His feet were bare, and Ben passed him the pair of trainers.

'Sorry, I didn't know whose shoes they were, or clothes.'

'It's fine, we're the same size but all of these are Theo's not mine. Can we go, please, Ben. If he dies and I'm not there to hold his hand and tell him how much I love him, I will never forgive you or me.'

Ben nodded. 'Come on.'

He didn't need to tell Declan to not walk over the scene. He was a seasoned professional and instinctively walked around the perimeter of it to Ben's waiting car with the engine still running.

TWENTY

Theo had been whisked away from Morgan, and she stood there staring after the empty space where the trolley had been moments ago feeling helpless. She wanted to cry and scream at the unfairness of it all, but she didn't. She felt a warm hand on her arm as the paramedic who had put Theo's line in was standing next to her. 'Let's get you out of the cold and into a waiting room.' He guided Morgan inside of the emergency department to the family room and opened the door.

'Can I get you a tea? It's good for shock.'

She shook her head. 'I don't drink it.'

'Be one minute.'

She sat down on one of the blue chairs. There was a box of tissues on the table and lots of leaflets about bereavement, sudden deaths and instructions on what to do when a loved one dies. She wanted to scoop them all up and throw them into the bin. Ben would bring Declan here soon, and she didn't want him looking at them. The door opened and the paramedic came in with a paper cup and passed it to her.

'Hot chocolate, it's better than the crappy tea anyway. It's about the only thing that's drinkable. Do you need a blanket? Can I call someone for you?'

She wrapped her fingers around the cup, not realising how much she was shivering until he'd pointed it out. 'I'm good, it's just shock but thank you for this.'

'We're going to need to fill out some paperwork. Can you answer the questions?'

The door opened and she saw Declan's distraught face. 'I'll do the paperwork; Theo is my partner. How is he?'

'He's gone for a CT scan then surgery, I think.'

Declan nodded. He came and sat down next to Morgan. 'Thank you.' He clasped her frozen hand in his much warmer one. 'Theo would be grateful that he didn't have to be alone in that ambulance.'

Morgan opened her mouth to tell him not to be so daft, that there was no need to thank her and all that came out was a huge sob as she burst into tears. Declan wrapped his arms around her, rocking her. She held him tight and rocked him back.

Ben slipped out of the room and went to fill in Theo's paperwork the best he could to give them a moment. As he was leaning over the desk to answer the questions, two officers came in, and Smithy made a beeline for him.

'What the hell, Ben, weren't one of us supposed to travel with the victim? And the suspect is supposed to be in custody, not here.'

Ben smiled at the receptionist. 'Sorry, that's all I have.'

'It's fine, we can fill the rest out.'

He turned to Smithy and the student officer who was standing next to him.

'Theo is our friend; Declan is not a suspect.'

'He's not? He was covered in blood and holding the victim when we arrived.'

'He found him like that. He's his partner, what else is he supposed to do?'

Smithy shrugged. 'Fair point. Well, we'll have to sit with him until we know what's happening so he can be interviewed.'

Ben knew all of this; he also knew that Smithy was just pissed because sitting up at the hospital for hours meant he didn't have to answer any other jobs that might come in. It was an easy shift and some officers enjoyed it; some hated it. Smithy enjoyed it a little too much.

'Fine, they're in the family room. Give them a minute before you go striding in there and putting your foot in it, and remember that Declan is not some scumbag off the street. He is the forensic pathologist for the entire area, a very well-respected doctor. He's not a suspect and he's my very good friend.'

'Oh crap, I didn't realise it was Dr Death.'

'Smithy, if I hear you call him that in public, I will drop kick you out of this department quicker than you could ever run, do you get me? It's Doctor Donnelly to you, don't screw this up.'

'Calm down, Ben, I won't. I'd leave you to it, but I have a student, and this is good to get ticked off the check list.'

Ben looked at the student, who looked as if he was fresh out of school and not old enough to shave, making him feel ancient. He scrubbed his hand across his face and his five o'clock shadow.

'Look, I'm here and Morgan is in with Declan. Go get yourselves a hot drink and give us ten minutes. No one is going anywhere. Can you do that?'

'No problem, we can.'

Ben turned and went back to the family room as Smithy began chatting with the receptionist to wangle them both a free brew, and Ben rolled his eyes before slipping back to be with his friends.

TWENTY-ONE

Raven Castle had never been a good sleeper; she loved the moonlight and preferred being out in the dark to the day. After the visit from those two detectives this afternoon her mind had been working overtime. She didn't want to get in trouble; she hadn't meant for any of it to happen. It had been a bit of fun that was all. It wasn't her fault it all went wrong and now she was scared she would get the blame for something that wasn't strictly all her doing. It had taken her just over an hour to cycle to Rydal Falls. She loved being out on her bike and never drove anywhere. It was cheap, she could always find somewhere to park her bike, for free, and it never needed petrol. Her mum had offered to buy her an electric one for her birthday, but she'd said no, she liked the exercise and how strong she felt pumping her legs and heart triple time to get up all the hills and fells around the area. It was the only exercise she did.

She couldn't believe she would never see Matt again. She hadn't known him long, but it had been long enough to fall in love with him, so when the detective had come in questioning her, she'd said too much too soon. She'd offered to pierce her ear to give herself time to think about how she was going to get out of this mess.

She turned into the quiet street full of beautiful Victorian semis and saw Matt's house all in darkness. Slowing down she cycled past it, hoping to see a light on. It didn't look like a major crime scene. She didn't see the police officer sitting in the plain car outside until she pulled up next to it and she saw her staring down at her phone, the glow illuminating the inside of the car and her luminous yellow body armour. The officer glanced up and started to see her staring in. Raven smiled and waved at her then carried on slowly as if she was in no rush to get away. She could feel the woman's eyes watching her from behind. She'd always been able to pick up on stuff like that, people's emotions, thoughts, feelings and she tried to act as normal as any teenage girl cycling around the street where a couple had supposedly been murdered in the early hours of the morning. It wasn't until she turned the corner that she speeded up enough to get the hell out of there. The last thing she needed was being pulled over by the cops.

She lived in Kendal, she had no reason to be here, at least not to anyone else's knowledge. Her heart ached at the thought of not seeing Matt again, not feeling his heart beating against hers as they lay naked in her single bed whilst her mum was working late. She knew he lived with a woman; he had told her that she was his house share, but a little bit of social media stalking after he'd mentioned Rosie a few too many times when they were a little bit tipsy off the wine he'd brought around had stirred something inside of her that made her think that Rosie was more than some woman he shared a house with. Her instinct had been right. Rosie Waite was definitely more than who he said she was judging by the number of photos of them together, arms draped around each other on holiday, days out, even at home. She had been furious, what woman wouldn't be? But she liked him and liked the way he screwed her as if he'd not had sex in months. It had only happened a few times, but it had been raw, passionate and unlike any other man she'd slept with, but he'd betrayed her, and she could never forgive him, and now he had paid the ultimate price. She wouldn't have wished death on him, but she had wished him harm and sometimes what is done can't be undone.

She headed in the direction of St Martha's; she loved the pretty church and its dark history that walked hand in hand with it. Dark history was her favourite. Another thing about Rydal Falls – you couldn't go five minutes without passing the place a body had been found. She was thinking about offering walking tours of all the local murder sites. They did it in York, Edinburgh, London, almost everywhere you could go on all sorts of tours. Only her mum had told her it was in bad taste because they were recent murders and not historical. Raven didn't think it mattered, because people were fascinated with the subject of murder and she bet loads of tourists would sign up for a murder walking tour with the dark goddess of the night.

Lost in her thoughts she almost crashed into the back of a parked police van in the narrow lane that led to the church, and she swerved around it to see another van and one with CSI emblazoned across it. She turned around smiling to herself and cycled in the opposite direction. Rydal Falls was on fire tonight with crime and cops. She was sufficiently tired enough to consider turning around and going home. She might actually fall asleep when she climbed into bed now after all the excitement.

TWENTY-TWO

Declan had insisted they go home. It was going to be a long night, and he had left them to go and wait outside the operating theatre for Theo to be brought out.

'Perks of the job, there aren't many but access to the places others can't counts as one.'

Morgan had told him they would wait, but he'd been reassured by the doctor's recent updates. Theo was in theatre having a metal plate put in his skull. He felt quite confident that he was going to be okay. Time would tell if there was any significant brain damage, but he'd be taken off the ventilator tomorrow or maybe even the day after.

The journey home was sombre, and they didn't even have the radio on.

'Do you think he'll be okay brain wise?' Morgan asked. Her tone was hushed.

Ben nodded. 'You were, you'll both be twins with matching metal plates in your skull. It's an exclusive club for people with extra hard heads.'

She smiled at him. 'It's a club I'd rather not be in.'

Ben's hand rested on her thigh. 'No, I wish you weren't a

member either. I'm sure Theo will be fine, he has God on his side, doesn't he? And Declan is there fighting his corner.'

'Yes, he does. I feel so bad.'

'Why? This is nothing to do with you.'

'What if he was attacked because of Declan working the case? He was at the scene, maybe they couldn't get to him and hurt Theo instead. I feel terrible for the way I always wanted to arrest him when he first moved to the area.'

'He was a pretty good fit for a few of those crimes and he's forgiven you for that.'

'I know, I really like him though and I hate the thought of Declan losing the love of his life.'

'Hey, I think we should be extra cautious, and we can't rule the note out as not being a target for whoever found it, but I don't know why they would target Theo. He has nothing to do with it. Where's the positive talking, Morgan? He's fine, he's in the best place being looked after by the best people.'

'Should we go back to the scene?'

'No, we can't do anything. CSI are there, and it's all locked down. We need to sleep at least a couple of hours and besides, I think that Marc won't let us work it anyway. He'll ask Gilly.'

'Really?'

'Yep, too close and personal to us both. What we need to focus on is why he was attacked.'

'You just said we wouldn't be working it.'

'I did, but it doesn't mean that we can't.'

She laughed. 'Oh boy.'

'What?'

'You're turning into me; I fear I'm a bad influence on you, boss.'

Ben laughed even louder. 'Yes, you are, Brookes. A very bad one, but I wouldn't have you any other way.'

As they turned into the street her eyes glanced towards Rosie and Matt's empty house. 'This is crazy, you know, like really off the chart. Who would do that to them? Who would do that to Theo? They have to be connected, two murders both with a heavy, sharp instrument and now Theo has a similar head injury. Did he know them? Had he ever talked to them? Maybe they were going to get married and had been to see him about it.'

'A lot of maybes, but who knows? Tomorrow we have a busy day. We need to find the motive for Rosie's and Matt's murders and then maybe we can find the reason for Theo's attack.'

'I hope so because for him to be attacked this late at night in his own church, someone had to have known he'd be going into the church; they couldn't wait around forever on the off chance.'

They got out of the car and Ben spoke quietly in case anyone's doorbell cameras or dashcams were recording. 'It was premeditated. How did they know Theo would go back to the church in the middle of the night? That wasn't something they stumbled upon. Whoever it was, they were waiting for him. What made him go back out?'

'Did he hear a noise, get a phone call maybe?'

They went inside Ben's house where they discovered he hadn't set the alarm before they'd run out. Morgan stared at the keypad with a heaviness in her stomach that made her feet reluctant to move. They had tried to not focus on the fact that they might be the targets but Theo's attack had cast doubt on everything they had thought. She reached forward and flipped on the lights, and Ben opened the hall cupboard where they kept their coats and shoes. He pulled out the old wooden cricket bat that had seen better days, and gripped the handle tight.

'We are going to check this place from bottom to top, every inch of it. Keep your phone on 999 ready to press call.' His voice was so quiet she barely heard it, but she nodded.

Ben didn't call out and they silently checked each downstairs room, leaving the lights on until the entire downstairs was lit up. About to go upstairs they heard a heavy thud come from their bedroom and both of them held their breaths until Kevin appeared at the top of the landing, staring down at them in disgust for waking him up. Morgan giggled and Ben laughed too. 'That bloody cat will be the death of me. I crapped myself then, I thought it was some hammer-wielding nutter coming for us,' said Ben.

Morgan couldn't stop laughing. 'Oh God, this isn't even funny, he might be a decoy.'

They didn't bother trying to be quiet as they climbed the stairs; instead, they checked each of the bedrooms, the bathroom and then they stopped underneath the attic. The hatch was closed.

'I'd say forget it, but I can't stop thinking about Rosie and Matt being spied on in the bathroom.'

'You're right, I'll go up there and check.'

'I'm coming with you, Ben, don't be such a hero.'

Ben got the pole with the hook on and caught the catch, pulling the loft ladder down. The entire house was lit up, bulbs burning in every single room. The only void of darkness was up there and it felt menacing.

'Is anyone up there? I'm warning you now, I have a weapon and I'm not afraid to use it.'

Despite it all, Morgan giggled at this, the attic was clearly not as scary as Ben sounded, not sure if it was nerves or the fact that Ben sounded ridiculous, but he went up and she followed. Inside the attic he turned the single bare bulb on and there was nothing that stood out. Between them they checked the corners and every place there could be for a person to hide.

'Nothing,' said Ben, and the relief was palpable in his voice.

'Thankfully. Actually, why would someone be up there in the first place?'

Before they went back downstairs, Ben closed the hatch behind them.

'It's the proximity to the crime scene and the fact that you are like a beacon to every psychopath in the country. I'd rather be assured we were under no threat. I'm also tired, but I'm too stressed to sleep.'

'It's the shock; what a day it's been. Should we have a glass of wine or something to help us relax?' Morgan didn't really want anything, but they did need to rest. Right now there wasn't anything they could do for anyone except take care of themselves, ready to put everything in to finding answers when they got to work. It would be a long shift but neither of them would complain because this was too personal.

'Yeah, okay. Just a small one, I want to be able to drive if Declan needs me.'

She smiled at Ben. 'You're such a good friend.'

'I wasn't always, and Declan taught me how to be. He never gave up on me after Cindy despite me giving up on myself, and I owe him so much for always being there for me. I doubt I'd still be here if it hadn't been for him.'

The thought of a life never knowing this kind, funny, wonderful man made her heart ache, and she was so grateful that she did. They went back to the kitchen where Kevin was sitting by his food bowl. Ben squeezed some cat food out of a pouch whilst Morgan poured them two small glasses of her favourite rosé wine. She passed Ben's glass to him and looked at the clock, it was just gone three a.m., and felt a coldness creep down her spine.

TWENTY-THREE

The office was already full, and as they walked through the door Gilly came dashing down the corridor after them.

'Morning, sorry I'm late.'

Ben smiled at her. 'Are you?'

She shrugged. 'No idea, but it sounded good.'

Morgan smiled at her, and she winked. 'Sorry to hear about your friend, it's hard to believe someone would attack a priest in his own church. What is the world coming to?'

Ben answered, 'No idea, but it's not good.' His phone began to ring, and Morgan saw Declan's picture flash up on the screen.

'Excuse me.'

He turned around and walked back out of the office and a little further down the corridor where there was no noise. Morgan's heart began to beat double time. She was desperate for an update yet at the same time terrified it could be bad news.

She followed Gilly in, giving Ben some space. Cain and Amy were sitting hunched over her computer reading the incident log from last night, and Morgan could see the address at the top of it.

Amy looked at her. 'This is awful. How is he?'

'Ben's on the phone to Declan now. He was going to theatre when we left to get a metal plate in his skull.'

For once Cain didn't say anything, no witty comments, no sarcasm, and Morgan wished he would. She wanted work to be as normal as possible even though they were under a great strain with two murders and an attempted murder. Officers in Barrow had spoken with both victims' families and passed on the sad news, which had been a relief for Morgan, as it took so much out of her whenever they had to pass on a death message. Matt's dad had taken it better than poor Rosie's parents according to the FLOs. Morgan was scrolling through Rosie's Instagram page, looking for pictures of Matt to see if he was wearing the medallion that had been found, but with no luck.

Madds walked through the door, took one look at their solemn faces, and rolled his eyes.

'Blimey, you lot look happy.'

Cain nodded at him. 'What's up, Sarge?'

He turned to Cain and crossed his arms. 'I'll tell you what's up, Cain, where are the biscuits you took yesterday? I thought to myself I'll have a nice cup of coffee to start my shift with and a couple of digestives. Only, guess what? The milk is off, and the biscuits are nowhere to be found. I have a reliable source who told me you were rifling through the downstairs brew cupboard.'

'That's not very nice of you, Sarge, accusing me of nicking your biscuits.'

'I'm not in a very nice mood. Have you got fresh milk and any biscuits up here?'

Amy stood up. 'Yes, we have, I brought some in this morning, Sarge.' She disappeared then came back less than a minute later with a fresh packet of biscuits and a carton of milk.

'Thanks, appreciate it. Oh, where's Benno? Is he around?'

'He's on the phone out there somewhere,' replied Morgan.

'Tell him I have a prime suspect in the cells for him, ready to interview.'

Everyone stared at him, mouths open. It was Gilly who answered.

'You do, for what?'

'The attack on the priest last night and probably the murder victims too. She was cycling down your street last night, Morgan, in the early hours, past the murder victims' house. Amber was on scene guard and noticed her staring at the house. Then she went to the church because one of the CSIs saw her almost crash into the back of a van then do a sharp turnaround to get out of there.'

'Who is she?' asked Morgan.

He shrugged. 'Not sure, I don't know her, never heard of her.'

He looked at Gilly. 'Why are you here?'

'I'm dealing with the attempted murder; Marc phoned me an hour ago to ask if I could help out.'

'I'd wear some kind of body armour if I was you, hanging around with this lot is like putting a death wish on yourself. Myself and Morgan will attend the PM if that's okay with you, Gilly, seems pointless you going when you need to deal with Theo's attack and put all your focus on that.'

Then he was gone, leaving them all looking at each other. Gilly who hadn't even sat down yet, left the room too. Morgan assumed she was going down to custody, to speak to whoever was the duty sergeant. Ben walked in and smiled at her; this was good news.

'Theo is stable and has been since coming out of surgery. He's in ICU but they don't intend to wake him for a while yet. Declan said he's had a couple of hours' sleep in his office and if we give him another hour, by the time we get there he'll be ready to do the post-mortems.'

'That's brilliant news about Theo, phew.' Morgan felt so much better now. Theo was made of strong stuff.

'Oh, Madds has just been in, they have a suspect in custody for Theo's attack. Gilly has gone down there to speak to the custody sergeant.'

'Really? Blimey, that's brilliant.'

'Should we go down too?'

Ben was already out of the door, and Morgan followed, leaving Amy and Cain in the same position they were in when she walked in.

Amy tutted. 'I could have told them her name, it's right here on the log, if they'd asked.'

'Leave them to it. Who is it? Anyone we know?'

Amy scrolled down the page and pointed to the name.

'Well, I never.' Cain sounded genuinely surprised. He stood up and walked out of the office, leaving Amy alone nibbling on the other packet of biscuits she'd brought in.

TWENTY-FOUR

There was quite the crowd of them around Eric's desk, and the custody sergeant didn't look too amused.

'Who invited you lot to this party? Why are you all here for one prisoner? It's overkill.'

Ben spoke first. 'Who got brought in last night for being at the crime scenes?'

'She's only a kid. If you ask me, you're barking up the wrong tree with this one.'

Gilly smiled at him. 'We didn't ask you. Her name, please?'

'Raven Castle.'

Morgan gasped, and everyone looked at her. 'Sorry, did I do that out loud?'

Gilly's eyes were studying Morgan now. 'Do you know her?'

'Sort of, well I didn't until yesterday when I visited her mum's shop in Kendal.'

Morgan wondered if now was the time to admit about her getting a piercing in work's time, but decided to keep quiet until she had to.

'She seemed nice enough. Why was she at the crime scene? Did she say?' Morgan asked.

'More like how did she know about the crime scene at the church? It wasn't public knowledge, and if she lives in Kendal, it's not as if she could see it out of her front window.'

Ben nodded and Morgan agreed; Gilly was right. How had she known about Theo?

'Has she got a brief?'

Eric shook his head. 'Doesn't want one because she hasn't done anything wrong according to her. She hasn't said anything else, except she wants to speak to Morgan, but I told her she wasn't here.'

Gilly nodded. 'Silly girl, come on, Ben, let's go put her straight and see what she has to say for herself.'

Morgan left them to it. As she crossed the atrium, she heard a familiar voice calling her name.

'Morgan, you have a visitor.'

She turned to look at her, confusion clouding her eyes. 'I do, who is it?'

'Gina LoBue.'

That was her second surprise of the morning, and she couldn't wait for the third. Her aunt Ettie had told her everything, whether good or bad, comes in threes and she believed her. Which reminded her, she needed to give her a ring, it had been too long, but the days slipped by so fast and turned into weeks, and before she knew it, it was months. She headed out to the reception area and saw Gina sitting there, headphones on listening to something. When she realised Morgan was watching her, she lowered them.

'Hi, can I help you?'

Gina shrugged. 'I don't know, but I thought I'd come and see you for an update personally. I didn't want to spend hours on the phone trying to get through to you.'

Morgan's shoulders sagged a little. She had nothing to update her with. She couldn't tell her about Matt visiting Raven and her being arrested, as it was all confidential. She opened the nearest interview room to her and waved Gina inside.

As Morgan sat down, she smiled at Gina who looked as if she'd stepped out of the pages of *Cosmopolitan* magazine, she looked so glamorous.

'I'm afraid I don't have much I can tell you. I'm sorry, you should have rung and saved yourself the journey here.'

Gina sat down. 'Nothing, it's been twenty-four hours. These are the golden hours and you're wasting them.'

'We haven't wasted them at all. There have been some interesting developments, and we currently have a suspect in custody. I'm afraid I can't say much more.'

Gina's eyes were wide open. 'You do, oh. I'm sorry, forgive me for being so forward. I couldn't sleep last night thinking about them, and I feel so damn useless. We talk about murders all the time on the podcast, and you wouldn't believe how many times the cops dropped the ball and messed up so many cases over the years. I guess I assumed you would be no better. I was wrong, and I apologise.'

'Apology accepted; we have a lot of experience with murder cases unfortunately. While you're here, can I ask you some questions about Matt?'

Gina nodded. 'Ask away, though I don't know how much I can help you with him. Rosie was my friend.'

Morgan smiled at her. 'Do you know if he suffered with migraines a lot?'

'What's that got to do with him being murdered?' Gina paused. 'Sorry, I need to drop the attitude, don't I?'

Morgan shrugged; she didn't care about her attitude although it was beginning to grate on her a tiny bit.

'Yes, he had a lot of headaches. Rosie said he'd been suffering badly the last month, so bad that he hadn't—' She stopped.

'Hadn't what?'

'I don't know if this is relevant to your question.'

'Tell me and I'll be the judge of it.'

Gina sighed. 'I feel bad, it's like I'm betraying Rosie by talking about her relationship.'

Morgan felt a tingle in the tips of her fingers and sat up straighter, clasping her hands under the desk.

'Gina, she's dead and I am so sorry she is but if this is something that might help with the investigation then you're not betraying Rosie; you're helping to find her killer.'

'She said they hadn't had sex in over a month because he kept crying off, saying he had a bad headache, and Rosie said it was bizarre, as it was supposed to be her complaining about screwing with the excuse of a headache not him.'

Morgan wondered if their seemingly happy relationship was as picture-perfect as she had originally thought.

'Did Rosie ever suspect why?'

'No,' Gina said, going pale. 'We didn't have any secrets.'

'Well that's extremely useful anyway, Gina, thanks.'

Gina stood up. 'I'll let you get on, Morgan, I've taken up too much of your time. Will you update me if you charge someone? I might feel better knowing that the person who did that to them isn't walking around the streets.'

'Of course.'

Gina looked devastated, and Morgan felt bad for her. She knew how awful it was to lose someone you loved to extreme violence.

TWENTY-FIVE

Amy hadn't spoken to Jack, her now ex-partner, since she'd moved in with Cain, and she'd been avoiding him too, not leaving the office unless it was for the toilet or to brew up, so when he stormed into the office, tiny circles of angry red on his usually pale cheeks, his floppy fringe pushed back and his green eyes shining so bright his pupils looked huge, she could tell he was raging with her. He waved the hospital letter in his hand, and she felt her stomach flip.

'What's this?'

'What does it look like, Jack?'

'It's an antenatal appointment. You told me you were getting an abortion, that you didn't want the baby either. I told you I don't want a baby, not now or not ever.'

She stood up and snatched the letter out of his hand. 'I changed my mind.'

'You changed your mind? You selfish cow. What about me?'

'What about you?'

'I don't want a fucking baby, Amy. I don't want to be tied down for the rest of my life. I'm not ready for that and I don't think I ever will be.'

His voice was raised too loud, and she could feel her cheeks burning because the office in the police station was not the right place to have this conversation.

'Shut up and stop shouting, you're like a spoiled child, Jack.'

'Don't tell me to shut up.' His face was getting redder, and she could feel the heat radiating from his cheeks. He took a step towards her, just as Cain walked in. Cain took one look at Amy's pale face and Jack's beetroot red one and held out his hands.

'Calm down, Jack. What's up, bud?'

Jack spun around to face Cain. 'Calm down? Fuck off. I bet it's not even my baby. She's shacked up with you, pregnant, and I bet she's going to take me to the child support agency for every penny I have when it's not even my kid, and I don't want anything to do with it if it is.'

Cain lunged for Jack who rushed towards him, fists flying everywhere. He smacked Cain in the face.

Cain said to Amy, 'Did you see that? He hit first.' Then he drew back his fist and smacked Jack back, much harder.

They continued to tussle, Cain had hold of him and was dragging him away from Amy, out of the door, out into the corridor. The next shift had all just started and were standing downstairs brewing up ready for the briefing. Eight coppers all looked up to see Cain and Jack scrapping above them. Madds came rushing out of his office, swearing under his breath, just as Ben walked out of the custody suite and Morgan came back into the atrium. It was carnage, the noise bringing every single person in the station to come and look at the spectacle that was happening above them.

Ben and Morgan ran up the stairs, and Madds who had sprinted up already had hold of Jack's shoulders. Ben ran towards Cain and shoved him hard with both hands away from Jack. Morgan stepped in-between the men to separate them.

'What the hell is going on?' asked Madds as he pushed Jack

towards the lift to get him away from Cain. 'My office now, Jack.'

Jack stopped fighting and looked like he now realised the enormity of the trouble he was in.

Madds turned to Ben. 'No idea what this is about, but you sort him out.' He was pointing in Cain's direction.

Cain held up his hands. 'It was just a laugh; we were just messing about.'

Ben arched an eyebrow at Cain who had a trail of blood trickling down his nostril. Morgan passed him a tissue, and he blotted at his nose. Ben opened the office door and pushed Cain inside.

'What the hell were you doing, Cain? In front of the whole station too, take your pick of witnesses.' His finger pointed towards the crowd. 'How many did you want?'

He shrugged and sat down.

Amy rushed towards him. 'Are you okay? Oh God, I'm sorry.'

Ben looked at her. 'Why are you sorry? You didn't hit him.'

She bit her lip. 'It's my fault, I was arguing with Jack and Cain tried to stop him.'

'That right, Cain?'

He nodded. 'It was still just messing around.'

'You could get suspended for this, Cain, it's serious.'

'What? For play fighting? Come on, Ben, it was just a laugh.'

Ben rolled his eyes. 'Wait there, do not leave this office until I've spoken to Madds.'

He let the door slam behind him.

Amy looked ill. 'Thank you, but you didn't need to. I can handle Jack.'

'He looked as if he was going to punch you. I'd rather he punched me, Amy. I'm not pregnant.'

Morgan had opened the first aid kit and torn open an antiseptic wipe for the small cut across Cain's eyebrow. She put on a pair of gloves and began to dab at it.

'Cain, you're a sweetheart, but what if you get suspended?'

'Morgan, I am never going to stand by and watch a guy intimidate a girl, especially not a pregnant one who I work with and respect.'

Amy began to sob, burying her head in her arms, and Cain lowered his voice. 'If Jack has any sense, he'll say we were messing around. He might be a dick, but he's a good copper. I wouldn't want him to get sacked because his head's a shed and he's lost it.'

Morgan smiled at him. 'Not as good a copper as you, though. We don't want to lose you either.'

'Then be a good friend and go make me a decent cup of coffee. I think I need caffeine or something.'

'Do you need a Snickers, Cain, are you hangry?'

Amy looked up and began laughing, blotting her eyes at the same time. 'Hahaha, good one, Morgan. That's what he always says to me, and why are my hormones so unreliable? I don't cry in public and never have.'

He nodded. 'I'm always hungry. Did he break my nose? It's only just been fixed.'

'Nose is good. You have a small cut on your eyebrow, but it's nothing.'

'Okay, story is we were messing around, unless you want to tell the truth about him, Amy?'

'No, he's never been like that before. I don't know why he's so against me keeping this baby. The more he tells me he doesn't want one the more I do, and I never thought I'd say that in a million years.'

'Can't believe he accused me of being the dad.'

Morgan burst out laughing. 'You two are more of a liability than I am.'

Amy shook her head. 'I can't believe he thinks I've slept with you, Cain.'

'And what is that supposed to mean? I'm not some vile creature out of the bog.'

When Ben walked in and looked at the three of them sitting there drinking coffee as if the whole debacle out on the corridor hadn't just happened, he crossed his arms and glared at them. 'Unbelievable, you lot, no wonder I have a bad heart.'

'*Had* a bad heart. I thought it was okay now, boss,' said Amy.

'Jack said he was messing around with you, and it got a bit out of hand. Is that true?'

Cain nodded.

'Yeah, well I walked out of custody to the iconic fight scene out of *Step Brothers* happening in full view of the police station like it's some alternative universe. What I can't figure out is, which one you is Dale or Brennan?'

Amy laughed. 'He's definitely Brennan.'

Cain gave her the finger.

'Cain, do not go near Jack, do not get yourself in any more trouble. I don't know what's going to happen, if you're both going to get suspended or what, but the good news is the CCTV is down because it's getting updated and none of the afternoon shift said they're giving statements because they also thought you were messing around. If you ask me, you have got off lightly.'

Cain shrugged, but there was no mistaking the look of relief on his face. 'Cheers, boss, sorry about that but it wasn't really my fault for a change.'

Ben rolled his eyes at him. He turned to Morgan. 'Morgan, that woman Raven won't speak to me or Gilly unless you're present. Can you go down and help Gilly interview her?'

Morgan stood up and walked outside. Ben followed her,

asking, 'Why is Raven so keen to talk to you? Did you know her before yesterday?'

It was now or never. 'No, that was the first time I ever met her. What did she say?'

'Nothing and that's the problem; the only words she said was your name.'

'Maybe she trusts me.'

Ben looked at her, furrowing his brow.

Morgan lifted the strands of hair covering her piercing which wasn't quite as angry-looking today. 'I asked her to do this...'

'Yesterday? Why?'

'I thought she might open up a bit and be more talkative if she pierced me. If she thought I was a customer. It worked, that's why she told me all about Matt's visit. Speaking of which, Gina just told me Matt and Rosie hadn't slept together in a while. I think there is more to Raven and Matt's relationship too. What if Matt mentioned something to Raven? What if Raven is more involved in this than I thought?' Morgan stopped for a moment. 'What if Matt was asking questions about the piercing equipment because he intended to kill Rosie, to muti-late her. What if he's the killer? He could have shared his disgusting ideas with Raven, convinced her to be an accom-plice... and then Raven double-crossed him.'

'Well, that's quite a stretch,' Ben replied, slightly shocked.

Morgan shrugged. 'How did Raven react when you told her Matt and Rosie were murdered?'

'She was calm, she never missed a beat. I would have thought she barely knew him to be honest. Maybe she's a classic sociopath, that could explain a lot.'

'Maybe, it doesn't explain what she was doing at the church though or why she would have a reason to attack Theo.'

He leaned closer to look at her ear. 'Is that sore? Are you mad, Morgan?'

She grinned at him. 'It's not too bad and probably, we're all mad here. I'm mad, you're mad.'

'*Alice in Wonderland*, I might not read much but I know the classics and that cat was right: you'd have to be mad to work in this office with you lot. Go find me a killer, Morgan, and let's put this to bed.'

As she walked to custody she couldn't help wondering if Raven could be a sociopath or was she a jealous lover who had lost control?

TWENTY-SIX

Raven looked exhausted. She had yesterday's make-up on and her eyeliner was a smudged mess. Morgan thought she may have been crying. Her hair was still in two – now messy – space buns. Gilly was sitting sipping from a mug of coffee, and there was a plastic cup of water in front of Raven.

'Hello, Raven, did you want to speak to me?'

Raven nodded. Gilly leaned forward and said, 'Interview recommencing. Detective Morgan Brookes has just entered the room.'

Morgan sat down wishing she'd brought her coffee with her. 'Why did you want to speak to me and not my colleagues?'

Raven sighed. 'I like you, you're cool. How's the ear?'

Gilly interrupted. 'How do you know Detective Brookes?'

'She came into Mum's tattoo shop yesterday asking me questions.'

Gilly nodded, and Morgan replied, 'The piercing is good. Raven, why were you cycling past Matt's house last night?'

'I just wanted to see where he lived. We have his address on the database, like I showed it to you yesterday, and to make sure you were telling the truth about his murder.'

'Why would I lie about that?'

She shrugged. 'I don't know, I couldn't stop thinking about it after you left and then I couldn't sleep, so I went out for a bike ride and found myself there. It's not a crime to cycle down a street, is it?'

'No, it's not. But you knew it was an active crime scene.'

'I always go out on my bike, I'm a good cyclist. I didn't know it would cause so much trouble, and besides I like cycling at night, hardly any crazy tourists driving like they're taking part in a rally. People go out doing stuff like this all the time and they don't get arrested for it. Why am I here?'

'Do you know the vicar from Saint Martha's church? Theo?'

Raven shook her head. 'No, why would I?'

'Why did you go to that particular church after you visited Matt's house?'

An even louder sigh escaped Raven's lips. 'Look, I'm not sick in the head or anything I just like looking at places where people have died, and that church has had a couple of murders happen there. I also think it's a really pretty church. It's my favourite and that was before the bodies turned up. I love the creepy graveyard, the atmosphere. I'm a spooky gal, what can I say? I find graveyards and cemeteries peaceful, I'm drawn to them.' She leaned back and crossed her arms.

'Did you know that the vicar had been seriously injured in an attack last night when you cycled there?'

'What? Wait a minute, no, I did not know that. Hang on, I didn't do it; I didn't have anything to do with that. Why would I?'

Morgan thought she sounded convincing, but there were so many holes in her story.

'Were you having an affair with Matt?' The question had come to Morgan's mind almost immediately when she'd heard Raven had been by the house. But she wanted to use it effectively. Get her timing right. And it had worked.

Raven's lips formed a straight line, but her eyes gave her away and she looked like a kid caught with their hand in the biscuit tin does. She looked stunned. 'Who told you that? I think you better get me a solicitor,' she said bluntly.

Morgan nodded and gave her a half smile; she couldn't help it.

Gilly stood up. 'Interview suspended at 10.27.' She walked out of the room leaving Morgan in there with Raven.

'I didn't do anything, Morgan; I swear I didn't.'

'Look, talk to a solicitor and tell them what you just told us, Raven, and anything else you think they should know.'

She nodded. 'Can you let my mum know where I am? She will be panicking. She'll think I've had an accident or something when she realises my bike isn't in the shed.'

'Of course. When you've spoken to the solicitor and Gilly comes back in to interview you, do what he says. Then you will be released on bail, and you can go home.'

'Thank you.'

Morgan smiled at her. 'No problem.'

Sharon, one of the detention officers, came in the room. 'Raven, I'll take you back to your room until the solicitor gets here. I'll get you some breakfast too. You need to eat something, you didn't touch the food I brought in earlier.'

Raven nodded and followed her out.

Morgan was torn, on one hand she really liked the girl, but a part of her was sure she was hiding something from them, which made it hard to be objective when dealing with Raven. However, liking someone didn't mean they were innocent, it meant they were charming, and Morgan knew she was going to have to dig a little deeper into Raven's background to see if she wasn't as innocent as she seemed. If she had psychopathic traits she could be charming and lack any kind of empathy with anyone. She could have killed Rosie and Matt without any remorse.

Morgan went back to tell Ben the bad news that they couldn't pin anything on Raven at the moment – not that she was involved in the murders or in Theo's attack; at least there was nothing in what Raven had said to prove she was. Unless they could find some evidence, she was going to be released pretty soon. A search of Raven's house might help them secure something to either make her talk or keep her in custody, but they needed to get a warrant for that.

TWENTY-SEVEN

Susie greeted them with the most vibrant copper and green hair that Morgan had ever seen. Ben did a double-take but kept quiet. It amused Morgan how Susie's hair shocked him every time despite him knowing that it was going to be magnificent.

'Love, love the hair, Susie.'

'Thanks, Morgan, it's in honour of you.'

'Wow, it's amazing, isn't it, Ben?' She jabbed him in the ribs with her elbow.

'Yeah, it's truly something. How's Declan holding up? Is there any update on Theo?'

Susie glanced over her shoulder. 'He's better than I expected.'

'Declan or Theo?' asked Ben.

'Well, both of them. Declan is a bit quiet and looks like shit. I don't think he should be here but he's insisting he's fine and doesn't want to be anywhere else. Theo is still stable, no news from ICU, which is good news I suppose. They promised they'd phone Declan if there's any change.'

They followed her down to the changing rooms, then into the mortuary where Declan was fiddling with the radio he kept on the shelf at the back. A noughties station began to play, and he turned around. Morgan couldn't help herself and before she knew it she was hugging him. He held her tight, swaying her from side to side then kissed the top of her head.

'Away with you, you're going to make me cry.'

She had tears in her eyes already and blinked to clear them. 'How is he?'

'He's good, amazingly good. I guess he has a head as tough as yours, thank the good Lord Jesus.'

Ben smiled at him. 'That's brilliant news.'

Morgan went back to stand by Ben's side. She looked at Ben and wanted to hug him too, but restrained herself. Ben had been in this situation with her far too many times, and he knew how heartsick it made you feel with the worry, and she wondered how he stayed on the force, or with her for that matter, when trouble seemed to follow her around.

'I thought we'd start with Rosie,' Declan began. 'Call me old-fashioned, but I like to do the ladies first and I'm sure her partner wouldn't object.'

Morgan wasn't so sure Matt would have cared. If her hunch was right, then things weren't as happy in Rosie and Matt's house as their outward appearance suggested.

The sound of the body bag being unzipped brought Morgan back into the room. She had drifted someplace in her work mind and, faced with the other option, she figured she'd kind of liked to have stayed there.

The team had already carried out all of the preliminary observations on both bodies. Wendy and Joe were both working diligently to document everything. Morgan smiled at Joe. She'd given him a hard time over the last case when he'd unknowingly become party to two teenage girls' reckless plans. He'd forgiven her though, his easy going-manner was just as well.

Her eyes finally rested on Rosie's deathly white face. She had once asked Declan why the skin went such a pale colour so fast after death, and he'd told her the medical term for it was pallor mortis. She had spent her teenage years trying to achieve that look with the palest of foundations and now preferred a little more colour. Morgan could not tear her gaze away from the thick black nail through her lips. Rosie's honey-coloured hair was matted with dried blood, and she didn't envy the job of the funeral director who would have to wash it all out when her body was released, to make her look presentable for her grief-stricken family. As if conjuring them up there was a commotion from somewhere outside of the mortuary. Loud voices and lots of shouting.

Declan looked at Ben. 'What in the name?' He ripped his plastic apron off then tugged off his gloves. Both Ben and Morgan did the same, following him out where there was a man tussling with a security guard and a hospital porter.

'Let me see her, you have no right to stop me. I have to see her because I think it's all bullshit.'

The security guard looked way out of his depth. 'Call the cops,' he yelled in their direction.

They both ran to help and with one swift move, Ben had his legs out from under him and was kneeling over him with Morgan cuffing his hands in front of him. Declan and Susie were both staring at the guy who was still trying to wrestle Ben off him. Morgan pulled a can of CS gas from her pocket.

'Carry on and I'll spray you, you need to calm down and then we can help you.'

He looked at her, his eyes ablaze with a light that went out when he realised his predicament.

'Where the fuck did you two come from?'

'The mortuary, who do you want to see?'

She thought he was going to say Susie, or maybe some other staff member, but she didn't expect his reply.

'Rosie Waite, she's my girlfriend. I have a right to see her, someone said she was dead and it's bollocks. Why would she be dead?'

Ben looked at Morgan, who was staring down at the guy on the floor. Joe and Wendy were watching too, and Wendy had her radio in hand ready to call for backup if he started to get out of hand again.

'Your girlfriend? Who are you?'

'I just told you, are you lot having a laugh? Is this all some joke at my expense because it's not funny. I hate the police, you're all useless.'

Morgan caught Declan out of the corner of her eye, miming eating popcorn to Susie, and she had to turn away from him quickly to suppress the smile.

The security guard and Ben helped him off the floor, sitting him on one of the hard, blue plastic chairs in the waiting area.

'What's your name?'

'Matt Smith.'

The look of confusion on Ben's face mirrored Morgan's. But then Morgan looked closer at him. His dishevelled hair. His dark eyes. He had a longer beard, but, he looked so much like the man sitting on the mortuary table...

'Where do you live, Matt?'

'I own the house next door but one to you, but I've been working in France the last year so haven't been back much.'

Morgan didn't recognise him. 'You can't, I know the Matt Smith who lives near to us and you're not him.'

'No, that arsehole is my twin brother Max. He's been staying at my house whilst I've been working away. I felt sorry for him because he lost his job in the hotel. He lived in it, so I said he could stay there and keep Rosie company, temporarily, only it turned into months. They don't really like each other, but she said she was happy for him to stop there as it saved her being on her own. I've been tied up for months and not able to get home.'

'He's not an identical twin to you?'

Matt rolled his eyes at her. 'Well, obviously not. I'm better looking.'

Morgan sat down on the chair as Ben took Declan to one side. She looked at Matt.

'Have you got any ID on you?'

'In my back pocket, but I can't reach it.' He held out his wrists with the cuffs on.

'Stand up, the security guard will get it.'

'No, he bloody won't, he's not touching me. You can get it though.' She saw his wallet sticking out of his pocket and plucked it out. Taking out his driving licence she held it up in Ben's direction.

'I don't understand, who told you to come here?'

'I got a pissed-up phone call off my dad who asked if I was dead, then asked if Rosie was, and said some copper that looked about twelve had been around to give him a death message about us both.'

'Is he aware that your brother was staying at your house?'

He shrugged. 'Probably not, none of us really speak to him. He prefers to spend his money and company with a bottle of Bell's whisky instead of his kids. What is going on? I went home and can't get in. It's been locked up and I left my spare key under the plant pot for Max months ago. He was supposed to get one cut.'

He held out his wrists and shook them at her. 'Am I under arrest?'

'No.'

'Then can you take them off. Please, I'm sorry for acting like an idiot. It's just all a bit of a shock. I've been travelling for hours to get here, and I'm knackered.'

She glanced at Ben who nodded, and she pulled her keyring out, unlocking them with the tiny key.

'Thank you, I'm sorry. But nobody is telling me anything. Is Rosie here? Is she dead or is my dad winding me up?'

'I'm afraid she is. I'm terribly sorry and I'm sorry about the confusion.'

'So, Max is dead as well?'

'Yes, well actually, we can't say for sure until he's been identified. Can you do that?'

Matt lowered his head, his shoulders sagged, and every bit of fight he had left his body as it seemed to shrink and collapse in on itself.

'What the hell is going on?'

Morgan patted his arm. 'I wish we knew.'

Morgan had never been so surprised in her entire life. She had not seen this coming and by the look of pure confusion on Ben's face, neither had he.

TWENTY-EIGHT

Susie and the security guard took Matt into the viewing room, and she got him a coffee before disappearing to go and make Rosie look presentable. She rushed into Declan's office. 'I mean, like what the heck is happening?'

Everyone's shoulders shrugged at the same time.

'I've given him a coffee, and Stuart is watching him, but he's obviously a bit worried about him kicking off. He's a big strong guy. Someone is going to have to warn him about her face.'

Declan nodded. 'I will speak to him first; can you throw a sheet over her and do the business, Susie?'

Susie smiled. 'Of course.' Then disappeared into the mortuary.

Declan turned to Ben. 'What a mess. Who identified our body as Matt Smith then?'

Morgan answered. 'Gina, Rosie's best friend. And we met him at a neighbour's barbeque not that long ago. I had no doubts.'

'Does Gina actually know the real Matt then? Or did she only ever meet Max?'

'We need to ask her what she knows.'

Declan sighed. 'This is a first for me and there have been some situations I tell you.'

Ben radioed control to send some officers over to wait outside. He was worried Matt would decide to fight the world again when he'd seen Rosie. Had Raven been sleeping with Matt or Max? Which one entered her tattoo parlour that day? Was Matt feigning shock? Was he their killer? She studied him as he cupped his mug of coffee. He looked upset. There were so many questions that only Rosie and Max could answer, but they had taken their reasons and secrets to the grave with them.

Ben's phone began to vibrate, and he answered it. 'Boss, you might want to get yourself to the mortuary, we have a situation.'

Declan whispered to Morgan. 'Mary mother of Jesus, it must be bad if he's calling Marc down here. I mean I'm not being funny, but does he think that blundering idiot is going to help the situation? I mean, he's a bit volatile out there and right-fully so, but still.'

'My head has gone into meltdown and, to make matters worse, we're going to have to bring him in for questioning. He's a suspect,' whispered Morgan.

Declan's gasp was loud, and he cupped a hand over his mouth. 'You think he could be the killer? But what about Theo? Why would he try and kill him?'

'I don't know, sorry, Declan, but we will figure it out, I promise you.'

Susie rushed back in. 'Done the best I can, what if he kicks off?'

Ben ended his call. 'There are two officers outside in a vehicle waiting in case we need them, but hopefully the shock of seeing Rosie and then his brother will take all of that fight out of him.'

Susie arched an eyebrow. 'Let's hope so.'

'Me and Morgan will be in the viewing room with him, and Marc is going to wait at the station for us to get there.'

'Why?' asked Morgan, who was more than a little relieved Marc wasn't going to come blundering in here and make the situation worse.

'Because we are going to have to take him in for interview. We can't let him leave here, he's like a ticking time bomb and there are a lot of questions that need answering.'

Morgan had already called that one, she just didn't fancy fighting with Matt for a second time, but she would if she had to. They stood up and looked at each other then went to the visiting room where Matt was pacing up and down.

'What's taking so long?'

Morgan spoke. 'We were about to start Rosie's post-mortem; your arrival has kind of thrown us. As far as we were aware you were dead.'

He looked at her. 'This is like some weird nightmare; I'm waiting to wake up any moment now.'

Morgan felt bad for him. 'I'm sorry, I wish it was too.'

Susie came in. 'Are you ready? If you stand at the glass, you will be able to see Rosie. I'm sorry, there is something on her face that we can't remove until the post-mortem, and it will be upsetting for you.'

'Like what?'

'It's best that you see for yourself.'

'I'm ready.'

Everyone in the room tensed, ready to spring into action should Matt lose it again. He pressed his face against the glass viewing window.

'Oh my God, she's really dead. I thought this was some big mistake, and what is that through her lips?'

Declan stepped forward. 'I'm sorry for your loss, Matt. I'm Declan Donnelly, a home office forensic pathologist, and I'll be dealing with Rosie. Whoever killed her put that large iron nail through her lips.'

He cupped a hand over his mouth and turned away. 'I can't look at her, that's awful, why?'

'We don't know that yet, but these fine officers are doing their very best to find that out so you need to work with them and help them, okay? It will do you no good fighting with them. It's not their fault, they didn't do this, they are trying to find the person who did.'

Matt's voice was barely a whisper. 'If that's Rosie, then you better show me the other body.'

Declan nodded. 'That would be a good idea, if you are up to it, and then we can sort out this mix-up in identification. It will take us a few minutes. Can we get you anything?'

His voice croaked. 'No.'

Declan and Susie left the room, which was too stuffy and claustrophobic with three men and Morgan inside of it. Morgan and Ben never took their eyes off Matt who was now slumped on the sofa, his eyes full of tears.

TWENTY-NINE

Matt was unable to speak after staring at the body of his twin brother; he just nodded. Then walked out of the viewing room with its muted lights and comfortable chairs into the stark, white corridor. Ben and Morgan followed him, unsure of what his next move was going to be. There was a small window that looked out onto the rest of the hospital, two parking spaces outside of it. One was occupied by a police van.

He turned to Ben. 'Why the van?'

'We didn't know how you were going to react after. I'm sorry for your loss, I can't imagine how hard this is.'

Matt nodded. 'Thanks, so now what?'

'Ideally, we would take you to the station for an interview so we can clear the confusion, it's all a bit of a mess.'

'Do you think I did it, that I killed them?'

Ben shrugged. 'I don't know anything, what little I did know has now been blown out of the water by finding out that you are alive and that's your brother.'

He nodded. 'Okay, that's okay. Can we do it now and get it over with?'

'Do you need to go in the van, Matt, or are you going to be able to stay calm and travel in the back of the car with us?'

'I'm in my car, can I not drive myself there? I don't need babysitting, I'm not going anywhere. I have questions for you too.'

'I'm afraid not. I'm going to be honest with you right now, you are a suspect and I'm not going to take the chance of you changing your mind and driving off into the sunset, and to be even more brutally honest I would rather you went in the van after your earlier outburst.'

Morgan felt her shoulders relax at hearing this. She was thinking Ben had forgot how volatile Matt was.

Matt nodded. 'Fine.'

Ben smiled at him. 'Thanks, appreciate it. I'm going to arrest you, Matt, not for earlier but for the murders.'

At hearing this Morgan's shoulders stiffened again. Was he mad and purposely trying to wind the guy up?

Matt's gaze that had been staring down at the floor, snapped up to stare Ben in the eye.

'I didn't do it, and I can prove that. When did they die?'

'Let's get this sorted out at the station. I want to be able to prove that you didn't. Come on, this is all a formality but a necessary one.'

Ben pointed towards the door and the two men walked out towards the waiting van. She heard Ben quietly read Matt his rights before leaving him with the two officers who, after searching his pockets, helped him into the cage at the back of the van.

When Ben came back in he didn't look particularly happy about arresting Matt.

'I thought you were trying to get us all killed then.'

He smiled at her. 'I figured he'd lost all of his fight; he knew he was going to be our number one suspect. What's the point in not wanting to clear his name?'

'What about the post-mortems?'

'Can you manage if I go back and interview? I can send Cain down, but I don't want to make Declan hang around longer than he has to when he's upset and wanting to be with Theo.'

'Of course.'

'I'll leave you the car; I'll go back in the van.'

Morgan went back to the mortuary where Declan and the rest of the team were waiting. He nodded. 'Well, that was a bit of a surprise. I would never have called that one.'

'Me either, I wish I could interview him. I need to know where the hell he's been for so long, where exactly in France. There are some many unanswered questions.'

'Ben should be able to uncover Matt's secrets,' Declan replied.

Morgan nodded. 'Should we continue?'

———

Everyone followed him, and Declan soon removed the sheet from Rosie's body. Morgan couldn't stop staring at her, wondering how deep the secrets she'd been keeping went and if they would ever find out the truth about this whole mixed-up mess.

Declan held the tweezers with the thick black iron nail sandwiched between them to the light. 'This looks really old; I've seen similar ones before, I'm sure I have. I think there are some like this that hold the church door together.'

Morgan felt that fizzing in her stomach at the thought of connecting the dots. 'Has there been any vandalism at the church, did Theo say anything?'

Declan shook his head. 'No, but I suppose there are a lot of doors inside the church. The door to the vestry is a smaller version of the old oak entrance door. If you had a pair of pliers they could be pulled out without much fuss.'

Morgan knew that as soon as she left here she had to go to the church and check for herself. If she found any missing nails, that was the connection to Theo's attack. It meant the killer must have visited the church before killing Matt and Rosie. Had the killer come back to get more nails and been caught by Theo? It was a very plausible explanation as to why they attacked him.

'Are you thinking these came from St Martha's, Morgan?'

His voice echoed inside of her head full volume, making her start a little.

'Yes, well I can't say for certain until I've had a look myself, but it would give us a reason why Theo was attacked if he caught the killer red-handed taking nails.'

Declan, who had been doing so well up until this point, looked as if he was going to cry at being reminded about Theo. Morgan wanted to hug him so hard. Only he was holding up a nail that he had carefully removed from a dead woman's lips, so she didn't; she stayed where she was and said a silent prayer for Theo.

Susie had put the block under Rosie's neck, ready for them to start the internal investigation. Declan put the nail into a silver dish and passed it to Wendy, ready to be bagged up for forensic testing. Picking up his scalpel he began the Y incision. Starting above the breastbone he carefully traced the blade from left to right before moving it down the body to form a large Y-shaped cut.

Morgan tried to focus on what he was doing, but her mind kept going back to St Martha's. She was desperate to go there so she could make some sense of why Theo was involved in a murder case he had no business being dragged into. Everyone was worried the note in the attic meant she and Ben were being targeted, and she had wondered if that was why Theo had been hurt. But it would rationalise all of that. It was far more random.

The sound of Rosie's ribs being snapped apart with a pair of pruning shears made her focus on the body, and she grimaced as Declan removed the bloodied breastplate that protected Rosie's heart.

The rest of the post-mortem was seamless and very quick. Rosie's internal organs were in perfect condition, and there were no underlying diseases that contributed to her death.

'It seems senseless having to make her endure an internal investigation when it's blatantly obvious that her cause of death was the head injury, but thorough I am and that's what the law requires of me, so here we are.'

Morgan thought he was talking more to himself than to the rest of them, and she knew he was right; there had been no other injuries except for the nail.

'The nail was put through moments after she stopped breathing due to the minimal amount of blood and swelling around the lips. I would have expected a lot more had her heart still been pumping. I still can't decide how they were put through though. If they had been hammered, I would think there would be some bruising around that area. I mean, how hard is it to hammer a nail into the wall? It's very rare they strike home on that first attempt and if you're anything like me, I end up with a wall full of holes and more bent nails than I can count. This was precise. I would say it was likely done with a single needle.'

'I thought it was expertly done,' Morgan confirmed.

'It's like a Medusa piercing.' Everyone turned to look at Susie who was staring down at the hole above Rosie's lips.

'Expand on that please, Susie.'

She pointed to the middle of her lip. 'They're getting really popular. My last girlfriend had it done, and she said it hurt like a bitch though and cried, which was a total show up.'

Morgan tugged off her glove and was already typing

Medusa piercing into her phone's search bar. She looked at Susie. 'Does it mean anything specific?'

Susie shrugged. 'I didn't ask, she said it hurt so that was the end of my interest in that one.'

'It's also known as the philtrum piercing, but there's not much about it. It says most people have it done because it brings symmetry to the face. Bloody hell, I thought it was going to tell me it had some great mythological meaning.' Morgan felt a wave of disappointment, but everything was leading to this being carried out by someone who had knowledge of body piercing and the equipment. Her theory was correct. She squeezed her eyes shut for a moment, trying to release the building pressure inside of them. Lately she was getting more and more headaches, but hers weren't migraines, or she didn't think they were. They were stress related, work related. She wondered if a daith piercing could solve them, but she knew who she wouldn't be going to for that. Raven was looking more and more like a suspect...

THIRTY

Matt Smith had gone from volatile to mute. He had struggled to tell Eric his name as he was getting booked in. The shock of seeing his girlfriend and twin at the mortuary had taken its toll on him. Ben had messaged Marc to say they may need a welcome party of officers at the station in case he kicked off, but he hadn't said a word and had let Ben lead him into the custody suite with no bother. He was in a cell with a plastic cup of sweet tea and some biscuits whilst they waited for the duty solicitor to turn up. The duty solicitor was having a busy day. Ben wondered if he was regretting going back to his office in Kendal only to be dragged back to Rydal Falls once more.

When everyone was present who needed to be, Matt was escorted into the interview room. He sat on the chair, hands folded in his lap, and didn't say a word.

'How are you holding up, Matt?' asked Marc.

Matt looked at him and shook his head. 'How do you think?'

'Terrible, I can't begin to imagine how you're feeling. So we should cut to the chase and get this over with so you can go home.'

Ben glared at Marc. They hadn't released the scene, and Matt had no home to go back to at the moment; anyway, would he really want to go back to the house that had decomposing blood-stains all over the living room, stairs and bathroom floor? It was going to need a major clean up before he could go inside again.

The solicitor looked around. 'A quick word with my client, please.'

Ben and Marc stood up, leaving them to have a little privacy, and waited in the corridor.

Ben whispered, 'He can't go home, so don't mention that again unless you're happy to release the scene.'

'Ah, Christ. What was I thinking? I was just trying to make conversation. He looks almost catatonic, what are we going to do about him? I was expecting a huge fight on our hands, and it was a bit of a let-down if I'm honest.'

'You wanted to fight?'

Marc shrugged. 'No, but a bit of excitement now and again gets the old blood flowing, doesn't it?'

Ben tried not to roll his eyes at his boss. 'Well, I'm glad he was angry enough at the mortuary. I feel bad for him now. Imagine working away and coming home to find out your girl-friend and twin are both dead in your house, and your twin has been pretending to be you. It's so weird.'

'It's definitely weird. Do you think he did it?'

'At this point, I would not be surprised if it was the woman from the corner shop. I'm that confused about it all.'

The door opened and the solicitor nodded.

Taking their seats once more they began the interview with Ben leading the questions.

'When was the last time you were home, Matt?'

'Nine months ago.'

Ben worked it out. 'Christmas and New Year?'

Matt nodded.

'That's a long time to be away, did you not want to see Rosie?'

'Of course I did, but I work in France, and it was a difficult job. I couldn't just leave.'

'What are you doing out there?'

'I'm in charge of a big building project. It's been one disaster after the other. I couldn't walk away. I had to stay to make sure we weren't losing any more money or days on site.'

'How did Rosie feel about this? Was she not bothered you couldn't come back?'

'Well, probably, but she has always liked her own company and done her own thing. She was happy enough and she came out to visit me once a month, so we were good, or I thought we were.'

'When did Max move in?'

'Christmas, we'd only had the house a month. He turned up Christmas Eve and told us he'd lost his job and his flat that went with it. I should never have said he could stay.'

'Why?'

'Isn't it obvious why? He stole my girlfriend and my life.'

Ben was shocked. This was quite an admission.

'He was always so devious and all he cared about was money. He was always jealous of my relationship with Rosie too.' He stopped as if realising he might sound harsh talking about his murdered brother that way.

Ben looked at Marc.

'When did Rosie and Max's relationship start?'

'Honestly, I don't know.'

'Has he been pretending to be you?'

Matt shrugged.

'Did Rosie's friend Gina know about this?'

'I never met Gina; Rosie met her not long after I moved out to France.'

'So how do you know Rosie and Max were having an affair?'

Matt leaned back. A moment of silence went by. 'He never moved out. It was supposed to be a temporary stay, and Rosie became more distant; she didn't seem bothered that I was stuck over in France. She stopped complaining about him whenever she phoned. It wasn't hard to figure out what was going on.'

The solicitor spoke. 'Have you got anything to prove he was at the scene of the crime or any evidence to link him to the murders?'

Ben shook his head. 'Well, we've just established quite the motive. How did you feel about your twin brother and your girl-friend shacking up behind your back?'

Matt looked angry.

'I'm going to tell you now that my client has proof he was in France and has only just come back into the country.'

Matt slid a passport and plane tickets across the table towards Ben, who arched an eyebrow at him.

'Where did you get those; I thought the officers searched you?'

Matt patted his stomach. 'I wear my grandad's old money belt when I'm travelling, saves me the hassle of worrying where my stuff is.'

Ben smiled at him, his grandad had a money belt too, then looked down at the documents. The tickets were in his name, for a flight that arrived at Manchester earlier this morning.

'Very good, do you have anyone in France who can verify you were there all day yesterday?'

'My colleague, François; I ate supper at his house with his wife and children. As I got home, I got the drunken phone call off my dad checking if I was dead, and I knew that something was wrong. I phoned Rosie, but it went to answerphone, Max's too. I tried emailing and messaging her on Messenger. When you check her phone you'll see them.'

'That's good. Do you have a number for François? We'll need to speak to him to corroborate your alibi.'

'It's in my phone you took off me.'

'It's okay, we'll get that.'

The solicitor smiled at them. 'I think it's at this point you both agree there is nothing you can hold my client on; you should release him on bail.'

Marc nodded. 'Yes, that's true and we will do that very shortly. Thank you for being so open with us, we appreciate that.'

'What have I got to hide? I didn't kill them.' He smiled.

'Do you have someplace you can stay until we release the house? It's a major crime scene and we haven't finished with it yet.'

Ben's voice was apologetic and that was because he felt bad for the guy.

He shrugged. 'I suppose I can stay at a hotel for a couple of nights until I can go home.'

'We can arrange to drive you there.'

'No, thanks. I'm not turning up to book a couple of nights in The Inn with a police escort, for one thing they won't let me stay there.'

'You have a fair point.'

'Someone can take me back to get my car?'

'That's not possible. I'm afraid it's been taken away to be examined by CSI.'

Matt's cheeks began to turn red. 'You took my clothes, my car, I can't go home despite having proof I only arrived in England this morning. Are you having a laugh? Is this all some big joke to you lot?'

'Why has the scene not been released yet?' the solicitor asked.

'Excuse us for a moment whilst we sort things out,' said Marc, smiling at them.

Ben followed him out.

'Why are we not releasing the scene? Wouldn't it be better to have him staying here where we can locate him?' asked Ben.

'I suppose so, but the house is a mess.'

'I'll take him home, walk him through and tell him we can get professional crime-scene cleaners in if that's what he wants.'

'I don't know, I'm not happy but not sure we have much other choice. Okay, let's do that.'

Ben went back into the interview room, and Marc left him to it.

'We are going to release the scene, but the house is a mess. I don't think you will want to stay there.'

'I have nowhere else. Am I free to clean it up? I'm assuming by the way they were killed there is a lot of blood.'

'There is and if you think you can, then yes, that's fine, but we can get in touch with a specialist cleaning company from Carlisle who will come down and do it.'

'In the next two hours? And who pays for it?'

'You, sorry, and it's unlikely to be tonight unless you're willing to pay the call-out fee.'

'Just let me get my car and I'll sort it out.'

The solicitor left, shaking hands with everyone.

Ben nodded at Matt. 'Come on, let's get you released. You will be on bail but still, you're free to go home, just don't try go back to France, okay?'

As he said that he realised he should have kept hold of Matt's passport in case he did try to run. He was certainly a suspect. His refusal to answer questions was a major red flag. But then again, he had been in France. His alibi sounded solid. Ben knew Morgan wouldn't be happy. The interview had created more questions than it had answered.

THIRTY-ONE

Morgan was weary. Standing still for hours on end was nothing new to her, she could handle scene guard, but when it was watching people get sliced open and their internal organs removed, it got that little bit harder. She needed coffee and wondered if The Coffee Pot was still open as she drove into Rydal Falls, taking a detour down the main street. It was pleasantly busy with tourists but not overly so and she managed to park the car a short walk away. The bell above the door tinkled as she pushed it open, and she was surprised to see Jade cleaning the tables.

The woman looked up at her, smiling so warmly it made her eyes light up.

'Morgan, how are you?'

Morgan wasn't normally much of a hugger, but she rushed over to Jade and wrapped her arms around her. 'Oh, I'm okay. More importantly, how are you?'

Jade's only daughter had been murdered a few months ago and yet here she was, still running her business, still carrying on with life despite the heartache running deep inside of her.

'I'm getting by, it's tough. I miss her so much; I even miss arguing with her in a morning about how long she was taking in the bathroom. It's so crap.'

Jade lifted a sleeve and blotted at the corner of her eye. 'How's things? You look exhausted.' She pointed to a chair. 'Have you got five minutes to have a break?'

Morgan nodded, and Jade turned the open sign to closed on the door and locked it so no one else could come inside.

'Let me make you a coffee. I miss having normal conversations. It still feels as if everyone is treading lightly around me and whilst I appreciate it, I hate it. I want my life back to normal. I want to go back to the time when none of this was a reality.'

'I bet you do, it's so hard. Are you managing with work and everything?'

'It keeps me sane, stops my mind going into overdrive. Why are you looking so tired? I worry about you.'

Morgan laughed. 'You're such a sweetheart, thank you for thinking of me. I guess you heard about the double murder.' She didn't want to talk about murders with Jade, but it was hard not to – it was her job.

'I did, it's so horrible. What is this town coming to? It's like someone plucked us up from the Lake District and plonked us down in the middle of *a crime drama*. Who was it or can you not say?'

Morgan debated but then thought as it had been twenty-four hours, it would already have been on the news and in the paper, not to mention all over Facebook.

'It was a couple who lived next door but one to me, Rosie and.' She paused. 'Max.'

Jade put two coffees down on the table then looked her in the eye. 'Not Rosie Waite? She's the only Rosie I know. Comes in here for her coffee, is a bit rude most days.'

'Yes, Rosie Waite. How rude?'

'I shouldn't judge, and I definitely shouldn't be gossiping

about a dead woman if it's her. I mean who am I to do that when my own daughter was murdered, but...'

'But?'

'There was something about her. You know when you think you should like someone, but you can't because they rub you up the wrong way. I'm so awful, I'm not usually a gossip.'

Morgan thought about all the statements they'd had from friends and family. Everyone else claimed she was a sweet and kind-hearted teaching assistant. She smiled at Jade. 'You're not being awful; in fact, you're being very helpful. What about her partner? Did you meet him?'

'I didn't know him to talk to. I knew the first one more, and then she shacked up with his twin brother and started hanging around with a woman called Gina. Well, that was it, she began to look down her nose at everyone else and I never did understand that because she didn't exactly have a good reason to be doing that, not the way she was carrying on behind her own front door.'

'Was it common knowledge that she was going out with her partner's twin?' Morgan was thrilled to finally have confirmation of one of her theories. Rosie and Matt's relationship was over, and Rosie was in fact having an affair with Max. She couldn't wait to tell Ben.

Jade shrugged. 'I did, but then I've always been very astute. Not sure if anyone else noticed to be fair. I bet Matt is devastated. I haven't seen him in such a long time; I think he moved away.'

Morgan didn't gossip about things, but this was all very interesting. 'Did Matt know about her and Max?'

'He must have done. He's never been back since that I know of, or I haven't seen him since. I assumed it was the reason he left.'

Morgan wondered whether Gina knew all of this. Had she

spent time with Max, thinking he was Matt? 'Did Rosie call him Max or Matt?'

'I don't know, now I'm confused. It doesn't take much.' Jade laughed and sipped her coffee. Morgan did the same, trying to make sense of things inside her head and finding it impossible.

'What do you think was going on between them?'

'Who knows, maybe she was in a relationship with the both of them.'

'Do you know Gina?'

She shook her head. 'No, never met her or, if I have, I didn't know it was her.'

'Why was Rosie so rude?'

'I don't know, she often never said thank you or please. She'd come in to order a cappuccino to go and that was it. No conversation, no manners, no tip for the staff, not even at Christmas. Always on her phone, I mean it was glued to her ear most days, which is kind of strange because most people avoid answering and making calls these days.'

'You'd make a good detective, if you ever get fed up with rude, entitled customers.'

Jade smiled. 'I couldn't do it; I couldn't do your job for all the money in the world.'

'Someone has to do it.'

'Yes, and thank goodness you do.'

Morgan stood up and pulled a five pound note out of her pocket.

Jade shook her head. 'Don't you dare insult me. If I can't give a friend a coffee when she needs it then there's no point to all of this.'

Morgan smiled at her, she liked the thought of Jade being her friend. She didn't have many and it wasn't for the free coffees either. 'Well, thank you. I appreciate it more than you could ever know.'

'Take care of yourself and don't leave it so long between

visits. I'm here most days now. I take Wednesdays off to mope around and feel sorry for myself but that's it. You should come round to the flat one Wednesday and we could have a bottle of wine, order pizza, gossip and get drunk.'

'Thank you, I'd like that a lot, and thank you for the coffee. Cain is going to be so jealous when I turn up with it. Bye.'

Morgan unlocked the door and stepped out onto the street before Jade offered to make drinks for the whole team. She was so kind Morgan knew that she would. Next stop was the church to examine the doors for any missing nails. Probably a waste of time, but she had to know if there was a connection between Theo's attack and the murders.

THIRTY-TWO

Morgan phoned Ben. She needed to update him and figured he'd be out of interview now. She was staring at the entrance door to St Martha's with a coffee in one hand and her phone in the other. There was nothing obvious from the outside, nothing looked to be missing. It went straight to voicemail, and she tutted; he'd probably forgot to switch it back on. As she crouched down to study the bottom of the door, a voice behind her echoed in her ear.

'Can I help you?'

She straightened up, almost spilling the lukewarm coffee all down herself. She didn't recognise the man standing in front of her; he was wearing a dog collar and a long coat though.

'Hi, I'm looking to see if there are any nails missing.'

He squinted at her and took a step backwards, and she thought that sounded a little weird even for her.

'I'm Detective Morgan Brookes.'

'Ah, you're a policewoman?'

'Yes, I am.'

He held out the palm of his hand, and she wondered what he was doing.

'Can I see your credentials, please, my colleague was badly attacked last night and I don't believe the police have caught the attacker yet. I'm Gordon.'

'Yes, of course.' She tugged the lanyard with her warrant card out of her shirt and held it up for him to read.

He nodded his head many times. 'Yes, good. Thank you, can't be too careful these days. I mean who would think a priest would get attacked on the front step of the church just a few feet away from their house?'

'Are you Theo's replacement?'

'Theo?'

'Father Theo.'

'No, well not right now. I've been sent down by the archdiocese from Carlisle to see what needs to be done. We can get cover from one of the other churches for now. I was expecting more of a mess to be honest with you.'

Morgan looked down at the uneven stone flagstones beneath her boots; she could make out dark-stained traces of blood on the lighter coloured ones, but the majority of them were slate and the blood would have cleaned off easily, and because it's a public place they would have had the scene sorted out as soon as the cordon was removed. Unlike poor Rosie's house which would still be covered in dried blood. She didn't envy the person who got the job of cleaning that up.

'Do you have a key for the door? I really need to check the inside and then the other doors.'

'Well, yes, I do, but why?'

She heard herself say *because I think someone stole the nails out of the church door to pierce through the lips of a dead man and woman.*

'It's relevant to the investigation.'

'Oh, okay, then yes.'

He stepped towards the door, pulling a key out of his

pocket. Pushing it open he held it back for her to walk inside. The entrance was dark.

'Let me find the lights.'

Seconds later the church flickered into a bright warmth. Morgan thought how creepy it was in here in the dark, and she wondered what Theo had been doing last night. Whoever attacked him had been hiding in here waiting for him to come inside. She carefully began to study the door and drew a sharp intake of breath as she saw a gap between the nails on one side near to the hinge. She took a couple of photos and kept on checking until she found another opposite.

'Yes.' She would have fist bumped the air if the vicar hadn't been watching her so carefully.

'Found something?'

'I think so. I'm going to ask you not to touch the door and step back, if that's okay?'

He grunted but did as he was told. 'I'll be in the vestry if you need me.'

He left her to it, and she felt a tingle of excitement that her hunch had been right. She rang Ben again and was relieved to hear his soothing voice.

'*Hey, how did the post-mortem go?*'

'Bad, look I know where the nails came from, and I think that's why Theo got attacked. It has to be connected, there's no other explanation for it.'

'*Amazing, please put me out of my misery.*'

'Those are really old nails, not just the sort you can pick up at a hardware shop. I mean they are antique kind of old. The same as the ones that keep the church door at St Martha's together. I'm at the church and there are two missing from the inside, two gaps. I think that for whatever reason Theo came out to the church last night, he disturbed the killer who may have been trying to remove more nails. He could identify the killer so that's why they attacked him.'

'Blimey.'

'Yes, blimey. It makes sense because why else would someone attack Theo? And if they were using the murder weapon to remove the nails then they had it handy enough to use it on him. We need CSI back here to fingerprint the door. What if they weren't wearing gloves and there are prints on here? Was this why Raven came by the church? To collect more nails? Why would someone want to use these nails, specifically?'

'I love you.'

'Hahaha, go get me a CSI and come here if you can. You can update me on the interview.'

'On my way.'

The line went dead, and Morgan felt a sense of hope that maybe this nightmare could end in the next couple of hours and whoever was responsible would be locked up before anyone else got hurt.

Morgan opened the door wide and, kicking a wooden wedge underneath it so nobody would touch the inside of it before CSI got here, she sat on a stool and waited; she was protecting it at all costs, and she just hoped that nobody had touched it or tried to clean it on the inside.

THIRTY-THREE

Wendy stared at the huge oak door then over at Morgan.

'I don't know how good they'll be. That's if I get any prints off it, and I'm not being funny but how many people do you think have touched this in the last week, not to mention the weather?'

Morgan thought probably not as many as there could have been. Church wasn't exactly popular, although Theo was doing a great job of bringing people here with his weekly soup and a sandwich lunch meetings and a clothes bank for anyone in need. She shrugged.

'Ah, but I don't want you to print the outside, do I?'

'Don't you?'

Morgan shook her head. 'No, it's on the inside and let me show you, it's easier.'

Kicking the wedge away she pushed the door shut and pointed to the holes left by the missing nails.

'I found where those nails came from.'

Wendy and Ben both peered at the empty spaces the nails had once filled, and Ben clapped his hands. 'They certainly look the same.'

Wendy nodded. 'Yeah, they do. I'm going to need to remove another for comparison though. Do you think the vicar will mind?'

'The vicar will mind what?' Gordon's deep voice echoed behind them, and all three of them who were crouching down to look at the door straightened up as if they'd just been caught doing something they shouldn't be. Morgan turned to him and smiled.

'Is it okay if we take another nail? We need to send one off to forensics to see if it's a match for the ones found at the crime scene.'

He shrugged. 'As long as the door doesn't fall down. I should probably say no because it's a very old door, but all I keep thinking about is Father Theo being attacked so viciously on his own doorstep by some maniac. If it will help then you can take the whole door.'

Morgan thought he wasn't as stuffy as he'd seemed when she first met him.

'Is there any news? I phoned the hospital, but they said because I wasn't family, they couldn't talk to me. I mean he's a vicar, we don't tend to have a lot of family which is often why we turn to the priesthood in the first place.'

'If you can give me a moment, I'll find out for you. The last update we had is that he was stable.'

'Thank you, I suppose stable is a good thing, isn't it, when everything is uncertain.'

She smiled at him as Ben typed a message to Declan. Instantly a reply flashed back from him.

He's good, eyes open, bit groggy and confused but awake.

Ben relayed Declan's message, and Morgan let out a whoop of delight that echoed around the church, but Gordon's eyes lit up and he placed his hands together in the prayer position. 'Thank you. That is brilliant news.'

Wendy was smiling too. 'Phew, what a relief. I'll just grab some pliers out of the van.'

After some tugging, she finally managed to get one of the thick old nails free and held it in the air. 'Looks the same to me, but Declan would be able to confirm that if you showed it to him.'

Gordon was watching them. 'I have to ask, and tell me to mind my own business, but what on earth would somebody want to use those for?'

It was Ben who answered. 'We are trying to figure that part out, Father. When we know, we will let you know too. I'm sorry I sound so evasive, but it's all part of an ongoing investigation and I think perhaps you will sleep better if you don't know the reason why.'

'People are strange, they do the weirdest stuff. I have seen some things over the years doing this. You wouldn't believe how many people think they live in haunted houses or think that coming to church will absolve them of their sins if they're sleeping with someone who isn't their spouse.'

Morgan said to Ben, 'I think we should take this for Declan to have a look at.' She pointed to the evidence bag Wendy was holding.

Ben nodded. 'Okay, let's go do that. Thanks, Wendy, for coming so fast and thank you, Gordon. I'll tell Amy to bring Cain to pick up the car you were in.' He passed the keys to Wendy to keep safe.

When they were in the car Ben waited until he'd driven away before asking. 'What was that quick exit about?'

'I'm desperate to tell you what else I found out. Jade, from The Coffee Pot, said she'd heard that Rosie and Max were having an affair.'

'Yes, Matt made the same admission.'

'He did?' Morgan was getting excited.

'But he has an alibi for the murders. He was in France. And he refused to answer any more questions.'

Morgan let out the breath she was holding.

'Do you think he's lying?'

'I kind of think there's more to it than that.'

'Like what?'

'Give me time, I'll figure it out.'

The drive back to the hospital was slow, but it was so worth it when they went straight to ICU only to be told that Theo had been moved onto a ward. Morgan felt as if the heaviness that had been weighing her down had lifted off her shoulders. The relief that Theo was going to be okay made her feel better about the way she had treated him the first few times she'd met him. He'd come across as a little weird, but that was before she got to know him and discovered he was one of the good guys. The way he and Declan were so in love with each other melted her heart and she hoped they never lost that spark. She glanced at Ben. She felt the same, and she didn't ever want to imagine a life without him in it. She had lost everyone she loved except for him, and she had a sudden urge to ask him to marry her. Only not here, in a hospital, probably not ever because she had never thought she'd feel the need to marry anyone. But being so close to death all the time made you appreciate your own mortality, and she knew Ben would say yes in a heartbeat. He'd hinted enough times to her that he would love to. Then they were at the desk, and she heard Ben asking the nurse which room Theo was in.

She pointed to a side room, and they were almost there when Morgan whispered, 'We should have brought flowers or a balloon.'

'We're working, we need to talk to him and get a statement, but when we come back we will.'

She nodded, forgetting for a moment they were working. Ben knocked on the door, and Declan opened it. He smiled warmly at them, hugging Ben first then pulling Morgan in and closing the door.

Theo was asleep, a bandage around his head. His pallor looked awful, but he was alive which was more than they had hoped for.

'How is he?' Ben asked.

Theo opened one eye; his other was swollen.

Morgan rushed to kiss his cheek. 'I'm so glad to see you.'

'Can't get rid of me that easily.' His voice was croaky, and Declan lifted a glass of water with a straw to his lips. He greedily sucked at the water then closed his eyes again.

Ben reached out and touched his shoulder. 'I'm glad you're awake, and I'm sorry to be asking this so soon, Theo, but can you remember what happened? Did you see the person who attacked you?'

Theo looked at Ben. 'No, it was too dark. I forgot to lock the church earlier, went back to lock it. Someone had left the light on in the ladies. I turned it off but felt as if I was being watched. Couldn't see anyone, checked the church, then, as I was leaving, I felt something smash into the back of my head. It floored me and then I woke up here. No idea what was going on.'

'Did you see anyone at all?'

'No, I wish I could say that I did.'

Ben gently squeezed his shoulder. 'Don't worry, just concentrate on getting better.'

Declan nodded. 'That's easy for you to say. Our quiz team is doomed now. We have no idea how many brain cells he's lost on the church step. We may as well give up because we never won when he was firing off all cylinders.'

Ben's mouth fell open in shock, but Morgan began to laugh.

'Oh, yes. You pack of losers were reliant on Theo's general knowledge expertise to make you not come last. You'll never recover from this now.'

Declan laughed so loud the ward sister, Danielle, opened the door to see what was going on, and she frowned at the three of them. 'Are you all supposed to be in here?'

She asked Theo, 'Should I tell them to leave?'

'No, I like being made fun of. It makes me feel better.'

Morgan giggled, and Danielle gave her a death stare. 'Sorry, we'll be quiet.'

Danielle turned to Declan. 'You said you'd look after him.'

'I am, laughter is the best medicine of all. Don't worry, Sister Gaskell, he's fine. I promise not to make any more jokes at his expense.'

She shook her head. 'Doctor, I am holding you to that.'

Morgan caught the smile on her face as she turned to leave and smiled back at her.

When she closed the door Declan pulled a face. 'Well, that's me being told to mind myself. Theo, even lying in a hospital bed, you are getting me in so much trouble.'

Theo's eyes closed and he began to drift off to sleep, and Ben whispered, 'We'll get going, call if you need anything at all.'

'Oh, we almost forgot. Do you think this is the same nails that were in—' She stopped herself, not sure if Theo was aware of what Declan had been dealing with in the hours before he'd been attacked. Morgan pulled the evidence bag out of her pocket to show Declan because he'd pulled the ones from both Rosie's and Max's lips.

Declan took the bag off her and held it up, and he studied them closely. 'Looks like it could be, they are certainly identical to those I removed earlier. Where did you find this?'

'They are holding the church door together.'

He frowned. 'Theo's church door?'

She nodded.

'There's only one way to tell for sure. Have you got time to come to the mortuary with me?'

'Yes,' they both spoke at the same time.

Declan leaned over and brushed his lips across Theo's cheek. 'Back soon, sleep well, my prince.'

Then they were out in the corridor walking out of the department. Morgan smiled at Danielle, who looked up from the desk with relief in her eyes that they were leaving so soon.

————

Declan swiped them into the long hospital corridor that led to the mortuary. It was all in darkness. 'I'm glad you two are with me. Have you ever seen something so scary in all your life as this corridor to hell?'

Morgan looked at him. 'Where are the lights and why are you referring to it like that?'

'Tell me you don't think it's creepy. The lights all blew earlier, and they can't find the fault. I told them to replace the bulbs, and they did, and they blew again, so they weren't too happy with my non-electrical advice.'

Morgan felt a chill down her spine. She was being creeped out by a dark corridor, which was stupid because she usually was the first to go barging into a dark house without a second thought when chasing suspects. She felt an elbow poke her in the ribs, and with the flick of a switch some of the lights blinked into life. She glared at him and heard Ben laughing.

'Declan, you're not funny, have you never watched those horror films where they go into abandoned hospitals and never come out?'

He shook his head. 'No need to, I already work in a hell hole. Sorry, I guess I'm a little hyper now that Theo is okay and responding well, no permanent brain damage. Although when I asked him about Birmingham, he looked confused so he may have a touch of amnesia, but the consultant will monitor it. I'm just happy he's alive and not lying in one of my fridges like Rosie or Max.'

As they went into the mortuary it struck Morgan how eerie it was. The lights were off, it was dark, and there was none of the usual background noise she was used to whenever she had to come here. The radio being silent was the worst, as every footstep echoed.

Declan tugged a pair of gloves and a plastic apron on, then went to the drawer with the name *Waite* written on it in black block capitals. Opening the drawer, he pulled Rosie's body out and looked to them both. 'Can I remove this from the evidence bag?' He was waving the small bag with the nail inside in the air.

Ben shrugged. 'Well, it's not technically evidence. We brought it as a comparison, so yeah I can't see a problem with it and we can bag it up or get another.'

'Good, because I want to see if it fits the hole the other one came out of.'

Declan peeled back the white sheet, exposing Rosie's face. She looked a lot better with all the dried blood washed off and the nail removed from her top lip. Picking up a pair of tweezers he held the tip of the nail from the church door near to the small, open wound.

'Bingo, it's a perfect fit. Look, I don't want to force it in and damage her face any further, but this would go straight through that hole if I put a little pressure on it.'

He turned to Morgan, still holding the tweezers with the nail in the air. 'You clever thing, I'm impressed.'

Ben was smiling at her too, and she felt her cheeks turn pink. 'It was just plain old detective work.'

Declan winked. 'You've trained your protégé well. I fear one day, Benjamin, she will be running the place and you'll be underneath her.'

Ben shrugged. 'Underneath Morgan is not a bad place to be.'

Declan let out a loud guffaw and turned back to push Rosie back into the drawer. Morgan was glaring at Ben, his turn for the pink cheeks.

'I, erm, I didn't mean that like it sounded.'

'Please children, no domestic on my watch. I have no popcorn.'

Morgan was still mortified. She snapped, 'Can we at least try and figure out what all of this means? Why are the nails important? How old is the church, does it signify some weird religious thing and that's why they have been taken from there, or is it some jealous person telling the pair of them to shut up like forever?'

'Not for me to say, I have no thoughts on it. Except to say that it looks as if Theo was more of a snap decision. Whoever was at the church thought that Theo may recognise them. This has nothing to do with us, or the note in the attic.'

'Yes, this is what I think. Theo disturbed them and they panicked, attacked him so they could get away and not be iden- tified. But why did they think he would be able to identify them? Is it someone he knows, has met briefly; he might not remember them, but they clearly knew him.'

'He would have told us if he'd met anyone recently who seemed suspicious. Did you mention the murders to him when you went home, Declan?' asked Ben.

'A little, I never told him names though, that would have been unprofessional of me, and you know I'm not like that. Maybe Rosie and Matt had been to him to see about getting married?'

'Rosie and Matt or Max?'

He shrugged. 'Are we done here, I want to go and sit with Theo for a little while before I go home.'

'Yes, of course. Thanks for this.' Ben smiled at him.

'You don't have to thank me; I want you to catch whoever did this to those guys and Theo. Not one of them deserved it. Oh, by the way, have you had any luck finding the murder weapon? I think it's one of those little ice axes. They have a sharp point and if you hit someone hard enough with them, you're going to do the kind of damage both victims sustained. I can't say about Theo's injuries, though, as I haven't seen the scans yet. I'm going to ask Philip when he does his rounds if they are similar, but I bet you a round of drinks they are. Only I don't think they meant to kill Theo, maybe deter him, and they hit him a little too hard.'

They walked out of the cold mortuary into the badly lit corridor, and Morgan didn't know what was worse, the fridges full of dead people or the corridor that looked longer every time she saw it, like one of those stretching tunnels out of a funfair fun house that gave you the creeps just thinking about it.

THIRTY-FOUR

Ben told Morgan to order everyone's usual from the Thai restaurant and they picked it up on the way back to the station. Morgan's stomach rumbled loudly sitting with the box on her knee, and she was so hungry her mouth was almost salivating. They scooted in the back way and jumped straight into the lift.

'Why the lift? Thought you were keen to get your steps in.'

'I want to avoid anyone and everyone, Morgan. Is it too much to ask to be able to eat a long, overdue meal without any added drama?'

She smiled at him. He was almost as grouchy as Amy when he was hungry. He took the box containing the cartons of food into the office, and she nipped back out to grab cutlery; they would eat out of the cartons – what a team they made. It would be okay if they all got something different so they could share, but every one of them always ordered the same chicken pad Thai, so there wasn't much to share out apart from the chips and spicy crackers. As she walked back in Amy and Cain were peeling the lids off the containers.

'Morgan, I'm going to marry Ben because he brought us food, I hope you don't mind.' Cain winked at her.

'Marry away, I'm not sure he will share your sentiment though.' She peered through the gap in the blinds in Ben's office.

'Where is he?'

'In no uncertain terms he said to leave him the fuck alone whilst he eats.'

'Hahaha, he didn't say that.'

Amy took a fork off Morgan and shook her head. 'No, he didn't. He said he was eating his tea in peace and didn't want to be disturbed for at least ten minutes. How did you get on?'

Morgan thought Ben had the right idea. She could do with a breather to process everything that had happened in the last couple of hours.

'Theo is awake and on a ward.'

'Yay, that's such good news. I've been so worried about him and for Declan. It's so nice that those two are genuinely happy together.'

Morgan nodded. 'I know, it's such a relief. He's a bit groggy, couldn't remember much, said he didn't see who attacked him.'

Cain shovelled the biggest forkful of noodles she'd ever seen into his mouth, and Morgan thought it would only take five of those and he'd have finished his. He tried to talk, and she held up her hand.

'Did your mother never tell you it's rude to speak with your mouth full, Cain?'

He shrugged, but stopped trying much to her relief. Peeling the lid back off her container she turned away from Cain. She loved him but watching him eat like he hadn't been fed in weeks made her stomach turn. Instead, she logged on to the computer and the incident logs to see what had been happening around Rydal Falls whilst they'd been off air the last couple of hours. Which was not much, two minor road traffic accidents, a shoplifting at the off-licence of a bottle of vodka, which meant they all knew who the culprit was; there was only one woman who ever stole vodka from shops, and she would be picked up as soon as they could find her. A complaint from a tourist about having a camera stolen out of the back of their car and that was it.

Cain's radio burst into life as a voice asked,

'Nearest patrols to an IR down on Kendal Road, break-in in progress.'

A chill ran down Morgan's spine, and she waited to see the address; they lived on Kendal Road. The small amount of noodles she'd eaten lay heavy in her stomach, and she stood up. She knocked on Ben's door and opened it.

'Are you listening to the radio?'

He shook his head.

'There's a break-in in progress on our street.'

'What address?'

Morgan shrugged but she knew what they were going to say, they were going to say number thirteen, their number, she could feel it deep inside of her. Ben turned the volume button all the way up on the top of his radio.

'It's at thirteen, neighbour reporting that the police officers who live there are at work.'

Ben was up and running towards the door, and Morgan followed. Cain also stood, took one last mouthful of noodles then shouted to Amy, 'Put the lid on that and don't eat it.'

Amy mimed being sick. 'As if, you've gobbed all over it.'

Ben was out of the back door in record time, and even Morgan struggled to keep up with him. He had the car running before she'd got into the passenger seat.

Cain threw open the back door and clambered inside.

'Go, go, go, boss.'

And go he did, the huge metal gates that led into the rear yard of the station were just sliding shut and he put his foot down, speeding through them with centimetres to spare before they jolted to a stop when the automatic sensor kicked in.

'How do they know about a break-in at our house? Who phoned it in? The security company? Because it could be a false alarm.'

Morgan was waiting for the log to update, but it was too slow and she grabbed her radio that she'd forgotten to take out of the glove compartment earlier.

'Control, who rang this in?'

'*Mrs Walker from number fifteen, said she saw someone dressed in black creeping around the back garden and the officers are at work.*'

'Yes, we are. It's Ben's house, we have an alarm system. Has the alarm company phoned anything in?'

'*Negative, just the neighbour.*'

She looked at Ben. 'She could be mistaken?'

'I doubt that, she doesn't miss a trick.'

Morgan wished she hadn't eaten now; her stomach was churning. *If you find this, you're next.* She heard the words from the note clearly inside of her mind as if Ben or Cain had spoken them out loud. They'd all assumed the note put Morgan at risk, but what if it was just the killer playing with them? Was this the murderer taunting them further? Showing them how they could get close to the crime scene? Ben slammed the brakes on as he almost rammed into the police van that was already parked in the middle of the road, blue lights illuminating the dusky sky. Cain was out before either Morgan or Ben and sprinting towards the officers at the front door.

'Stay here, please, Morgan.'

'No, I'll go speak to Annie.'

Ben didn't reply. He was out of the car, and she was too. She watched them as Ben unlocked the front door and Kevin dashed out, darting off into the bushes.

Before she'd reached the gate Annie's front door was open, and she waved her in.

'I'm sorry, Morgan, I was upstairs, and I looked out of the window and there was someone in your garden. Gave me the fright of my life, all dressed in black. I knew it wasn't you even though you dress in black most of the time.'

'How, how did you know it wasn't me, Annie? And thank you for phoning it in so fast.'

'They had their face covered, had one of those face masks covering everything but their eyes. I'm so glad you weren't at home, I kept thinking about next door and—' Tears came to Annie's eyes, and Morgan gently took hold of her elbow, leading her to the sofa to sit down. 'I feel so bad I never saw whoever did that to them. I've been extra vigilant and I'm so glad that I saw this person.'

'Annie, you have no blame in any of this whatsoever, the only person who should be carrying any guilt around with them is the person who killed Rosie and...' Morgan wondered if Annie had any idea it was Max who had died, as she knew Matt had returned home by now. Had he told Annie he was alive? 'But I can guarantee you they don't feel one little bit guilty about it because most killers have no conscience. Please you wait here, I'll be back shortly.'

Morgan couldn't stand not knowing what was happening; it was her home too. She left Annie on the sofa and ran into her own house. Ben appeared at the top of the stairs.

'Nobody's been inside, everything is okay.'

'What about the attic?'

He stared up at the hatch above her head and lifted a finger to his lips, then pointed to the officers who appeared behind her. He then pointed at the attic, and they nodded, walking as quietly as they could in their heavy Magnum boots and heavy body armour to join Ben. Cain came out of the kitchen, his cheeks red and out of breath a little. She lifted a finger to her lips to stop him before he started talking.

He whispered, 'Garden's okay, checked the shed and in all the bushes, nobody hiding out there.'

'Thank you,' she whispered back.

Ben was lifting the pole that unlatched the attic, but she guessed there was no way anyone could be up there unless they had been super-fast and managed to get in there, then pull the ladders up in the time between Annie phoning the police and them turning up. She checked the log: four minutes. Was that enough time? Four minutes was a lifetime if you were bleeding to death from a serious head wound, and she wondered how long it had taken Rosie to die after she'd been hit on the back of her head so viciously her blood had sprayed and seeped every-where. The noise from the loft ladder being pulled down was enough to wake the dead, then the two officers were up there, torches in hand checking out their attic space whilst they all watched on.

'All clear, nobody up here.'

Her shoulders dropped with relief. The two officers made their way back down.

'House is clear, all good, no sign of anyone breaking in. All windows and doors are secure, sir.'

'Thank you so much.' Ben smiled at them. 'I appreciate that, did you check all the bedrooms?'

They both nodded.

'Thanks.'

As they were standing around Morgan realised that the burglar alarm hadn't gone off.

'Ben did you turn the alarm off?'

He shook his head. 'No, it wasn't armed.' He rolled his eyes at her, and she felt a tiny gnawing inside of her stomach. Who could have got away so quickly from their house without the chance of getting caught after snooping around? She turned and walked back out, and taking the few steps to the murder house, she hammered on the door with her fist.

The door opened and Matt stared at her. 'Problem?'

'Were you just in our garden?'

He looked confused. 'Why would I be in your garden?'

She looked down to see he had on a pair of big yellow Marigold gloves. There was a fine sheen of perspiration on his brow.

'Annie thought she saw someone.'

'And she told you it was me?'

'No, she didn't say that. I was just checking, I'll be asking everyone and maybe you should speak to Annie, as she thinks you're dead.'

He frowned at her. 'Okay, you do that. I'm busy trying to clean bloodstains from almost every part of my house. I'll speak to her when I have time.'

'Sorry, I'll let you get back to it.'

She walked towards his front gate then turned back, feeling his gaze burning through the back of her neck.

'Do you need a hand?'

This threw him and his eyes clouded over. 'Are you offering to help me clean up their blood?'

She shrugged. She actually just wanted a chance to ask him questions. 'I bet Annie would help too, and between the three of us we might get it done quicker.'

All the animosity left his face as he shook his head. 'Thank you, but no, it's okay and I couldn't expect the old dear next door to start scrubbing at this mess, it might finish her off.'

She shrugged. 'She's a lot tougher than she looks, but if you change your mind let me know. I'm going to be home for a couple of hours.'

'Thanks.'

He closed the door on her, and she wondered if he had been in their back garden. He was sweaty, he was also dressed in black joggers and a black tee. It would explain how the suspect had got away so quickly, but it didn't explain why he would be snooping around their house though, which was the frustrating part. Despite his alibi for the murders, she had a gut feeling that Matt was hiding something. Was it the relationship with Raven? Or something even more deadly?

THIRTY-FIVE

The two officers stood down and left Ben, Cain and Morgan inside the house.

'It must have been the killer. We know they are devious, and like playing with us. Hence the note in the attic. Why else would someone be snooping around here?' she asked.

'Burglar, stalker, killer, thief, take your pick.' Cain couldn't help himself, and Morgan smiled at him despite the desperateness of the situation.

'I think someone needs to go and talk to Annie next door about the whole Rosie and Matt, Max thing. I asked Matt if he would, to let her know he was still alive, but he said he was busy cleaning up the bloodstains.'

Ben nodded. 'Yeah, that's fine but I don't really want to leave you on your own.'

'I'll be fine, I'll make sure the alarm is on. I can't believe we didn't do it before we left.'

Cain pointed to it, just as Ben's phone began to ring. She saw Declan's picture and hoped it was good news.

'You paid all that money for a fancy alarm and didn't set it when there's a serial killer on the loose in your street.' Cain tutted loudly.

'He's not a serial killer.'

'No? I thought two victims were now classed as serial? And if the priest had died that would have made a definite three, the intent was there so technically I think we can assume they are a serial killer, and I can't see them stopping now.'

'Gee, thanks, Cain. You sure know how to make a girl feel safe.'

He reached out for her arm, clasping it gently. 'I'm sorry, I get all worried about you both and say stupid stuff.'

Ben tucked his phone in his pocket, and his face was serious. 'Theo has taken a turn for the worse and they've taken him back to theatre to drain a clot. I'm going to the hospital to sit with Declan for a bit. He would do the same for me. Are you sure you're okay here, Morgan? Cain can stay with you.'

'Cain can go home. I'm busy and I don't need him to watch over me.'

'She's touchy tonight, isn't she?' said Cain to Ben.

They both ignored him, and Morgan asked, 'Do you want me to come with you?'

Ben shook his head. 'No, but thanks. I think he needs to let a bit of steam off and he won't do that if you're there.'

'Of course, give him my love.'

Ben smiled at her, then kissed her cheek. 'And you be careful, any funny business you ring 999, okay, Morgan? Don't be your own hero and go out snooping if you hear a noise outside. I don't care if you mistake a cat for a person, if they're rustling around just call, okay?'

'Pinkie promise. I'm going to sit with Annie.'

Ben set the alarm, and they left the house to the beeps. Kevin appeared at the top of the steps and began to rub himself against Morgan's legs, weaving in and out of them.

'Sorry, cat, you missed your chance. I won't be long, or you could actually go out and use the cat flap we had put on the back door for you.'

Kevin looked up at her in disgust and turned away.

Cain laughed. 'I swear to God that cat is Des reincarnated. He's so like him.'

'I would agree with you, but Des had the cat before he died, so impossible really for him to come back as a cat,' Ben said. He was already getting into his own car, leaving the div car for Cain.

Morgan waved. 'Drive safe.'

Ben nodded and shut the door, and Cain turned to her. 'I can stay here with you, it's no problem.'

'No, you get back to Angela. Anyway, how did it go? Did you get a ring and did she say yes?'

Cain grinned at her. 'She did and after all that she picked an antique engagement ring out of the display case, it fit her perfectly and she said she liked the thought of giving it a second chance.'

Morgan had to blink away tears, when had she turned into such a romantic. 'Aw, Cain. That's so sweet and adorable. I think you two make a wonderful couple. You get back to Angela, we've worked over twelve hours already. Does she mind about Amy moving in?'

'She really is amazing and no, she's not bothered one little bit. And besides, I tend to stop at hers three or four times a week, and Amy is no bother. She's a lot quieter than I imagined and spends a lot of time in her room watching Netflix with tubs of Ben and Jerry's. She's also a bit of a neat freak so she's always tidying up and washing stuff. I can't complain about her at all.'

Morgan smiled at him. 'You really are a good guy, Cain, underneath all of that muscle. We're lucky to have you on our team.'

His face lit up and he was literally beaming. He drew her in for a hug and she hugged him back. 'Morgan, please, please if

you think there's anything wrong phone it in, then phone me.
I'll keep my mobile on loud.'

She laughed. 'I will, I'm not stupid. I don't fancy an ice axe
through the back of my head.'

'No, your head is on its last legs the amount of damage
you've done to that. I'm surprised you can still string a sentence
together.'

He rubbed the top of her head then bounded down the path
back to his car before she could do anything. She waved at him
then followed him and went next door to speak to Annie about
the confusion and update her.

———

Annie opened the door and shooed Morgan inside to the
kitchen; it was warm and it smelled of fresh bread. It was
amazing and Morgan imagined eating a thick slice of it covered
in butter. There was a glass on the table with ice and clear
liquid in it. Annie picked it up, downed the liquid then took a
bottle of vodka out of the freezer and waved it in the air.

'Fancy one? Surely, you've finished work now. How long
have you been there? It's been hours and hours.'

Morgan did fancy an ice-cold shot. 'I'd love a small one,
please.'

Annie grinned at her. 'About time. I take it by the lack of
activity you didn't find anyone in the house or gardens?'

'No, but thank you for ringing it in.'

'You're not annoyed with me for being an old busybody?'

'No, I am not, and neither is anyone else. It's thanks to kind
people like you we manage to keep the crime rate down a little
bit. Did Rosie or Matt ever wear a St Christopher necklace?'

Annie shook her head. 'No, I can't say I ever saw them
wearing one of those.'

Morgan felt a tingle, it must have belonged to the killer.

Annie took a crystal glass out of the cupboard, a bag of ice out of the freezer and took something out of the drawer to hammer the bag with and break it up, then she got a lemon out of the fridge. Morgan watched as she poured the ice in, and the sound of it clinking against the side of the glass and then cracking as the cold liquid was poured on top was soothing to her soul.

'Lemon?'

'Yes, please.'

'I prefer lime myself, but the shop only had lemons so here we are.' She expertly sliced some lemon and added it to the drink, passing it to Morgan. She topped her own glass up and sat opposite her. 'Cheers.' She clinked her glass against Morgan's.

Morgan wondered what they were celebrating.

'Oh, that sounded crass, this is a commiseration drink not a celebratory one.'

Morgan sipped the neat vodka and felt it burning down her throat, but the warmth inside made her begin to relax for the first time in a couple of hours. The sound of something being rubbed against the wall made Annie turn and stare.

She whispered, 'Are you searching the house again?'

'Not exactly.' Morgan began to tell her about Max.

Annie was shaking her head, and Morgan could tell she had no idea it wasn't Matt living with Rosie for the past few months.

'You are kidding me, so the Matt I knew isn't the real one. Why did Rosie lie about that, I don't understand?'

Morgan took a big sip this time, savouring the heat as the vodka burned her throat. 'Honestly, I don't know. I'm confused, I'm tired and I literally have no idea what the hell is going on.'

'I bet you don't. I watch all the TV shows, *Midsomer Murders*, *A Touch of Frost*, and I would have never pegged Rosie as the kind of person who can commit fraud on that level.'

Morgan sat up. 'Fraud?'

'Well, what else could it be?' Annie reached across the table and patted her hand. It was comforting and Morgan wished her own mum had lived to be Annie's age. She could do with her advice and hugs now and again; she missed her terribly.

'You'll figure it out. Do you want another drink?'

Morgan had that soft buzz a drink of alcohol gave you when you had one glass, and she was tempted to say yes, but also aware that she needed to figure out what the hell was going on with this case.

'I better not.'

'Oh, just a small one, then you can tell me all about the real Matt.'

She smiled at her. 'Okay, a small one.'

Annie unscrewed the cap off the bottle and poured a large one into Morgan's glass.

'Oops, sorry. I was never very good at measurements.'

'It's okay, I'll try not to drink it all.'

'You better had, that stuff is expensive. I treated myself to a bottle to see what all the fuss was about and why it's so dear compared to the supermarket brands. You know what, it's the biggest mistake I ever made.'

Morgan took another sip; it was smooth and it went down perfectly. 'Why?'

'Well, now I can't abide the cheap stuff so I have to buy this.'

Morgan laughed. 'You're funny, I never thought I'd say that about you.'

'No, you thought I was just the nosey old bat from next door with a sad little life and no friends.'

She shrugged. 'I didn't think you had a sad life, but nosey I'm afraid so and I'm sorry for being so judgy, I had no right to be. Especially not when you buy expensive vodka and bake your own bread, which smells divine by the way.'

Annie pushed herself up. 'Oh shoot, my bread.'

She took a tea towel off the side and opened the oven door, taking a loaf tin out with the nicest smelling bread in the world. She placed it on the side. 'Thank you, I forgot about it. Would you like to try it when it's cooled a little?'

Morgan smiled. 'Yes, please. Fresh bread is one of my favourite smells, reminds me of being a kid and passing the bakery next to the school.'

'Ah, mine too. I used to be a baker. Before that I worked in the butchers, but I hated the smell of all the blood and meat. So, I trained to be a baker, and it was the best job I had. I got to eat lots of nice things. I sell my own bread to make a little pocket money, these houses aren't cheap to run, and my pension doesn't seem to cover the necessities any more.'

'I couldn't be a butcher, turns my stomach. So, are we thinking about Rosie and how she was committing fraud, if you're my new assistant detective?'

Annie laughed. 'So, I'm certain Rosie was pretending Max was Matt, just so you know. I don't see why, but I distinctly remember hearing his name being called while I was in their vicinity in the front garden. Do you think it *was* Matt?'

Morgan squeezed her eyes closed. 'Why would he risk getting caught and then go clean up the crime scene?'

Annie shrugged. 'I'm a little tipsy, forgive my rubbish ideas.'

Morgan stood up. 'Me too but thank you for having a go at figuring it out. I better get home; I can't keep my eyes open. I just need to have a nap or something.'

She stood up and wondered why she could feel so drunk after so little alcohol. She'd only taken a few sips of her second glass, then she realised it was because she'd hardly eaten and left her takeaway at work.

'That bread smells so good.'

'I'll bring you some around when I can get it out of the tin. It's got to cool off or it will be a mashed-up mess.'

'Thank you, Annie, you're very kind.'

Annie lifted her glass in the air to her. 'Just shows how wrong we can get people, but I won't hold it against you. Sleep tight, Morgan.'

Morgan smiled at her neighbour and wobbled her way out of the front door and down the steps. She was tempted to climb the low wall that separated their properties but if she fell over and smashed her brains in Ben would never forgive her. Why was she so drunk? She glanced over at the lights on in Rosie's house and wondered how Matt was managing with his cleaning. Well, he better not come get her now, she was no good to anyone. She best remember never to drink with Annie again. She didn't have the stomach for it.

Morgan opened her front door and managed to reset the alarm without it going off and disturbing the whole street. She realised Kevin might still be outside and opened it again to see a guy standing by her front gate. He stared at her then carried on walking, making her feel a little bit uneasy until he called out, 'Buttons.' And she saw the white poodle that was sniffing at their gate. She didn't shut the door and called out, 'Kevin, chchchch.'

A loud miaow from next door's garden and then he was running towards the door before she shut him out again.

Morgan laughed. 'You've got no street cred whatsoever. Have you been hiding under there for the past thirty minutes?'

He followed her down to the kitchen where she opened another pouch of cat food for him. Then she swayed her way upstairs, feeling as if her feet didn't belong to her body and wondering if Annie had spiked her drink, then pushing that thought out of her head. Why would she? It was stupid.

THIRTY-SIX

Ben wasn't sure where to go when he reached the hospital entrance to the emergency department, so he ducked in there and messaged Declan. He was so used to attending the mortuary he didn't know the rest of the hospital that well. Ben tried not to look at the people waiting to be seen, he hated hospitals, hated that he spent almost as much time in them as he did the police station. He messaged Morgan too, and she replied instantly telling him she was home. Annie had given her the idea that the murders were to do with some big fraud scam, but she couldn't figure out what it could be. Kevin was fed and she was going to lie down because she felt a bit queasy after accepting a glass of straight vodka on the rocks off Annie. He'd only been gone forty minutes, and she was drunk, good effort.

Hey, did you set the alarm?

Yes, love you night.

Then.

Sorry, I feel so bad.

Get some toast down you, a large glass of water and two parac-etamol, you'll be right as rain in the morning. It's exhaustion and hunger, you've hardly eaten or slept for a couple of days.

She sent him a blowing a kiss emoji.

'Ben.'

Declan's voice was so close it sounded as if he'd shouted down his ear.

He looked up. 'How are you?'

'Ach, I've had better days. Come through, we'll go sit in the staff lounge near the theatre.'

He swiped them through the double doors into another long corridor. 'Where's Morgan?'

'Drunk, at home and going to bed.'

'Get away with you. Are the pair of you not working?'

'It's a long story, have you got time for this?'

'Time is all I do have.'

'We've been working since early this morning. I left her at home after next door reported seeing someone in the back garden, our back garden, and she was going to update the woman who rang it in, only she's given her neat vodka and now Morgan sounds pissed, and I've told her to go to bed and sleep it off.'

'Good effort, Morgan, bless her.'

'Bless her, I've only been gone forty minutes.'

Declan let out a loud guffaw that filled the entire corridor and made two staff nurses who were walking ahead of them turn around to look. They grinned at him then turned back. He was bent almost double laughing.

'What's so funny?'

'I, she, it's just I don't know but everything she does it's kind of extra, isn't it?'

This made Ben laugh. 'Yeah, extra for sure. I worry about her so much, it's like I'm constantly thinking about where she is, what she's doing, if she's safe, has she eaten, does she need a break.'

'Oh, that's not worry. That's true love. She'll be fine when she's slept it off. What happened about the guy in the garden though? That's a bit of a worry.'

'Patrols flooded the area, officers checked all the gardens, no sign of anyone or anyone being there. I think maybe the woman next door might have been at the vodka long before Morgan went around.'

Declan snorted. 'As long as everything is tickety-boo. Can I get you a coffee? I do have a bottle of very expensive whisky in my bottom drawer in my office. I'm loath to drink when Theo is in such a bad way, but you're welcome to one.'

'No, I'm good. I need to drive home at some point, coffee would be greatly appreciated though. And anyway, enough about me and Morgan, I'm here for you and Theo. Any news?'

Declan's warm hand squeezed Ben's shoulder tight. 'Thank you, I appreciate it. I just love hearing about yours and Morgan's antics, they make my shit show of a life seem a little better. It's a bit worrying to be honest, they found a blood clot and needed to remove it. His brain was swelling too fast. Hopefully they've managed to get the clot out and removed a small piece of his skull to allow his brain to expand. You know he was talking only an hour before he slipped into unconsciousness again. I thought he was okay, just shows how wrong and presumptuous it was of me to believe that.'

'It's not presumptuous at all. He seemed okay when we visited. I mean not okay, but he was certainly better than I imagined he was going to be. You must be so worried.'

Declan pushed a door open to a room filled with sofas, a table with mismatched chairs, and a galley kitchen that ran the full length of the wall. It was empty, the TV was on Sky news and Declan strode to pick up the remote, switching it off and plunging the space into darkness. Ben felt around for the light switch, and finding it the fluorescents sputtered into life.

Declan sighed. 'I'm beginning to dislike hospitals and their creepy vibe. Was it me or did it feel scary as fuck when the room went dark?'

Ben smiled. 'You're almost as bad as Morgan. She gets creeped out way more than I thought she would in this hospital. Yet, she's happy to wander around the house in complete darkness and doesn't hesitate to take off running into a dark alley or anywhere where some six-foot guy with a ball pein hammer might be waiting for her.'

'Women, huh.'

This made Ben laugh so much his side began to ache, even though he hadn't been joking about Morgan putting herself in danger. Declan was grinning and it warmed his heart to see his friend still able to smile despite the desperate situation he was in. Declan made coffees then passed a mug to Ben and sat opposite him.

'Thank you.'

'You don't need to thank me.'

'I know, but I do. I keep wondering what if this is Theo's time to go, maybe his God has called him home or whatever they believe in. I've never been so happy, Ben, or felt so settled. I don't know what I'd do if he doesn't make it.'

Tears glistened in the corners of Declan's eyes. Ben leaned over and squeezed his knee.

'Look, how many times have I been where you're sitting because Morgan was hurt?'

Declan smiled. 'Far too many.'

'Yes, far too many but she managed to pull through. Theo will be okay, Declan; you've got to believe that. It's not for us to throw the towel in before giving him a fighting chance. He's fought to stay here up to now, why would he stop fighting when he has you?'

'I hope you're right, Ben, yes. Why would he want to leave me? He's stronger than he looks that's for sure.'

'Yep, before we know it Theo and Morgan will be comparing the size of the scars on their heads to see who has the biggest.'

'I hope so, I really do. So, have you got anywhere with the case?'

'Not really, it is completely mind-blowing. Our strongest suspect is someone with an air-tight alibi. Morgan has a theory about Raven Castle, the body piercer, but if this was a crime of passion, I don't understand who was hiding in the attic...'

Declan put his mug down on the coffee table and sat back on the sofa. Placing his arms behind his head he closed his eyes for a few seconds then looked at Ben.

'You could be looking at this with too much depth. The attic could have been set up to confuse you. It could be really straightforward. Perhaps Rosie just didn't want the hassle of having to explain to everyone that she preferred sleeping with her boyfriend's twin brother and, maybe, Matt knew about it. Who is going to argue that she had never split up with him? Are you sure he wasn't around at the time of the murders? What do we always say, the number one suspect is the husband or the partner?'

Ben thought about it, could it be that simple? Had Rosie told Matt about Max, and he'd lost it in a fit of jealousy? It made more sense this way. If he had killed the pair of them, that would mean he got his house back and any life insurance money or pension that Rosie might have. Had Raven helped? Was everything in the attic a ruse to distract them?

'Declan, you are brilliant.'

He shrugged. 'I've heard that before.'

They sat in comfortable silence for the next hour, Ben

wondering if they should be watching Matt more closely. They also needed to interview Raven again, more thoroughly this time. She had lied or had failed to inform them about the affair she was having with Max.

The door opened and a woman dressed in scrubs smiled at Declan. 'He's okay, it went well. Obviously, he's going to have to go back into ICU to be monitored, and I think it's better to keep him sedated and give him a chance to heal. Are you happy with that?'

Declan stood up and grinned at the doctor. 'Sacha, I'm forever in your debt. Yes, I'm happy, thank you.'

Sacha beamed at him. 'He's in good hands, Declan. Why don't you go home and get some sleep because you look like shit, and I don't want you having a heart attack and in the next bed.'

Ben said to Declan, 'If you don't want to go to yours, you're welcome to come back to mine.'

'I don't think I could stand listening to Morgan snoring all night, and she said you snore even worse, thanks. I'll go home, have a hot shower and hopefully get a few hours. If you could do your best not to send me any bodies for the next twenty-four hours that would be greatly appreciated, my friend.'

'I'll do my best not to.'

Ben stood up and hugged Declan. 'See you tomorrow.'

'Yes, without a body in tow, please.'

Ben waved his hand at him and began the long walk through the hospital to get back to the car park.

He was ready to call it a night if he could. First thing tomorrow the whole team was going to have to revise the strategy around Matt and Raven. There was a lot to discuss with them all, and they were running out of time to catch the killer. He felt as if they were risking too much. He didn't want this one to get away. Up to now the team had a pretty good success rate, but it happened and he didn't want this case to go cold.

THIRTY-SEVEN

Morgan had eaten her toast, drank her water and taken two painkillers like Ben had told her. Undressing she'd pulled on her pyjamas and collapsed into the bed, feeling way too woozy and dizzy off a glass of vodka than she should have. Her eyes had closed the moment her head hit the pillow, and she should have slept soundly, but there was something scratching away in the corner of her mind that wouldn't let her rest so easy. She was lying there not quite in a deep sleep, but not awake either, she was in-between and it was as if she was floating between two worlds. She could hear movement above her, but didn't know if it was her dream state. Turning on her side something underneath her pillow crinkled. Opening her eyes she blinked a couple of times to let them adjust to the dark and reached underneath the pillow with her fingers, wondering what had made that sound.

Her fingers brushed the edge of a piece of paper. Had she left it under there? No, she hadn't had time to write in her journal all week.

A thud from somewhere inside the house made her heart begin to beat way too fast. Wide-awake now Morgan sat up and looked at the piece of paper clutched between her fingers. Her mouth dry and head pounding she turned on the lamp beside her bed and read the two words, each capitalised.

YOUR TURN

Then there was another noise from somewhere inside of the house. She couldn't figure out where it was coming from. It wasn't the attic, was it? But someone couldn't be in here, she'd set the alarm like Ben told her to. Maybe it was Ben who was home and banging around. The air inside of the bedroom felt fraught with tension. Whoever it was, she got the feeling it wasn't Ben. He whistled, hummed and, despite trying his best to be quiet, made enough noise for three rowdy teenagers stomping around the place. He would have called out and told her he was home.

She frantically looked for her phone, but it wasn't here. Morgan didn't know what to do. Should she go and investigate, or should she arm herself and wait it out here? The wooden floorboards in this room creaked near to the doorway, and they would give her away if she tried to get out. She looked around and a thought occurred to her: how many bedrooms had she hid in in the past and been injured? Too many. Behind the bed was Ben's old cricket bat. She stood up and leaned behind to grab it. Whoever it was, she wouldn't go down without a fight. Gripping the handle tight she crept to the door that she hadn't closed properly and tried to tread lightly on the offending board, so it didn't make too much noise. Throwing open the door she stepped out, and Kevin miaowed so loudly she screamed, scaring the crap out of him, and he darted back downstairs. Cupping a hand over her mouth she began to laugh, that bloody cat was going to be the death of her, and she sat on the top stair, still holding tight to the bat in case someone was actually inside the house. The light turned on and she screeched again.

'Morgan, what the hell's wrong with you? Are you okay?'

Ben was standing at the bottom of the staircase with a plate of toast in one hand and a mug in the other.

She shook her head. 'Losing the plot, sorry. I heard noises and then I found a note under the pillow.'

'What note?'

She stood up, not letting go of the bat in case she was having some weird dream and Ben morphed into an ice-axe-wielding maniac. She went back to the bedroom and retrieved the note. He followed her and she held it up so he could read it.

'Someone has been inside the house and left that. How, who and why? Put it down on the bed, Morgan, it's evidence.'

'Ben, is someone inside of here now? Am I having a nightmare?'

'No, you're not. How much vodka did Mrs Walker give you, Morgan?'

'Not enough to make me feel the way I do, that's for sure.'

'I'll call it in.'

'No, don't. What's anyone going to do now? Bag that up and take it away? Search the house then tell us it's okay? We can do that ourselves. Why don't we search everywhere and then sleep in the spare room, so we don't mess this one up for Wendy. Although I've been in the bed and touched the note. Ben, why would someone come in here?'

He lifted a finger to his lips to shush her as he turned around to listen. She wondered if he could feel it too, the vibes were off, something wasn't right. They both stood there, breathing a little too hard as they tried to keep quiet.

Ben whispered, 'I think we should call it in.'

Morgan shook her head, they'd already had police here earlier for a false alarm. If they did it again then people in the station would start talking. Ben looked over at the wardrobes that ran across one wall and walked towards them. Morgan lifted the bat ready to strike first and ask questions later because if she found someone hiding in her house, she wasn't about to engage in a polite conversation with them. She was going to beat their brains in. He pulled all the doors open and began rifling through the coat hangers. She stood next to him poking the bat inside. There wasn't any boogey man hiding inside, thank goodness.

They made their way from room to room repeating the process until every nook and cranny had been checked, poked, and they were happy nobody was inside the house. Kevin watched them from the bottom step, and she wondered if it had been him thudding around after all, but that didn't explain the note. When the house was deemed safe from an intruder they went into the lounge. Ben retrieved the plate of toast that was cold, but at least the butter had soaked into it. He offered a slice to Morgan who took it and began to chew on it.

'Do you think Annie spiked my drink?'

Ben had taken a glug of his tea and he spat it all over himself, spraying toast and cold tea everywhere. 'What the hell, why would she do that?'

Morgan shrugged. 'I don't know, I just felt so weird after she gave me a drink. I mean, I don't drink a lot of alcohol, but we have the occasional glass of wine on our days off, don't we? and I've drunk vodka plenty of times in the past in the days before my job when I was at college. I've never felt so out of it after one shot, and I have the worst headache from hell.'

He shrugged. 'You're tired, stressed, how's your head? It's only been a month or so since you got smashed in the brains. You haven't eaten much, and I know you haven't because you look a bit drawn.'

'Oh, wow, thanks so much. So, basically, you're saying I look a mess. Do I look like a walking corpse?'

Ben laughed. 'That's not what I meant at all, you are beautiful, but you don't always take good care of yourself like you should.'

'Fuck, Ben, thanks for that. Anyway, how's Theo? Is Declan holding up okay?'

'Surgery went well, he's back in ICU to give him a full chance of recovery. Declan is good, it's you I'm worried about. How the hell did that note get under your pillow, Morgan?'

'That's such a relief, poor Theo and Declan. What a nightmare for them both. Maybe the note's been there a while. I haven't changed the bedding for a few days.'

'We need to be ultra vigilant with the alarms. We can't slip up no matter how much of a rush we are in.'

'Did the killer put the note there when we were busy at the scene? The alarm wasn't set then, maybe they managed to slip inside whilst we were so busy, and nobody noticed. If they did, they have some front. Who would feel comfortable going inside our house when the street was full of cops?'

'Another cop?' said Ben incredulously.

She shook her head. 'Annie would have known exactly what was happening. She doesn't miss anything, Ben. She waits and she watches. She's always watching, and she probably knows our alarm key code. She sits in that window for hours every single day.'

'No, why would she want to do that? I thought she was good friends with Rosie.'

'That's what she told us, but was she? We take what people tell us at face value. We trust that they're being truthful because of the badge we carry, but not everyone is a good person, and I thought I was being mean by judging her but maybe my internal instincts were right to be wary of her.'

'Wow, that's deep and if you truly think your drink was spiked, you need to do a urine sample. I can send it in tomorrow. We also need to get your blood tested although it depends on what was used as you know some drugs are out of a person's system in twelve hours, but others last up to seven days – and what the hell would she gain by stalking Rosie and Max, then trying to scare you off?'

'Same as any other person who behaves that way. It's the thrill, isn't it? She said herself she's bored, hasn't many friends, no place to go, maybe this is all some elaborate game for her own entertainment.'

Ben yawned, his mouth stretching wide. 'I'm shattered. Should we sleep down here? I'm too tired to go move all the clutter off the spare bed, and I can't think straight, that's a lot to process.'

Morgan nodded. He went to get changed out of his suit trousers, and she went to grab the spare sample pot she had in the bathroom cabinet to pee in; it would prove one way or the other if Annie had drugged her. When she'd managed to do that she curled up on the sofa and tugged a throw on top of her. She was so out of sorts and feeling off, but what if she was right and Annie had some ulterior motive that none of them was aware of?

THIRTY-EIGHT

Ben had called a briefing for nine o'clock in the blue room. Gilly was on her way, and Marc had turned up with a blossoming bruise forming under his right eye, which everyone had stared at, but nobody had the courage to ask him how he'd got. Morgan looked at Cain's empty chair, no doubt he would put them out of their misery and ask him outright; he always had been a little outspoken.

She looked back to the app on her phone. She was going through the recordings from their doorbell on the day of the murders again, where they had not only left their house unlocked but also hadn't set the alarm. The camera had been going wild for the first few minutes then it had managed to stop recording. Whoever had gone inside must have known this, but that was if they had gone in through the front door. Would Annie be confident enough to walk into their house when there were police crawling all over the house next door to her? That was the question. She had viewed Annie Walker as an elderly woman who had nothing to do with her time, but she could have stepped over the low wall that separated their front gardens and stayed close to the steps. Nobody was looking in that direction because all eyes were on Rosie and Matt's house. Morgan wished they had internal cameras now. Ben had talked about it when they got the alarm system installed, but she had refused point-blank to be recorded walking around their home in her underwear or wearing nothing but a towel. So that had never happened. Now though she wished she had said yes.

Cain finally appeared, and Ben began to clap his hands together.

'Thanks for coming, Cain, nice of you to put in an appearance today.'

Cain glanced at the clock on the wall. 'Erm, I'm officially on a late so you're very welcome, boss.'

Ben grinned at him. 'You're forgiven.'

Cain looked across at Amy. 'Yeah, thanks. She isn't though, she's the one who rang me and told me to come in as there was important shit going down. Is there, have I dragged myself out of my warm, cosy bed for something?'

'All will be revealed shortly at the briefing because I'm not repeating myself ten times.'

Morgan pointed to a cardboard tray with one remaining coffee cup in it. 'That's yours, might need reheating.'

Cain rushed across to Morgan and kissed the top of her head. 'You are my angel, truly you are. You look like shit today, Morgan, what's going on with you?'

'Really? I give you free coffee and you talk to me like that.'

He leaned down and squeezed her. 'I'm worried about you. I dunno, you look a bit peaky that's all.'

The door opened and the custody nurse put her head through the gap. 'Morgan, I'm set up if you want to come down.'

Cain's face paled. 'Oh, crap. Are you ill? I'm sorry, I need to learn to keep my big mouth shut.'

'I'm not ill, I'm having a blood test.'

Cain screwed his face up but didn't speak, much to her

relief, and she slipped out of the office and followed the nurse down to the medical room.

'I've spoken to the doctor, and he told me which forms to submit, so ready when you are?'

Morgan rolled her sleeve up, displaying her floral and book-themed tattoos that now filled most of her arm.

'Nice tattoo, I bet that took some time.'

'It's been a work in progress, that's for sure. Can you still see to take my blood?'

'Yeah, no problem. I feel for your veins anyway.'

Within a couple of minutes, a tourniquet was tightened around her arm, which was wiped with antiseptic, and a vial of her blood was now on the tray next to her.

'Where did you get spiked? Was it in a pub or club?'

'No, I think a friend may have done it.'

'Really, wow. With friends like that you don't need enemies, do you? That's just mean not to mention dangerous. I don't get why people do it, so senseless and do they know what you do for a living?'

Morgan nodded.

'Wow, that's super reckless then.'

'I might be wrong. I may have just had a bad reaction to the alcohol.'

'How much did you drink?'

She held her fingers about an inch apart.

'Is that it? I thought you were going to say three quarters of a bottle of vodka not a single shot. Well, you'll know for sure in a few hours. I'll get it fast-tracked for you. If I was you I wouldn't drink with that friend again.'

Morgan smiled at her as she tugged her sleeve down. She wouldn't drink with Annie again – she didn't need warning about that. 'Thank you.'

'You're welcome.'

Morgan went back up to the office which had now been

deserted, and she realised they were all in the blue room. She looked to her desk to see her latte was missing and swore, if someone had drunk it – or worse still binned it – she would be so angry. Storming to the blue room there was an empty chair next to Cain. He pointed to it and to her coffee cup, which was on the table. She grinned at him, the anger dispersing into nothingness. Ben nodded at her and carried on talking.

'This is where we are at the moment. Rosie's partner Matt turned up yesterday. He said he's been working in France and only got home yesterday morning. His alibi has been checked, and for now... it's airtight. Now, up until this point we believed that the deceased male found in the bathroom at the house was Matt Smith, but it turns out it was his non-identical twin brother Max.'

A collective gasp went around the room.

'Confusing is not the word. We have been told by the neighbour, Annie, and Rosie's best friend Gina that Rosie was telling people the name of the man who was murdered was Matt; in fact, Morgan and I met him not that long ago at a barbeque and he told us his name was Matt. So, we need to figure out why Max was pretending to be his brother Matt; for what reason? Can someone speak to Gina about this, and get some clear answers from her? Did she know? Cain and Morgan, do you want to do that after we finish up here? I also want to reinterview Raven Castle and find out exactly who she was having an affair with – did she know Max was pretending to be Matt? – and what her involvement is, if any. I'm going to ask section staff to go find her and bring her in, and I think this time we're going to have to arrest her.'

They all nodded.

'We need to find out why they were deceiving people, it's so odd. Declan thought that maybe it was just easier to pretend Max was Matt instead of having to explain, but they were going to have to come clean about it at some point.'

Marc who hadn't spoken a word yet looked up from his phone. 'And this is clear motive for Matt, correct? You said you had a feeling the piercer was having an affair with Matt, this must have been recent. So how long has he been in the UK? And does this mean that the two of them could have killed Rosie and Max?'

Ben nodded. 'That's one of my theories.'

Marc stood up. 'Morgan, I'll go with you to speak to Gina. Cain, you can make yourself useful here—'

Ben held up a hand. 'Hang on, I'm not finished. Someone was in our house at some point during the last couple of days and left this under Morgan's pillow.' He waved the evidence bag in the air. 'A neighbour reported seeing someone in our back garden yesterday. And we have a slight suspicion she slipped something into Morgan's drink last night. So she may also be a suspect.'

Marc took the bag off Ben and studied it. '"Your Turn". That's a direct threat to you, Morgan, if it was under your pillow. I think you two should stay in a hotel or something, or you can stop at mine if you want. You know the place well, Morgan, you used to live there.'

'No, thank you. That place has far too many bad memories.' She stopped, realising everyone was watching her.

'I have been telling you that you're at risk ever since you found the first note in the attic,' Marc replied. 'That's why your priest was attacked.'

Ben leaned over to bring a photograph of the church door up. 'Actually, Morgan identified the iron nails that were used at the crime scene. They are from the church door at St Martha's, so we believe the attack on Father Theo was a coincidence. We are waiting on confirmation from forensics that they are an exact match, but they must be. There were two missing spaces, and Theo was attacked right by that door. The killer must have gone to get more nails, and Theo saw them, which is the only logical conclusion for him being attacked. We think he might have known them, that they perhaps frequented the church, but Theo isn't well enough to be interviewed further.'

Cain sipped his drink and tore his gaze away from Marc. 'I don't want to be the bearer of bad news here, but Morgan found the note at the crime scene, which we thought was a complete coincidence, but finding another under her pillow is a direct threat. Is the killer planning on smashing her to death with an ice axe and nailing her mouth shut?'

'Cain,' said Ben, who looked a little shocked at how brutal and blunt he had just been.

'If she's at risk we can't pretend it's another coincidence, can we? There is a very real threat to Morgan's life, if this is the case. We need to ask ourselves why Morgan would be a potential victim and there's only one reason I can think of.'

Morgan nodded. 'What's that?'

'I think you know the killer; I think you might not realise they're a killer, you might only know them in passing, but they certainly know you, and there is a chance they might try and silence you for good because they clearly see you as a threat.'

Everyone sat open-mouthed, and the atmosphere in the room was so heavy it made Morgan want to pull open the windows to let in some fresh air. She hated being the centre of attention, yet here she was again, right in the middle of an investigation that she had nothing to do with. She didn't know Rosie or Matt, Max, whoever other than to say hi to in passing.

'Around a month ago, we were at a barbeque in the street, and Rosie spent most of the time getting drunk. We should speak to the two women she was sitting with, as they may know something. First though, I'll speak to Daniel who lives on the other side of the victims, as it was his party, and he will know who they were.'

She stood up, eager to get out of the now claustrophobic room that seemed to be closing in on her rapidly. Ben nodded at

Cain, and she heard him lower his voice, probably hoping she wouldn't hear. 'Do not leave her on her own.'

The words stung, yet she knew he was doing what he'd do for anyone on his team. Taking care of them, making sure they were okay, but it felt suffocating to Morgan – as if he thought she was some delicate flower that couldn't handle a strong breeze, yet she had endured major storms and come out the other side.

'Wait up, what's the rush?'

She stopped, waiting for Cain to catch up to her.

'Why are you raging?'

'I'm not raging, just need some fresh air. It's embarrassing, you know, always being the centre of attention. Wouldn't you get fed up with it if everyone talked about you as if you weren't sitting there, smack bang in the middle of it, with your ears and cheeks burning?'

'Everyone talks about me, can't help themselves, I'm a legend.'

Morgan laughed. 'You're an idiot.'

'Yeah, that as well. Come on, Morgan, if we didn't care we wouldn't be having this conversation. See how nobody bothered to ask Marc how he got that shiner? Everyone wants to know, but they don't care enough about him to ask.'

'What's the plan? Can we maybe squeeze in a visit to The Coffee Pot whilst we're en route to speak to Daniel.'

'Daniel who?'

'Daniel hosted the summer barbeque for the neighbours. And we're going to speak to Gina before Marc does; in fact, talking of him, can we get out of here before he comes looking for me? I do not want to be stuck with him all morning.'

They walked briskly to grab a set of keys off the whiteboard and get out of the station before Marc realised they'd left.

———

When they were driving out of the gates with nobody stopping them, she felt a little better. She drove in the direction of the café.

Cain came out with coffees and a bag with spots of grease staining it. She leaned over and opened the door for him. 'Got you a sausage bun with tomato sauce and a latte. Don't say your uncle Cain doesn't look out for you.'

'Thanks, I don't know if I can eat a sausage bun.'

'Morgan, you need to eat something. You look as if you're hungover and a greasy sandwich always does the trick.'

'I'm not hungover. I think the neighbour spiked my drink last night. I gave a urine sample to the nurse but it was inconclusive, so she's sent a blood sample off.'

He looked at her with his eyes wide. 'What the hell? Hang on, which neighbour?'

'The older woman who lives in the house between ours and the victims'.'

He took a sip of the coffee, burning his lip on the hot liquid and swearing loudly.

'Right, let me get this straight. The woman who lives between you tried to spike you; why?'

She shrugged. 'I might be imagining things, but I went to talk to her last night, and she gave me a glass of vodka. It wasn't much but I felt so out of control after it.'

He lifted a hand to stop her. 'Why have we not arrested her?'

'Because she's old and she might not have. I could have had a bad reaction to the vodka.'

Cain was shaking his head. 'She's the one, she's the killer. She has access to both of your houses, and she knows your routines; if she sees you running out of your front door, she knows you will not be back for hours. We're talking about that nosey old bat who's always sitting in her window, yeah?'

'Yes.'

'Why are you and Ben acting so dumb about it?'

'She's old, there's no way she dragged Rosie up those stairs.'

'Then she's working with someone and, hang on, how do you not know that she isn't fitter than the pair of us and works out every day?'

'I don't.'

'See, you work long shifts. She could be doing all sorts. I can't believe it; we need to bring her in.'

'Should we get an arrest team together, or at least tell Ben your theory?'

'By the time they get an arrest team she could be on a flight to Benidorm. If I can't handle a seventy-year-old woman I'm losing my touch and resigning.'

'I don't know about this; I've got a bad feeling.'

'Sometimes we don't see things clearly if we're too close to it. What's it going to hurt to bring her in for an interview?'

'I live next door to her, awkward is what it will be.'

'Morgan, she spiked your drink, and she probably left that note under your pillow, and there is a good chance she killed the victims and attacked Theo who is fighting for his life. I bet she goes to church, and he knows who she is, so when he caught her trying to take the nails, she realised she was screwed so attacked him too. It's not impossible, in fact I think it's highly possible. You don't need to be a body builder to swing an axe at someone's head.'

Morgan shuddered at the thought of an axe swinging through the air. Her biological father had been killed by an axe, and she'd been there to watch the whole, bloodied death, grasping hold of his hand as his life drained away despite the fact that she despised him on a whole other level, but Gary Marks had never been human like her. He had been a monster.

'Okay, let's do it, let's go and ask her if she spiked your drink and see how she reacts. We can arrest her and take her in for questioning about the murders as well.'

Cain parked a little further along her street and they watched Annie's house for a while. She was there. She was in her usual place in the bay window, behind the net curtain. Morgan could make out her figure, and she wondered if they were doing the right thing. What if she was dangerous and tried to attack them both? She would see them walking down the street, know they were coming to her house.

Cain got out of the car and she followed him, her stomach all knotted up. She was letting her personal feelings get in the way. That and the fact that Ben was going to be pissed with the pair of them, but they were detectives, they didn't need his permission to make an arrest if they thought the suspect could be brought in; but working with him and telling him what they were doing felt a lot better than doing it this way. As they approached the gate to Annie's house the shadow behind the curtain never moved. She didn't step back and try to hide. She stayed there watching them as if she knew what was about to happen.

Morgan knocked on her door, while Cain watched the window. He whispered, 'She's not coming; she's ignoring us.'

Morgan lifted the flap on the letter box. 'Annie, it's me, Morgan, can I have a word with you?'

'Ooh, she's stubborn. Still not answering the door, hasn't moved yet, she's very good.'

Annie's door was a heavy wooden door, original to the house and lovingly looked after. There was a brass doorknob, and Morgan gripped it and twisted to see if it would turn. To her surprise it turned all the way and the door clicked open.

She looked at Cain. 'Now what? She may be waiting to attack us if we go inside.'

'I'll go first, how tall is she?'

'Same as me, maybe a bit taller.'

'Skinny, big?'

'Medium.'

Cain stepped in front of Morgan, who still felt terrible about what they were about to do. He pushed the door wide open.

'Mrs Walker, it's Cain and Morgan from the police, can we come in and talk to you?'

The hallway was so quiet Morgan could hear her own pulse pounding in the side of her head. 'Annie, it's me, Morgan, we're coming in, don't be alarmed, okay?'

She pointed to the lounge that looked out onto the street, where Annie spent most of her days and evenings watching the world go by. Cain pushed the door open – and they stepped into utter carnage.

Morgan smelled the earthy, metallic of the red liquid that coated the cream rug, and the pine floorboards were covered with it too – blood. Morgan's eyes fell on Annie, and she let out a screech. The woman was sitting propped up on a chair, facing the window, and the back of her head had been smashed to pieces with such ferocity there were spatters of blood on the ceiling and at the top of the net curtains in front of her.

'Oh shit,' muttered Cain.

Morgan pulled her radio out of her pocket, and she pressed the button.

'Control, IR to 15 Kendal Road. We have a confirmed Foxtrot and a murder scene.'

Before control could respond, Ben's voice filtered out of the radio handset she was holding in her trembling fingers.

'What's going on, Morgan?'

'It's Annie, she's dead.'

Everything after that became one big blur. Morgan stepped carefully across the room, avoiding any blood, until she could see a side profile of Annie's face. She had to know if it was the same. Through her lips was a thick black nail.

THIRIY-NINE

They checked the rest of the house to see if anyone was still inside. Once they were happy the rooms were empty, they waited in the front garden. Sirens were heading their way but for once Morgan didn't feel comforted to hear them. What she felt was numb, her entire body was frozen.

Ben jumped out of the passenger seat of the van that stopped in front of the house; it was déjà vu. History was repeating itself in the worst possible way, and Morgan felt bad for the relief she felt that everyone wasn't rushing to see her dead body with the back of her head stoved in, blood all over *their* house. It would kill Ben. He'd lost his wife Cindy inside of their home, and if he lost Morgan in there too, she didn't think he'd survive.

She felt his warm arms around her, holding her tight, smelled the subtle hint of his aftershave and, for once, instead of pulling away from him because there was an audience, she sank into his embrace. Letting him rock her gently from side to side. She knew he was imagining the same thing she had moments ago.

When he pulled apart, he nodded at her. 'You're good, you're okay and I think that we need to get you out of here.'

She shook her head. 'I'm okay, it was the initial shock of seeing her like that but I'm good. I don't want to go back and sit in the station feeling useless.'

'Then why don't you go and speak to Daniel? See if you can get the addresses of the women Rosie was chatting to at his party. Morgan, why did you come here? I thought that was the plan, you were going to Daniel's.'

'I told Cain about Annie, and he wanted to arrest her. He thought she was the killer.'

He nodded. 'And why wasn't I informed of this snap decision?'

He was back in boss mode, and she appreciated it more than he would ever know, because if he carried on being nice to her, she might just cry and that was not her style.

'Because it literally was a snap decision, there was no time.'

He shook his head and rubbed his chest. 'You guys are trying to kill me off, I swear it.'

'Sorry.'

'It's okay, if you hadn't come here, she could have been there for days. How long do you think she's been dead?'

'Not long, it doesn't smell like she's starting to decompose yet. We checked the house, apart from the attic, and it's empty. You can send task force up there; we didn't even attempt it.'

She left Ben wrestling to get a white crime-scene suit out of the bag to go and speak to Daniel, who was curtain twitching like a professional.

As she passed Rosie's house, she paused to look at it. The blinds were all closed, there was no sign of life, and she wondered if Matt was aware of what was happening outside of his door. More so she wondered if Matt could be the killer. He was there, right in the middle of it all. Who knew what he was capable of?

Before she even opened the gate, Daniel's front door was wide open and he was waving her inside.

'What is going on, Morgan? I can't cope with all of this. Is Annie okay?'

She shook her head, but didn't speak as he led her into his living room, where she purposely sat with her back to the window. Daniel, however, was sitting in a position where he could see out of it, watching all the action.

'Where's Annie?'

'She's dead.'

'She is getting to be a real nuisance for you all. She phoned the police yesterday and—' He paused, turning his gaze to stare at her. 'What did you just say?'

'I said, she's dead.'

He cupped his hand across his mouth. 'No!'

'Yes, killed the same way as Rosie and—' She stopped and changed tack. 'Daniel, did you know that the guy living with Rosie was called Max?'

He looked utterly confused, just how she felt. Her insides were in turmoil trying to get her facts straight.

'The man who was killed with Rosie is Matt, you mean?'

'No, his name is Max, or was Max. He had a twin whose name is Matt, but Matt says he's been working in France for months.'

He closed his eyes as if trying to process the information she'd just told him. Then he nodded. 'Actually, maybe you're right, when they first moved in, the guy with her looked a little different. Then he wasn't around and the guy who I saw a lot of was.'

Morgan sat back, considering what they knew.

'Daniel, at the party Rosie was drinking with two women. Do you know them, where I could I find them?'

'Shari and Taylor? They work in a boutique in Kendal, well they own it, but they live a couple of streets away. I used to live next door to them, which is why I invited them to the barbeque. Number eight Rydal Way, I think, or number four. I lived at six.'

Morgan stood up. 'Thank you, that's helpful.'

She left him still sitting in his chair at the window. They would go back for a statement later, but he clearly hadn't seen anything because he loved to gossip and he would have mentioned it. She hoped that either Shari or Taylor was home. Officers had strung tape across the road once more and she hurried towards it, ducking under to go to Rydal Way.

———

She knocked on number four, but nobody answered, so she tried eight and was relieved to hear someone in a pair of heels tapping their way to the front door. It opened and she smiled, recognising the woman. Taking out her badge she showed it to her. 'Can I come in for a moment? I'd like to chat with you about Rosie Waite.'

The blonde-haired woman nodded; she looked as if she was about to go to work.

'I'm sorry to disturb you. I'm a detective.'

'I know who you are, I've seen you around. You were at Dan's party the other month.'

'Good, I was, well then I was wondering if you could tell me how close you were with Rosie.'

She sighed. 'It's so horrid, isn't it? I don't know why anyone would do that to her or Max. It doesn't make sense.'

Morgan realised that she had said the name Max. 'I didn't catch your name?'

'Taylor Landon.'

'Taylor, there's been some confusion over Max and his twin brother Matt. Was Rosie in a relationship with Matt?'

Taylor screwed up her face and laughed. 'Yes, in the beginning, but he left to go work in France and his twin moved in and suddenly Rosie and Max were an item. Matt seemed to get pushed out of the picture, it was weird, but each to their own I suppose.'

'Why did everyone call Max, Matt?'

'Not everyone. Daniel who is a bit of a doozy called him Matt continuously, which Rosie thought was hilarious because Max and Matt both have a bit of a love-hate relationship with each other. She said she didn't have the heart to correct him, so then other people called him Matt and it kind of got a bit out of hand.'

'Did Max not mind?'

'He said he was used to it, been happening since they were kids.'

'Do you know Rosie's friend Gina?'

Taylor arched an eyebrow at her. 'Not really, heard plenty about her though. Rumour is she killed her husband for the insurance money and got away with it, which is why she's living in the UK in an apartment most of us could only fantasise about.'

'Is there any truth to that or is it just a rumour?'

Taylor shrugged. 'Who am I to say? Rosie joked about it at the party, but she was drunk and downing Prosecco like it was a juice and not alcohol. It wouldn't surprise me though.'

'Thank you, I appreciate your help.'

Morgan could feel something in the back of her mind. It was there, she just needed to put all the pieces together.

FORTY

Cain was standing outside of Annie's house looking up and down the street. When he saw her he shook his head. 'What the hell, Morgan, where did you go? I've been standing here debating on telling Ben that you were missing in action but didn't have the balls to do it.'

'Sorry, I went to speak to Daniel then a friend of his who lives around the corner. Ben knew where I was, that's why I didn't come get you.'

He mimed clutching his heart and stumbling. 'Ben is not the only one with a bad heart at this rate. I'm sure you're trying to kill me off for my police pension.' He laughed loud, and she felt everything slide into place.

'That's it.'

'That's what?'

She grabbed Cain by the elbow and pushed him towards the car. He let her and didn't say another word until they were inside.

'Hear me out, Rosie's partner was Max and they were a couple. Matt has never been in a relationship with Rosie. Who told us that the dead guy was Matt?'

'The friend Gina.'

'She told us that she could ID them and that it was Matt. Then Matt turns up the next day claiming he's Rosie's boyfriend. Why?'

Cain shook his head. 'Too complicated for my brain.'

'I think Gina and Matt are responsible; they set this up. I think Matt told us that he had the job but it was Max who had a good job, a good pension, and if he's dead it would all go to Rosie. However, if Rosie was dead, it would all go to Matt. I would bet you a thousand pounds he's named in his twin's will.'

'But why go to all this trouble giving misleading information?'

'To stall things, to give the real Matt an alibi. I think that Matt and Gina are lovers. I also think that Matt had a bit of a fling with Raven to set her up. She was never going to see the bodies after they died, so he could have purposely pretended to Raven he was Rosie's partner and she wouldn't know. She's young and the perfect decoy, and if he did that it means he's been in the UK longer than he said he was, we need to contact border control to get a definitive date of entry for Matt to the UK.'

'Why kill the neighbour?'

'I think somehow Matt talked Annie into leaving the note in my house. He probably paid her or told her he would give her some money if she did it. I think Matt was the one who hid in Rosie's attic to make it look like they had some crazed stalker. They didn't, they had a crazy, jealous brother who wanted the house and the money.'

'Phew, that's a lot. It sounds like the plot of a *Scooby-Doo* episode.'

'I bet if there are any prints from the church they will come back as Gina's. We need to bring her in. I think she was his accomplice; I think the pair of them killed Rosie and Max, or if she didn't kill them she was there or was involved somehow. I

would say she certainly attacked Theo at the church and probably Annie too. She wouldn't have wanted to fight with any of
the victims, so taking them out with a direct blow to the back of
the head would negate that possibility and make it quick.
Although Matt could have gone into Annie's, as she would have
a reason to let him in if she thought he was going to pay her for
leaving the note and making the false phone call yesterday
about the intruder in our garden.'

'Okay, so give it to me the easy way.'

'The killer or killers are Matt and Gina. They roped Annie
in to do their dirty work but realised she was too much of a
liability, especially after I was in her house drinking with her
last night. They had to silence her. Theo was in the wrong place
at the wrong time. This is all about money, greed, and the rest of
it is all some big set-up to make us think that it's far different to
what it really is. Clever stuff, if it had worked.'

'So, we get an arrest team and storm next door. Bring that
sick arsehole in and go after Gina?'

Morgan stared out of her window at Annie's house, feeling
sad for the woman who had probably been lured by the thought
of the money they offered her. Maybe she hadn't even realised
that they were going to kill Rosie and Max, and she had got
herself in over her head, too involved to say anything without
getting arrested herself.

'I suppose so, but I don't think he's there, there's been no
sign of him. We can get an officer to sit outside the house to
keep tabs on it in case he does come back.' She got out of the car
and was striding towards Rosie and Max's front door. Before
Cain could stop her, she hammered on it so loud the sound
echoed around the street. Putting an ear to the door Morgan
listened for movement inside and heard nothing. She turned to
Cain who had a look of panic on his face at her pure reckless-
ness. 'I bet if we went to Gina's he's hiding out there until it all
blows over.'

'Bloody hell, Morgan, what if he'd answered and come running out with an ice axe? Did you stop and think about that, and what are we going to do? Just walk into Gina's unannounced to see if he is and arrest them both? Without backup? You know that if they don't kill you, Ben will, right?'

She shrugged. 'Cain, this is just some hunch. I have no evidence to say any different. I'm running with my gut instinct.'

'Is it usually wrong?'

'No.'

'Fuck.'

'Ben knows I'm going to speak to Gina. Let me go in and take it from there. I won't be a threat. I can get an idea of what's going down. You wait outside.'

'And there we have it, another stupid I'll-go-get-myself-killed idea from Detective Brookes who is too reckless for her own good. I can't let you do that even if it is a good idea, and it's purely from a selfish point of view because if I let you go in on your own and something happened, Ben would kill me with his bare hands. Have you ever seen him in a proper fight?'

Morgan shook her head. 'No.'

'You're lucky because he's an animal. He would put a cage fighter out in less than thirty seconds when he's proper angry.'

'Don't be ridiculous, he's not a fighter.'

'Maybe not now. I'm sure I've told you this before, but back in the day when we were younger, working the streets of Barrow and there were fights every which way you turned on Cornwallis Street, he was there, wading in and fists flying. He's older now and turned into a right soft git because of you, but I know he would kill me so there you go; I'm saying no to that idea.'

She paused. 'We'll go in together then.'

'Go tell Ben your plan?'

'Can't.'

'No, you can't because he'll say no to you.'

'When did you turn so wimpy?'

'I like my life, what can I say.'

'You best get out of the car then and I'll go do what I was officially tasked to do at the briefing.'

Cain shook his head. 'There she is, my feisty, ginger friend who has been a little too quiet the last few days. I'll go tell Ben where we are going, to cover our arses when it all goes wrong.'

He got out of the car and headed to Annie's house, and she smiled, hoping that she wasn't leading either of them into a situation so dangerous it could end with one or both of them fighting for their lives.

FORTY-ONE

Marc had left the briefing and driven to Gina's in his own car, the big splashy Porsche that Morgan had almost written off a few months ago. He had been walking around with his head in the sand for the last six months since his wife had told him it was over and walked out of his life with the girls. It had hurt a lot more than he'd let her know, let anyone know. And then last night he'd decided to go for a drink in Kendal with a woman he'd met on a dating app. That was a disaster. She looked like an older, rougher version of the profile picture, and to top it off her disgruntled ex had turned up looking for a fight. He'd ended up smacking Marc in the eye when he wasn't looking, and Marc had delivered a blow back that had taken the guy down to his knees. He'd got out of there fast with a renewed hatred of dating apps and decided that he was staying single unless the woman of his dreams walked into his life without opening his eyes.

Gina LoBue had done just that; he'd taken one look at her in real life and knew he was smitten. The regret that he'd swiped left last month when her face had filled the screen on his dating app left a sour taste in his mouth. He'd realised at the crime scene it was her and could have kicked himself in the pants. The appalling date last night had sealed the deal, and even though it was highly unprofessional to hit on a grieving victim's friend, he was only going to talk to her, let her know he existed kind of thing. For once he didn't have his radio on full volume, he had turned it down. The department could manage without him for an hour.

Marc had put Gina's postcode into his satnav and had driven along the drive to the lakeside mansion with his jaw open as he admired the views of the lake, the formal gardens and the beautiful house. He parked next to another Porsche and sighed. This was the kind of place he'd always envisioned living in; unfortunately his police inspector's salary wouldn't stretch to this level of luxury. A lottery win could help, and he thought about seeing if the team wanted to set up a syndicate. They could all do with a little luck. He checked his appearance in the rear-view mirror; the bruising around his eye was unfortunate but he could blame it on work if she pointed it out.

He didn't know what he was expecting. She might not be interested in him, which was fine, but he had to see her one last time in her own surroundings to put him out of his misery. This was all it was.

The front door was unlocked, and he walked into the grand entrance and sighed. It was nothing like the flats and bedsits he was used to back in Manchester. He'd read the files and knew she lived on the top floor in the penthouse. He didn't take the lift, as he preferred walking and besides, it meant he could take in the splendour of this place, appreciating every fine detail. The staircase had huge windows that looked out onto the gardens. Marc paused to take in the views as a guy came jogging down the stairs.

He didn't turn to look at him but said, 'Good morning.'

The guy grunted back and carried on going down as Marc turned to go up.

There were only two doors on the third floor, one either side of the staircase. He went to the one which belonged to Gina and knocked politely, not his usual heavy-fisted police hammer. There was nothing and he thought that maybe she wasn't in. He didn't look for her car, hadn't taken much notice of what car she had driven the other day because he had been a little preoccupied with the murder scene. About to leave, the door opened and she was standing there, a dark-haired vision of beauty. Dressed head to toe in black, she reminded him a little of Morgan, only older, and with age comes a certain confidence that can make a beautiful woman light up the whole room, and once again the regret that he hadn't matched with her previously lay heavy. Now it was too late. He supposed he should be grateful; it could have made this all so awkward if he'd been speaking to her or even taken her out on a date instead of the woman who had been a disaster. Gina looked puzzled, and he realised that although he'd done nothing but think about her since he first saw her, she probably hadn't the slightest clue who he was, which brought him back to reality with a hard bump.

'Can I help you?'

'Yes, I'm Detective Inspector Marcell Howard and I wondered if it was possible to have a word with you about Rosie.'

She smiled at him and opened the door wide. 'Be my guest.'

He stepped inside the apartment and nodded appreciatively. 'This is beautiful, you have a stunning home.'

'Thanks, I like it.'

'It must be so nice having such good views of the lake and gardens.'

'It is. Even when it's raining, I like to sit and admire the views. How can I help you, Marcell?'

'Marc, Marcell is a bit of a mouthful.' He gave her his best smile, and she nodded.

'How can I help you, Marc?'

'Can we have a chat about Rosie and Matt?'

She pointed to the oversized velvet sofa. 'Take a seat. Can I get you a drink?'

He wanted this moment to last, and he nodded. 'Coffee would be great.'

She left him to go to the kitchen, where he heard the sound of coffee beans being freshly ground and thought that this was his idea of heaven.

Gina came back a couple of minutes later with a tray bearing two coffee cups, a milk jug and sugar bowl.

'I thought you Brits preferred tea?'

Marc laughed. 'Not when you work for the police. Tea is something to be enjoyed, it's a gentle drink. When your working life keeps you on the edge you need that quick hit of caffeine to keep your brain focused and alert.'

'But you're an inspector, shouldn't you be sitting in your office giving out the orders to the grunts below you and sipping your tea?'

He looked at her, his head nodding at her words, he found her completely mesmerising.

'I hosted a true crime podcast for a few years and now I produce them. I know a lot more about true crime than I'd care to admit. Same goes for the police in both the UK and back home. What I can say is that in a lot of the cases we've covered, the cops, and I don't mean to be rude but they are usually quite... how can I phrase this? Inefficient.'

Marc smiled at her. Putting his phone down on the table, with a Care Bear sticker on the back of the case his daughter had put on that he couldn't bring himself to remove, he poured some cream into his coffee and a dollop of sugar. 'I will give you that, Gina, a lot of the time you might as well send in some circus clowns, but not here. My team is exceptional, really exceptional, which I never expected in a million years. I used to work in Manchester city centre, and it was busy. I moved here to a more rural area thinking I could slow things down a little bit, and I was wrong on so many levels. If you've lived here for some time, then you're probably aware of the high number of murders that have happened. We have a one hundred per cent success rate at catching the killers. There are no cold cases on our books.'

Gina smiled. 'That's impressive. I was talking to my friend Shannon about this just the other day, and we're thinking of doing a series of podcasts on the area. Of course, I'm not sure if it's too painful for people but you know, murder is good business.'

Marc could have sighed with pleasure. The coffee was extremely good, it must be the heavy cream instead of milk, and the company was even better. He felt as if he could stay and chat with Gina all day. He glanced at the photos on the coffee table in front of him, there were three of Gina with different women and he noticed the necklace around her neck, it was a St Christopher. Alarm bells were ringing inside of his head but he had to play it cool, if that was the necklace Rosie had been clutching, then Gina was a very dangerous woman. She was smiling at him, and he took another large sip of coffee.

'This is good, I've never thought of adding cream.' His words sounded a bit funny; his tongue was tingling a little, but he dismissed it and carried on. 'This may seem like a strange question, but Rosie—' He stopped, his mind was spinning, and he felt as if he was going to pass out. There was ringing inside of his ears, and his line of vision was blurred and getting narrower.

He saw Gina reach over and take the mug out of his hand; her cool fingertips brushed against his.

'You were saying about Rosie?'

Marc knew something was very wrong. He tried to stand up and stumbled. He couldn't think of anything except getting out into the fresh air. He felt like he was about to pass out and then as he stumbled towards the door, his knees gave way and the room went a dark grey as he fell to the floor.

FORTY-TWO

Cain came back with a smile on his face. 'In the words of our esteemed leader, just get on with it.'

Morgan laughed. 'Ben said that?'

'Uhuh, said to stop wasting time, question Gina and get back here pronto. Ready for a shit ton of house-to-house enquiries.'

As she drove to Gina's, Morgan couldn't stop thinking about Annie. The vision of her with her head smashed to pieces was not how she wanted to remember her. Life was so cruel; she couldn't help wondering if Annie had spiked her drink. Was *she* supposed to be dead now? But maybe she hadn't been able to go through with it, so Annie had been killed instead. She turned into the drive, and Cain let out his low whistle he reserved for big posh houses. 'Nice digs.'

'Too nice for a killer.'

'Do you really think it's her, that she's the mastermind behind all of this?'

'Yes, I do.'

'Okay, good enough for me, but if you already had all of this why would you put yourself at risk of losing it all?'

Morgan shrugged. 'Some people are never satisfied with what they have and always want more, or maybe it's the thrill of being able to carry out something so daring that she likes.'

As she parked the white Ford Focus in-between two Porsches, Cain shook his head. 'Looks like a Porsche is a requirement of the rental agreement.'

They got out of the car, and he paused to look at the blue one. 'Hey, is that the boss's car?'

Morgan glanced at it. 'I have no idea.'

'Well, you should do you almost totalled it.'

'A car is a car to me.'

Cain looked at her in mock horror. 'One does not simply call a Porsche a car. It's so much more than—'

'Cain shut up, what's the plan?'

'Knock on the door, ask her if she's been screwing Matt and if she killed her so-called best friends, and then arrest her.'

'Might want a little more tact than that. She's rich enough to sue us.'

'Not if she's a killer she isn't. Come on, it's my turn, I have a bad feeling about this one.'

Morgan glanced back at the car, hoping it was Marc's and that he'd already questioned Gina for them. They took the lift up and when the doors glided open, Cain pushed her out first.

'You do the talking, I'll put my foot in it.'

She whispered, 'I'm not arguing with you on that one.'

She hammered on Gina's door, but there was no reply. So, she hammered even louder. This time she pressed her ear against the door, listening for any signs of movement. There was nothing. She turned to Cain. 'What's plan B?'

'Put the door through?'

'On what grounds? We better go see if we can get a warrant and then we can put it through officially.'

'You're no fun anymore, Morgan.'

It looked like they needed to go and tell Ben everything after all, and then find Marc to get them a warrant to break down Gina's door.

FORTY-THREE

Ben came out of Annie's house with an ice axe inside of an evidence bag, dried blood all over the sharp, pointed blade, not to mention hair and brain matter. Morgan and Cain arrived in time to watch him, and she shuddered. The thought of being hit with that was too much. Ben passed it to Wendy, then turned to the pair of them.

'That didn't take long, what did Gina say?'

'Nothing, she wasn't in. Look, I have a theory, and I think we need a warrant for Gina's address.'

'Go on.'

Morgan explained to Ben how she thought Gina and Matt were in it for the money, that Rosie had been legitimately living with Max and how they had dragged Annie into it, but scared she might talk to Morgan, they'd silenced her for good.

'Sounds plausible, have you seen Marc? I've been trying to get hold of him but he's not answering his phone or radio.'

Morgan thought about the car outside Gina's apartment. 'Did he go to speak to Gina?'

'Said something about that, but it all got a bit confusing

once you called this in. I really need him here and, as always, he's messing about somewhere else.'

She tried to stop the panic that was building inside of her chest, but she couldn't hold it down as it pushed its way to the top of her lungs, bursting out of her mouth.

'I think he's at Gina's. We weren't sure if it was his car parked outside.'

Cain, who had been talking to Wendy, turned to listen to Morgan, whose voice was much louder than usual.

'If he's not answering and he went there, he might be in trouble.'

Ben looked as if he was going to be sick. He began to issue orders down the radio asking for patrols to IR to Gina's address. At the same time, he was unzipping his suit, and Morgan tugged his arms out, then pushed it down to his feet so he could step out of it. Cain commandeered a police van and the three of them jumped in. Cain was a far more experienced van driver than Morgan and he set off at high speed with the sirens blaring and the blue lights strobing.

Morgan said to Ben, 'I might be wrong.'

'You might be right.'

She felt terrible, they had been there, outside of Gina's door, and had left without thinking too much about anything, to drive back here only to find themselves now blue lighting it all the way back. As they drove down the narrow driveway to reach the mansion, they could see only one Porsche in the drive, a black one, the blue one had gone, and Morgan wondered if they had overreacted.

'The car's gone, maybe it wasn't Marc's or if it was, maybe he was having a wander around the gardens and we missed him.'

Ben tried calling out to him over the radio airwaves again and was met with silence. He phoned his mobile only for it to go straight to voicemail. 'Then why isn't he answering when we're in the middle of a high-profile murder investigation? Surely, he wouldn't ignore me when it could be important.'

She stared at him. There was no way to answer any of Ben's questions. Cain stopped the van and slid open the rear doors to get the heavy red door whammer out of its cradle. He was supposed to wear specialist protective equipment when he used the whammer, but he didn't care – this could be life or death.

He followed Morgan and Ben inside. They were already sprinting up the stairs, and he followed them, out of breath and breathing heavy by the time he reached the third floor. Ben curled his fingers into a fist and beat them against the door.

'Police, open up.'

They were greeted with silence.

Ben nodded at Cain, who swung the whammer back and managed to break down the door with one precise, forceful hit against the lock. Pieces of wood splintered and sprayed all over, and then they were inside. It looked empty. Cain dropped the whammer and rushed towards the first door he saw. Ben did the same whilst Morgan looked around the huge living area. She saw the tray with two mugs on it, and next to it was Marc's phone. She recognised the kid's sticker on it.

Ben and Cain had checked every room, joining her as she pointed to the phone. 'That's Marc's, he has that Care Bear sticker on it.'

Ben tugged on a pair of gloves and lifted it up. The screen lit up and on the home screen in green were the messages and missed calls from Ben. 'We have a problem.'

Ben began issuing orders, calling for officers to come and secure Gina's apartment until they could bring in CSIs from other parts of the county because Wendy and Joe were busy at Annie's house. He also rhymed off Marc's number plate and put a *stop* marker on it. The last thing she heard him say was, 'Suspects are likely armed and dangerous.' Then he turned to Cain.

'I need you to guard the scene until officers get here and take over. When they arrive you take their car, okay?'

'What are you going to do?'

'Find Marc. Come on, Morgan.'

She turned to Cain. 'Will you be okay?'

He nodded. 'I have the whammer, go.'

Ben was already charging down the staircase, and she followed him, her heart racing, wondering if Marc was still alive or if they were too late.

FORTY-FOUR

Marc knew he was in a car, but he felt so out of it he didn't know who was driving. He wondered if he'd had a heart attack or even worse, a stroke. Was he semi-conscious on the way to the hospital? He couldn't see anything, and he couldn't open his mouth, and realised it was taped shut. He felt disorientated and the bumpy movement was making his stomach clench. He wanted to vomit but knew if he did, he would choke to death. His hands were immobile along with his feet. He wasn't even on the seat of the car. He was on the floor with the middle piece digging into his back. He smelled the smoky vanilla of a car air freshener and realised he was in his own car. Every bump in the road sent shockwaves along his spine, and his head felt as if it was throbbing so much his brain might explode out of his ears. Who was driving? What had happened to him? And then it came back to him: Gina, her coffee, the conversation.

'Why, Gina, why did you do this? You should have charmed the pants off him and sent him packing. Did you need to drug him so much you might have killed him anyway?'

Marc listened, keeping his eyes squeezed shut.

'He knew, he would have outed me and arrested me. I am

not going to prison. I told you if it comes to that I was leaving, and you'd never see me again.'

'Fuck.' The sound of a hand slamming against the steering wheel.

'Rosie and Max were part of the plan. Annie was a necessity. She was going to talk, that much was obvious; she was too friendly with the copper who lived next door, and the priest. Again, why did you take out the priest?'

'I told you, he talked to me earlier, and he would have been able to ID me.'

'How, did you go to his church?'

'He spoke to me when I was taking the flowers for my dearly departed husband.'

'You are sicker than I thought. Your husband is buried in the States.'

'I know, but I like to take him flowers and I can't, so I left them on the grave of a young boy who never seems to have any. If the priest had gone to investigate, he would have discovered that the kid was not my husband. He also might have realised that I was the one who had removed those nails in the first place. I needed two more and taking flowers was a good distraction.'

The voices stopped, and Marc realised that Gina was probably not the woman for him after all. The car stopped too.

'What are you doing here?'

'I'm going to drag him out and leave him in the church so someone will find him before he wakes up.'

'You can't do that, Matt.'

'Why not, Gina?'

'He can identify me and if he knows about me, you can bet your bottom dollar he knows about you too. Did you pass him on the stairs?'

'He didn't see me.'

'It doesn't matter, he isn't stupid, or he wouldn't be an inspector. We have to kill him, then we get the hell out of here.'

Marc played dead as the doors opened a few minutes later and he was manhandled out of the car and half-dragged, half-carried into a building he knew was the church by the smell of the candles and incense; the musty smell that churches seemed to have lingering in the air. He was dropped onto the cold hard floor and for the first time he risked opening his eyes to look around.

———

Ben drove back to Rydal Falls at speed, lights flashing, sirens blaring whilst Morgan was trying to figure out where they could have taken Marc. Everything focused on their street, but they couldn't take him there, as it was currently sealed off and had police officers crawling all over it.

'Does Gina have a podcast studio somewhere?'

Morgan shook her head. 'No, she has it all set up in the corner of her lounge.' She paused. 'The church, maybe they've gone there.'

'Theo's church?'

'Yes, it's the only other place I can think of. They took the nails from there and attacked Theo, so they will know that it's empty. There are no services, as everything has been cancelled for the foreseeable future until they know how Theo is.'

Ben swerved the van to head towards the church. He was five minutes away. Morgan leaned across to turn off the blues and twos.

'If they're there we don't want to alert them.'

'I know that, I'm panicking. Marc is only just beginning to fit in with us all. I'd hate for anything to happen to him.'

Morgan felt the same. She was beginning to warm to their strange, intense inspector and he had proven himself to be one of the team. They couldn't lose him now. Ben stopped the van further up from the church. Before getting out of it he asked for backup to St Martha's but with a silent approach. Then they were out of the van. Morgan had no protective equipment on her so reached in the back for a baton and tucked it into the waist of her trousers; it was better than nothing.

As they got nearer they saw Marc's blue Porsche parked in front of the gates blocking the view of the entrance to the church.

Ben whispered, 'We need armed officers.'

'We haven't got the time.'

Morgan withdrew the baton, Ben nodded and they ran towards the church door, slipping past the Porsche that was empty. Morgan peered through the rear window to check, but there was no sign of Marc. Ben went into the church first, with Morgan close behind. They saw Gina struggling with Marc.

'Stop, police. Let him go and put your hands up.'

Gina stopped and pushed Marc with far more strength than he would have ever given her credit for; there was a look rage in her eyes that told him he was in big trouble. He stumbled forwards, landing on his knees. She raised a hand that was holding an identical ice axe to the one Ben had brought out of Annie's house earlier.

'If you come any closer, your inspector's brains will be coating the inside of this quaint old church in seconds.'

Morgan didn't think that Gina was on her own, Matt must be somewhere, and she kept looking around for him, but then they heard the sound of the Porsche engine roaring into life and a look of fury filled Gina's face.

She turned her attention back to Marc, still wielding the axe above his head. Morgan took a step closer. 'Don't do it, Gina, there is no point, you're already in over your head and it looks as if your partner in crime has driven off and left you to face the consequences all on your own.'

Gina's dark eyes were staring straight into Morgan's as the vestry door opened a little, and Morgan realised that Gordon must be in there, oblivious to the situation out here. She carried on talking, louder, hoping that he might realise something was wrong. She didn't want to risk another innocent person getting hurt.

'We know everything, you can't get away with this. Even if you kill Marc, what are you going to do, kill us both?' Morgan had the baton extended, ready to run at the woman and strike her across the head if she had to.

The door opened wider and she saw Gordon step out, staring at the situation. Then he lifted a finger to his lips to shush her, and she wondered what on earth he was going to do. Ben was standing a little to the front of her, a look of horror on his face at their current situation. He fell to his knees, clutching his heart, and Morgan felt everything inside of her rip free as she screamed at the top of her voice. Gina's attention had gone to Ben and Gordon, who was holding a heavy wooden cross in his right hand. He ran at her, the cross swooshing through the air as it hit the hand she was holding the axe in.

Gina let out a screech of pain, the sound of the bone in her wrist cracking filled the church, and then Ben was up on his feet, and pushing past Morgan he dived for Gina and took her down to the floor. Gordon kicked the axe away from her and nodded as Ben restrained her. Morgan ran up to help as heavy footsteps on the gravel outside signalled the arrival of the backup they had requested what felt like hours ago.

Gordon looked down at Gina. 'That's for Father Theo. You're lucky I'm not a violent man or I'd have smashed you over the head with our good Lord Jesus and repaid the favour.'

Morgan couldn't help it, she grinned at the priest who looked very happy with himself.

Gina didn't fight; she seemed to have shrunken in on herself and was holding her hand that was clearly broken, close to her chest. Morgan bent down to help Marc; he was kneeling on the floor, his eyes wide. She ripped the tape off his mouth and set about trying to free his arms.

He stuttered, 'What, the, hell?'

Gordon pulled a penknife from his pocket to assist Morgan to cut off the thick tapes around Marc's arms. He nodded in agreement. 'Yes, indeed. What the hell is going on here?'

Marc looked at the priest who was a good twenty years older than him and nodded his appreciation at him. 'Thank you, Father, you saved my life.'

'It was nothing. I am sick of cleaning blood up out of this church. Are you injured?'

Marc shook his head.

'Good, that's one up for the Jesus crew. Handy things these heavy crucifixes, wouldn't you agree?'

The officers had Gina restrained and took her out to the van. They walked out as Cain ran in and took in the scene. Morgan smiled at him. 'Father Gordon saved the day.'

'Wow, good work. Erm, is the boss okay?'

Marc had been helped onto one of the wooden pews and he turned to him. 'Yeah, I've been better but I'm okay, thanks.' His words were a little slurred.

'Oh, that's great. You might not be okay at what I'm going to tell you though.'

'What?'

'Your car is parked inside of the Co-op; the driver must have accelerated around that bend too hard and went straight through the double-plate glass windows; it's currently embedded in a mountain of tins of baked beans that were on special offer. No one was hurt, thankfully. Except for the driver, and your car is probably a write-off.'

All eyes were on Marc, waiting for his reaction. They expected him to explode, but instead he shook his head. 'I bloody hate that car, it's been nothing but trouble. I'm going to get me a nice, sturdy Volvo.'

The laughter filled the church, even Gordon who didn't really understand what they were laughing about joined in. They watched as he closed his eyes and said a little prayer, all of them thankful for his help. Morgan couldn't help but wonder if he'd had some help from high above, a little divine intervention perhaps.

EPILOGUE

ONE WEEK LATER

Morgan, Ben, Cain, Amy and Gordon were in the vicarage waiting for Declan to arrive with Theo. Gordon had bought balloons and welcome home banners for the occasion, which Morgan thought was just the sweetest thing ever. It was role reversal, as not that long ago it had been Ben bringing her home from the hospital to a little welcome home party. Gordon had roped some of the women's group to bake some cakes and make sandwiches, and the little spread was on the pine kitchen table with a checked tablecloth underneath it. Theo walked in, took one look at them and laughed.

'Whose party is this?'

Morgan stepped forward and hugged him tight. 'Yours, we figured you earned it and, to be fair it was Gordon who organised it.'

Theo looked at Gordon who was literally beaming with delight. 'Gordon, thank you. This was very kind of you.'

'It's the least I could do, Father Theo, I've been worried about you. This is a dangerous place to be. I've only been here a week and it's been like an episode of *Father Brown*. It's very exciting though. I don't know if I'm going to be able to go back to my sedentary little village after all of this.'

Declan for once didn't have anything to say. Morgan let Theo go and hugged him next. 'I don't give these out freely by the way. I only give them to special people.'

He kissed the top of her head. 'Right, for once can we forget about who got the worst head injury and who nearly died, and just eat? I'm starving, you two can compare your notes later.'

There was a knock at the door and a voice called, 'Hello.'

They all paused, waiting for Marc to join them. 'Sorry I'm late, my car's in the garage.'

Cain winked at him. 'At least it's no longer inside the Co-op.'

Theo and Declan looked at Marc who shook his head. 'It's a long story, I'll tell you about it some time.'

———

After they left Theo's, the team went back to the station which was relatively peaceful. The office smelled of lemon furniture polish for a change not stale food; the cleaner had been in whilst they were out and even emptied the bins.

Ben waited until everyone was seated, and he was about to brief them on the enquiries that needed to be carried out. Raven had been cleared, she'd had the briefest affair with Max. Apart from her interest in the crimes there was nothing to tie her to them now that both Matt and Gina had been remanded into custody to await the murder trials of Rosie, Max and Annie, plus the attempted murder of Theo, as well as the drugging and abduction of the boss too, but Marc pointed to a chair, and Ben sat down instead.

'I have to tell you that I was sorely misled by Gina,' Marc said. 'I had found her attractive and very sweet, which goes to show I'm a terrible judge of character. Gilly said that when she interviewed Matt, he came clean and told her everything, trying to save himself. Gina is still no comment and hasn't admitted anything. Matt had a very good friend in France who he left his phone with to answer and send messages whilst he was over here plotting with Gina all the time; apparently, it was Gina who went into the attic to stage the scene that made us think they were being stalked and it was all very clever. Border control confirmed that Matt arrived in the UK a month ago. I just wanted to say, thank you all. You have worked so hard on this case, well not just this case, every case you work, and it's an honour to be a part of your team. Thank you for letting me stay. What can I say? Things are bound to get better.'

Everyone smiled. Morgan spoke. 'Fingers crossed.'

'Yes, fingers crossed. Anything you need, don't hesitate to ask. I've said it before, and I'll say it again, my door is always open.'

Cain nodded. 'I have a question.'

'Yes, Cain.'

'Who gave you that black eye?'

Marc grinned at him. 'Let's just say I'm not dating for the foreseeable future. I swiped right on a woman on Tinder whose ex turned up and well, you can guess the rest.'

Cain laughed. 'Thank you for your honesty, boss, nice one. I hope you gave as good as you got.'

All of them got back to work, glad for once to be working on the mundane stuff like CCTV and house-to-house enquiries until the next murder happened, and Morgan knew deep down that it would; there was something about Rydal Falls that drew in killers and couldn't keep them away, but they would be ready to hunt them down. That was what they did best, hunt down the bad people who committed despicable crimes and serve them the justice they deserve.

A LETTER FROM HELEN

I want to say a huge thank you for choosing to read *Their Dying Embrace*.

If you did enjoy it, and want to keep up-to-date with all my latest releases, just sign up at the following link. Your email address will never be shared and you can unsubscribe at any time.

www.bookouture.com/helen-phifer

I can't believe this is book fourteen. Morgan, Ben and the rest of the team have really been through it. I hope you found this one a little different. Poor Morgan needed to catch a break and Marc had to finally fit in with everyone else, and I hope that he's finally done just that. Thank you from the bottom of my heart for reading this, your support means so much to me.

Gina LoBue is the cohost of my favourite true crime podcast which I've mentioned many times: 50 States of Madness, and also one of the coolest, kindest women I know. Gina, you rock and it was pretty hard making you a killer, but I hope I did you justice! The formidable Gilly Mahaffy is one of my dear school friends and biggest supporters. We will be seeing more from Gilly, somebody had to keep Marc under control and she is the perfect woman to do just that.

I hope you loved *Their Dying Embrace*, and if you did I would be very grateful if you could write a review. I'd love to hear what you think, and it makes such a difference helping new readers to discover one of my books for the first time.

I love hearing from my readers – you can get in touch through my social media or my website.

Thanks,

Helen

www.helenphifer.com

 facebook.com/Helenphifer1
x.com/helenphifer1

ACKNOWLEDGEMENTS

As always, the biggest thank you to my amazing editor Jennifer Hunt. She is so fabulous at making these stories so much better than what I send to her, thank you, Jen, I really appreciate everything you do.

Thank you so much to the keen-eyed Janette Currie for her thorough copy edits. Also thank you to the lovely Jen Shannon for everything and thanks so much to Shirley Khan for her proofread.

Another huge thank you to the amazing team at Bookouture for all of their hard work. They never give anything other than a hundred per cent in everything that they do, and I appreciate every single one of them.

Noelle Holten is my amazing wing gal, always has my back for publication and cover release days, and I can't thank her enough for that. A huge thank you to the rest of the publicity team too, you're all amazing.

A massive thank you to the team at Audio Factory for bringing these stories to life and Alison Campbell for her brilliant narration, thank you, Alison, you are Morgan Brookes.

Where would I be without my readers, you are so wonderful, kind, supportive and I honestly wish I could meet you all and thank you in person. I appreciate you all so much, your reviews, kind and funny comments make me laugh so much, you also make my head swell too but I love you all so much for coming on this journey with me and seeing where it goes.

Thank you to all the book bloggers for being so amazing,

that you read and review my books when there are so many to choose from is an absolute honour and I appreciate it more than you know.

A debt of gratitude to the beautiful, glamorous, amazing Gina LoBue and Gilly Mahaffy for letting me put you in my book. It's been a wild ride writing about you both and I've loved it. Gina is one half of my favourite podcast 50 States of Madness, with her wonderful co-host Shannon, and I've talked about it before but if you love true crime then you really need to give it a listen. They are both so funny as well as brilliant and it never fails to brighten my day when a new episode drops.

A heartfelt thank you to our amazing support team Selena Clarke-Smith, Dan and Jenny for taking such good care of Jaimea so we can have much needed breaks. You are all beautiful souls and just wonderful.

Another huge thank you to the amazing staff at Mill Lane Day Care Centre for taking care of Jaimea through the week, you are all very much appreciated.

Lastly, thank you to my amazing, crazy, fun, loving family. I love you so much, I am so proud of each and every one of you and one day if you ever read these books, I'll probably have a heart attack, so maybe best if you don't *wink emoji*. I am so blessed to have such brilliant kids and grandkids that give me so much joy, well the grandkids definitely do!

Much love to you all.

Helen xx

PUBLISHING TEAM

Turning a manuscript into a book requires the efforts of many people. The publishing team at Bookouture would like to acknowledge everyone who contributed to this publication.

Audio
Alba Proko
Sinead O'Connor
Melissa Tran

Commercial
Lauren Morrissette
Hannah Richmond
Imogen Allport

Cover design
The Brewster Project

Data and analysis
Mark Alder
Mohamed Bussuri

Editorial
Jennifer Hunt
Charlotte Hegley

Made in United States
Orlando, FL
03 February 2025

58120152R00163